little b
· IT'S A C

Dear Little Black Dress Read

Thanks for picking up this Little Black Dress book, one of the great new titles from our series of fun, page-turning romance novels. Lucky you — you're about to have a fantastic romantic read that we know you won't be able to put down!

Why don't you make your Little Black Dress experience even better by logging on to

www.littleblackdressbooks.com

where you can:

- ♥ Enter our **monthly competitions** to win **gorgeous** prizes
- ♥ Get **hot-off-the-press** news about our latest titles
- ♥ Read **exclusive** preview chapters both from your **favourite** authors and from brilliant new writing talent
- ♥ Buy **up-and-coming** books online
- ♥ Sign up for an essential slice of romance via our **fortnightly email** newsletter

We love nothing more than to curl up and indulge in an addictive romance, and so we're delighted to welcome you into the Little Black Dress club!

With love from,

The *little black dress* team

Five interesting things about Jessica Fox:

1. I can't resist stopping to look at newly married couples emerging from churches.

2. My palm-reader told me I have a lifeline that is shorter than my heart line. I assume this means I will be with my husband Rob in this life and the next. I just hope he will have learned to pick up his socks by then.

3. I have a phobia of elevators. On our honeymoon, the Eiffel Tower was definitely worth it. Until I realised I'd left my camera at the top.

4. I was once on a hen night where the groom appeared in the early hours and started chatting me up!

5. If my house was on fire, and I could only rescue one thing, it would be my antique tarot cards. Sorry, Rob.

By Jessica Fox

The Hen Night Prophecies: The One That Got Away
The Hen Night Prophecies: Eastern Promise
The Hen Night Prophecies: Hard to Get

The Hen Night Prophecies:

Hard to Get

Jessica Fox

little
black
dress

First published in 2010
by LITTLE BLACK DRESS
An imprint of HEADLINE PUBLISHING GROUP

A LITTLE BLACK DRESS paperback

1

Cataloguing in Publication Data is available from the British Library

ISBN 978 0 7553 4959 3

Typeset in Transit511BT by Avon DataSet Ltd,
Bidford-on-Avon, Warwickshire

Printed and bound in Great Britain by
Clays Ltd, St Ives plc

HEADLINE PUBLISHING GROUP
An Hachette UK Company
338 Euston Road
London NW1 3BH

www.littleblackdressbooks.com
www.headline.co.uk
www.hachette.co.uk

With special thanks to Ruth Saberton

Acknowledgements

This one is for my husband, who's always believed in me. Thanks for putting up with the antisocial hours I keep when chained to the keyboard!

P.S. PLEASE can we get a puppy?

Charlotte Sinclair was pressed for time and much as it pained her to forgo her usual double espresso she knew being late for work would annoy her even more. Charlotte was never late anywhere and she had absolutely no intention of changing the habit of a lifetime. Even Superman might have struggled to make it from Lambs Conduit Street and through the gaggle of commuters to Farringdon, so when Charlotte made it to the Arts Council's offices with time to spare, it was nothing short of miraculous.

'You look stressed,' commented Richard, perching his neat Paul Smith-clad backside on the edge of Charlotte's desk and grinning at her.

Charlotte glowered back at him. She wasn't a morning person, never had been and never would be. Richard really ought to have worked that much out by now.

He was her ex-husband, after all.

'Care to share?' he asked.

'No, thank you,' Charlotte said coolly, booting up her ancient PC and taking off her jacket. 'I'm far too busy to chat.'

Refusing to meet his eyes she fixed her gaze on her computer screen. Charlotte drummed her fingers on the desk impatiently. She was rushed off her feet and every second counted. There were a million and one emails lurking in her in-box – everything from a troupe of juggling lesbians to a fire-eating opera singer – and the last thing she had time to do was exchange pleasantries with her ex.

'Come on, Lottie, don't be like that.' Richard crinkled liquid-brown eyes at her in a winning smile. This might work on everyone else but it had no effect on Charlotte. She'd be more won over by the sight of Alan Sugar naked than by Richard on a charm offensive.

'I'm not being like anything,' she said patiently. *Bloody computer!* A snail with a limp would've moved faster. She made a mental note to go and nag her line manager about getting the system upgraded. And if he continued to ignore her, she'd have to dig out her tap shoes from 1987, figure out a routine and approve her own Arts Council funding to pay for it!

'Relax!' Richard's strong fingers closed over her own frantically drumming ones. 'The computer will start in a minute. Just give it time.'

'I don't have time. Believe it or not some of us actually have work to do.' Charlotte yanked her fingers away, resisting the urge to squirt them with a big dollop of her antibacterial spray. Richard's whole touchy-feely 'we're good mates' routine drove her insane. After eighteen months, you'd think he would've realised she found it too difficult to be his friend.

'Hmm,' he said, 'I take it you've missed out on your double espresso?'

Charlotte frowned. Was there anything more annoying than a smart-arse, except maybe a smart-arse who knew you inside out? And how typical of Richard to assume it was lack of caffeine making her tetchy rather than the fact that he got on her nerves more than a dentist's drill. Shouldn't he be locked away in Accounting and Auditing, obsessing over a calculator?

'I'm fine,' she snapped. 'Or rather, I would be if I was allowed to get on with my work. Some of us have to, you know. We're not all sleeping with the boss.'

'That was below the belt, Lottie.' Richard's eyes grew dark with hurt but Charlotte didn't care. His poor-old-me routine didn't wash with her.

Not these days, anyway.

'Please don't call me Lottie. You know I hate it.'

'I'm sorry. I give up. I was only trying to be civil.' Raising both hands in surrender he slipped off her desk. 'But, seriously, you really need to stop frowning, Lot – err, I mean Charlotte. It's going to give you lines.'

'Being over forty, you're the expert so I'll take your word for it,' Charlotte replied calmly. Inside, though, she was seething. If she wanted to sit at her desk and scowl until the Grand Canyon appeared between her eyes, then it was up to her and nothing to do with anyone else, especially not Richard Sinclair.

'Anyway,' she continued smoothly as her computer finally woke up and allowed her into her emails, 'there's always Botox to sort out wrinkles. But as far as I know they haven't yet discovered a cure for hair loss.'

Richard's hands instantly flew to his temples where, despite his thick head of curls, he was starting to look a little thin. *Yes! Direct hit!* Many times Charlotte had watched Richard checking his hairline in mirrors, glass doors and any shiny surface he came across. She still knew his weak spots (or should that be bald spots?) just as he knew hers. She was just toying with the idea of winding him up a bit more when Suzie, their pretty blonde boss and also Richard's partner, joined them.

'Do you think my hair's thinning?' Richard asked her, looking worried.

Suzie ruffled his curls affectionately and dropped a kiss on to his cheek. 'Don't be silly. You're as gorgeous as ever.'

Richard swelled with pride as he basked in the warm sunshine of his boss's admiration while Charlotte rolled her eyes. This billing and cooing was all very well for them but it was pretty distracting for everyone else.

'Suzie, do you actually need me for anything? If not, I have plenty to do and I'd appreciate some quiet to get on with it.'

Two perfect pink circles appeared on Suzie's peachy cheeks. As though suddenly aware that she was in the office and not the bedroom she slipped her arm from Richard's shoulder. *It is pathetic the way she can hardly bear to be apart from Richard*, thought Charlotte. They were like Siamese twins joined at the tongue, just like her brother and his new wife Zoe.

'I'm calling a meeting,' Suzie said quickly. 'My office in five, OK?'

'Fine,' said Charlotte coolly. 'Now if you don't mind, I'm in the middle of a discussion with my colleague, so if you would . . .'

She locked eyes with Suzie, but Suzie looked away first. *All this time on and still she can't bear to look me in the eye*, Charlotte thought. But it no longer gave her the sense of satisfaction that it once had – in fact, it just made her feel sad. And very, very weary.

'No problem. Just be there please,' Suzie reiterated, trying to regain her composure. Her cheeks still stained pink, she turned sharply on her heel leaving Charlotte and Richard alone.

'Yes, boss!' Richard called after her, raising his hand in a mock salute but, once Suzie's slender frame had vanished back into her office, the smile faded from his lips and he shook his head despairingly.

'Do you really have to be so hard on her? None of this is Suzie's fault.'

Charlotte sighed. 'Ahh, the guilt trip. You must have a season ticket.'

'Don't be like that,' he pleaded. 'Can't we put the past behind us? We had our good times . . . You even used to laugh at my jokes.'

'I was faking,' she said, implying that her laughter wasn't the only thing she'd had to fake in their relationship. But she had to admit that she missed Richard's daft sense of humour.

'Ouch,' he said, smiling, but clearly hurt. 'Seriously,

though, we do have to work together. Can we be friends?' He held out his hand, tanned and strong, the nails well shaped and beautifully manicured, each with perfect half-moons. Suddenly a memory flashed before her vision like the glittering scales of a fish flickering through sun-dappled water. That same hand was cupping her cheek and tracing the curve of her lips before straying lower to caress her breast . . .

Oh no! Stop right there! Charlotte ordered herself. *You are not having these thoughts! No way!*

'Friends?' she echoed incredulously.

'Absolutely. We shouldn't let a silly falling out get in the way of our friendship.'

Inside Charlotte was screaming and stabbing him to death with a Bic biro, but outwardly she remained cool and collected. She'd done more than her fair share of screaming and crying when she'd been *married* to him.

'A silly falling out?' she repeated slowly. 'Is that really how you see it? Richard, we didn't have a row over what to have for dinner! I was your wife and you left me. Worse than that, it only took you three days to find someone else! *Friends* are supposed to be loyal to one another!'

'Lottie,' Richard sighed heavily, 'you'd finished with me, remember? You asked me to leave!'

'I asked you to give me some space for a while!' She bunched her hands into fists. She was not having a scene in the office. No way. Lowering her voice she hissed, 'You wanted us to have a baby, Richard, it was a major step. It wasn't like you'd asked me to go and pick up a pizza!'

'And what was so wrong about that?' he shot back. 'Most women in their thirties would be over the moon to have a baby with their husband, but not you, Charlotte. Oh no, that was one commitment too far for you, wasn't it? Were you worried about wrecking your amazing career or your figure? Or maybe –' his voice dropped and suddenly his eyes were filled with a wistful expression – 'you just didn't love me enough?'

For a second she was speechless, struck dumb by the unfairness of this accusation. If they'd had a baby, she knew that the tiny person would have owned her heart and soul. No baby could ever have been so wanted. But what about Richard? Would he have loved them both enough to sacrifice the freedom that he so enjoyed? To swap his latest impractical sports car for a Family Wagon or to collect nappies rather than vintage wine?

A baby was for life, not just for wet weekends.

She'd had to be sure, had to make certain that they both wanted the same things. What if he got bored once the novelty wore off and the colic kicked in? Or became so absorbed in his work that he never had time for them? *Or what*, a nasty little voice had whispered, *if you can't cut it as a mother?* What then?

She sighed. 'There's no point raking over this again; it's ancient history. Let's move on.'

'Like you did, you mean?' he said, eyes still doey.

'That's rather ironic,' Charlotte replied calmly, quitting her mailbox and shrugging into her jacket. 'It took you three days to go from wanting a child with one woman to shagging another. Has the *Guinness Book of Records* contacted you yet?'

'What about you? I blinked, and suddenly you were filing for divorce,' Richard shot back, his eyes bright with indignation. 'You never even gave me a chance to explain!'

As she fastened her jacket Charlotte's heart was doing a flamenco. She detested dirty laundry airing, loathed dredging up these horrible memories.

'There was nothing for you to explain. It was all very clear,' she reminded her ex-husband firmly. 'You proved beyond all reasonable doubt that my instinct to think things through was the right one. So actually, Richard, I owe Suzie, don't I? If it hadn't been for her I could have made one huge mistake.'

Richard stared at her. 'How can you be so indifferent? I really missed you when I moved out.'

For all of three days, thought Charlotte darkly. Then she sighed. He would never get it.

'Of course you did,' she said. 'The fridge didn't fill itself, dinners didn't appear by magic and – unless I'm very much mistaken – man might be able to land on the moon but he hasn't yet managed to give himself a blow job! Now unless you want to be in the bad books with your latest lover, I suggest you make a move to this meeting because we're late.'

And scooping up her notebook and pen Charlotte stalked off leaving Richard staring open mouthed behind her.

'How the hell did I ever marry someone so cold?' he said finally, but she chose to ignore him. So he had the impression she didn't care that he'd moved straight from her to Suzie without so much as brushing his teeth? And just like everyone else in the office he thought she was fine with the situation, did he? Well, good. She'd much rather they all believed she was a cold sarcastic old bag than that they knew about all the nights her pillow had been wetter than a British summer. No, it was infinitely preferable that everybody took her to be as tough as old boots because that way nobody would ever know the sad, pathetic truth.

Richard Sinclair had smashed Charlotte's heart to smithereens.

While Suzie banged on about the latest government subsidies and funding targets Charlotte zoned out, doodling on her notepad to look busy. Dredging up the unpleasant memories with Richard was the emotional equivalent of ripping off a scab. Perhaps she wasn't quite as over things as she'd believed.

How dare he try to blame me for the divorce? Charlotte thought furiously, her fingers gripping her pen so hard that her knuckles glowed through her pale freckled skin. That was a case of false memory syndrome if ever she'd heard it. Charlotte had loved Richard from the minute she first saw him to the second before he confessed his infidelity. The warm, tanned caramel skin, lean lithe body and those melting Maltesers eyes never failed to make her grow weak with molten lust. Richard had always been more than enough and she loved him totally and utterly, trusting him one hundred per cent to feel the same way.

What an idiot she'd been.

So much for forsaking all others. He'd only lasted

three days before his dick had got the better of him. Three days to forget seven years of marriage, the endless dinners, ego massages and passionate sex. Three days to fall into the arms of Suzie.

How could he ever imagine she could get over *that*?

So when Richard had pleaded for a second chance, Charlotte hadn't wavered for a nanosecond. As far as she was concerned he'd proven beyond any doubt that he wasn't committed to her or the family he claimed he wanted so much. On the fourth day she'd filed for divorce, wanting to put it all behind her as soon as possible, and Richard had moved in with Suzie on the fifth.

'Last item on the agenda,' Suzie was saying, her firm tone dragging Charlotte back into the present. 'The Yorkshire projects have finally been given the go-ahead from Head Office to move to stage-two funding – subject, of course, to approval.'

There was a brief ripple of applause from the people gathered in the office.

'You don't need me to remind you how vital it is that projects get stage-two clearance,' Suzie continued. 'Allocation of funding enables charities to continue the good work that they've begun. Richard and I will be visiting the projects in person. We'll be working hard to prepare some detailed interim reports.'

I bet you will, thought Charlotte, jabbing her pen nib into her pad. A few days cosied up in some plush hotel would no doubt be written off to expenses somewhere along the line, too.

Suzie shuffled her paperwork together. 'I have every confidence they'll both be approved for funding. The Hope Foundation and YORC appear to have done some excellent work.'

The word 'hope' made Charlotte smile in spite of herself as a silly memory flitted through her mind.

Love will come to you through hope alone.

A few months ago her baby brother Steve (Some baby now! He was in his thirties and over six feet tall!) had been about to get married and, to her great surprise, Charlotte had been invited to his fiancée Zoe's hen night. Although she liked Zoe, they weren't really close, being as diverse in personality as they were in looks. Charlotte was tall and angular with red hair and a natural inclination to keep herself to herself. Zoe, on the other hand, was a small and slender blonde with the face and personality of an angel. She was also very gregarious and loved nothing more than gathering her nearest and dearest around her at every opportunity.

I suppose I'm one of her nearest and dearest now, Charlotte had thought as she RSVP'd to her Hen Night invitation. Past experience had taught her there was little point making excuses. Much as she would rather be indoors, happy to be miserable and antisocial in front of the telly, Zoe would only find another way to include her. Maybe they needed a spectre at the feast? And if so, who better for the job than bitter and twisted old Charlotte?

So on the evening of Zoe's hen party she'd grabbed

a couple of bottles of red and dragged herself over to Richmond. She'd been resigned to a night of giggling, L-plates and nail painting. She'd even expected a stripper or a gorilla-gram.

What she hadn't expected was a visit from a psychic.

That little surprise had been the handiwork of Libby, Zoe's scatty twenty-four-year-old sister. A ball of uncontained energy, Libby could scarcely sit still for ten seconds at a time before bombing around on her skateboard, zapping hapless aliens on her Xbox or jumping about with the Wii Fit. Just looking at her made Charlotte feel exhausted and more ancient than Methuselah. Had she ever been that young and impulsive, so confident that life was brimming with great opportunities just crying out to be grabbed with both hands? As the hens sipped their drinks and bubbles of excited conversation had risen and popped like champagne fizz, Charlotte had felt herself becoming more morose by the second. Of course she'd never been as full of beans as Libby or as open and as loving as Zoe. How could she have been? Life had kicked her in the teeth when she was only twelve and, as far as Charlotte could see, it had been downhill from then on in.

But as the hen night progressed she'd (mostly) kept her cynicism at bay, watching as Zoe opened her presents and chatted excitedly about the big day. She'd felt almost maternal listening to the younger girls' conversation. They were all so hopeful that they'd find love and happiness, their lives stretching before them like fields of untrodden snow. Hers was all slushy and ruined, she'd thought bleakly, as would theirs be one day. But she had held her tongue, knowing that there was time enough for dizzy Fern, serious Priya and lively Libby to discover for themselves that Prince Charming invariably turned back into a toad once you'd kissed him. Her cynicism didn't quite extend to Zoe and Steve, though, because she knew that her brother loved his fiancée with all his heart. Steve was one of the good guys but, and here was the rub, he was still a man and therefore programmed to be a complete disappointment to womankind.

That came with having a willy, in her experience.

When Libby announced that she'd booked a tarot reader for a bit of a laugh (no strippers for Zoe which was clearly a big let down as far as Fern and Priya were concerned), Charlotte was more than ready to scoff at the clichéd predictions of love, marriage and children that she knew would be trotted out more times than the donkeys on Blackpool Beach.

She'd show that phoney psychic a thing or two.

Thinking back to the darkness of Zoe's conservatory on that warm June night Charlotte shivered in spite of herself. Although she'd been rather disappointed with how ordinary Angela, the psychic, had appeared – a curly grey perm and Marks and Spencer's slacks weren't quite in keeping with the hooped earrings and jewel-hued skirts she'd been expecting – the reading itself had been spookily accurate and many things had resonated rather too much for Charlotte's liking. *Get a grip*, she'd told herself firmly, *they're all lucky guesses*. The comments about being hard to get had been made because she was in her thirties and not wearing a wedding ring, and the bags under her eyes were a huge give away that she was tired and working far too hard. It was all standard stuff.

Or at least it was until the reading drew to a close.

'You doubt me,' the tarot reader had said with a sigh. 'I can see it in your face. But you doubt yourself even more, don't you, lovie? Underneath the control and the sharp tongue there's a lonely and very scared woman, a woman who thinks she's not good enough to love and to be loved in return.'

Charlotte had feigned a yawn. 'Right.'

Angela shook her head. 'It's a lonely path you've chosen to tread. Keeping yourself safe isn't the road to the happy family life that you long for.'

'It sounds great to me, nice and peaceful. I see enough of my family at Christmas,' she shot back. But the psychic just sighed, which really wound Charlotte up. How dare a total stranger feel sorry for her? Nobody was allowed to feel sorry for Charlotte Sinclair!

'Thanks for the reading.' She stood up, smoothing the creases out of her black wrap dress. 'I'll send in the next sucker – I mean hen – shall I?'

The psychic shrugged. 'You're not a believer but my guides don't care about that. Besides, they are never wrong. They have a message for you now and even if you choose to discard everything else I've told you, please listen to what they say.'

Derek Acorah had nothing on this!

'Go on, then. What is this vital message? Saturday's lottery numbers? Brad Pitt's email address? Please don't tell me George Clooney's proposing marriage. I hear he has a thing about Japanese pot bellies and I've already lived with one pig in my life.'

But Angela wasn't listening. Her eyes had gone all weird, kind of turning inwards on themselves, and when she started to speak her voice sounded completely different, all gravelly and low, with not a trace of her previous West Country burr. In spite of herself Charlotte's skin prickled.

'Love will be yours and love is waiting for you,' Angela rasped. Her eyes locked on to Charlotte's with burning intensity. 'Heed this, Charlotte Sinclair, and heed it well. Love will come to you through hope alone.'

Charlotte stared back at her. 'What's that supposed to mean? Love will come to me through hope alone? What the hell is that all about?'

The psychic didn't answer, or, more accurately, couldn't answer because suddenly she was slumped over the table, her curly grey head narrowly missing her crystal ball. Moments later, when she did raise her head, Charlotte was alarmed to see that she was a horrible shade of grey.

Oh Lord, please don't let the old dear be about to pop her clogs! That really will put a dampener on the hen night!

She stepped forward. 'Angela? Are you OK?'

'I think so,' Angela answered, her voice now weak and trembling. 'Would you be so kind as to fetch me a glass of water?'

'Of course!' Still slightly panic stricken Charlotte filled a champagne flute with iced water and moments later Angela was sipping it gratefully, colour slowly returning to her waxy skin.

Was all this part of her act? Charlotte wondered, crossing her arms and regarding the older woman through narrowed eyes. If so, it was bloody good. She'd really had her going there for a moment.

'I'm so sorry if I frightened you, love,' Angela said eventually, fanning her face with a pudgy hand. 'Sometimes my guides have messages that are so important they simply have to pass it on, regardless of how draining it is for me.'

That shattered the illusion right away. What a load of old cobblers! If these spirit guides of hers were so genuine, then why did they insist in speaking in riddles, rather than saying something specific like: 'Your perfect man will be in the fish finger aisle of your local Waitrose at one-thirty next Tuesday and his name is Adam'? These cryptic messages allowed for a wealth of interpretation, which was obviously the whole point.

Charlotte didn't believe it for one second.

But now in the office with the September sunshine streaming in slices through the blind, Charlotte recalled the prophecy and shivered in spite of the warmth.

Love will come to you through hope alone. As if!

Charlotte scooped up her things and trailed back to her desk. She wasn't even sure whether she believed in love, anyway. The evidence so far was rather shaky to say the least.

'It's good news about the projects going to second stage, isn't it?' Richard paused by her desk and gave Charlotte a smile of genuine delight. 'After all the hard work you put in at the early stages you must be over the moon.'

'Yeah, that's right. I'm overjoyed that yet again Suzie's taken something from me that I spent ages working on.'

'You put in the ground work for both projects, though,' Richard was keen to keep the conversation on a safer footing. 'Suzie would be the first to say that the credit goes to you.'

Charlotte pulled a face. The trouble was that Suzie probably would give her all the credit. The woman was never anything but fair and polite to her, in fact, she often seemed to go out of her way to be super nice. That was what a guilty conscience did to you, Charlotte supposed.

'I'm glad I put in all the grunt work so that my ex-husband and his girlfriend can slack off in a country hotel,' she said icily. 'I must remember to put that particular achievement on my CV when I update it.'

'I can't win with you, can I?' said Richard. 'Day in, day out I put up with your sarky comments and being made to feel like a leper in my own work place. Every attempt to be civil is thrown back in my face. And as for poor Suzie—'

'Oh yes, please let's hear about poor old Suzie!' countered Charlotte. 'My heart bleeds for her. Sleeping with another woman's husband is an act that really requires my sympathy. I tell you what, Richard, why don't I just go into her office right now and apologise for being so bloody unreasonable!'

'For God's sake, we'd split up!'

Charlotte was considering splitting his lip when a vibrating sensation in her jacket pocket announced a call. *Saved by the buzz, Richard.* Pulling her BlackBerry out she saw the word *Dad* flashing on the screen and her heart went into freefall. She loved her father, but their relationship was rather topsy-turvey: ever since her mother had walked out Charlotte had taken on the role of parent. While Geoff Kent found solace in the bottom of a bottle it had been left to his twelve-year-old daughter to worry about paying the bills, buying groceries and getting Steve and herself to school. Consequently she'd had to grow up pretty fast. There'd been no time for a teenage social life, so Steve and her father had become her whole world. Even now she felt a nagging sense of guilt for having moved out and for leaving Geoff to fend for himself.

'Dad! How are you?' she asked brightly, perching on the edge of her desk and pointedly ignoring her ex-husband.

'I'm very worried,' Geoff was saying. 'I've had terrible indigestion lately. What if I've got cancer, Charlie, like Mrs Cook from next door?'

'Dad, you've had indigestion for years. You

practically mainline Gaviscon,' Charlotte pointed out.

'That's true,' Geoff agreed, perking up and going on to recount the entire week's plot of *EastEnders* in minute detail. He didn't get out much so Dot, Phil and Ian Beale were like personal friends to him. Twenty long minutes later they felt like personal friends to Charlotte too, and her ear was throbbing from being pressed to the phone.

'That man,' Geoff tutted. 'He's a bad lot all right, isn't he?'

'Mmm, absolutely,' she agreed.

'Not like my Steve,' Geoff added. A pause followed and then he added petulantly, 'I never see Steve these days. He doesn't come and visit me any more.'

Charlotte closed her eyes wearily. 'Dad, Steve's been away on his honeymoon. He got married to Zoe a few months ago, remember?'

'Married?' Geoff echoed. 'But he's only fifteen!'

Here we go again, thought Charlotte. 'Dad, Steve's thirty. He's married to Zoe who wrote that *Jane Eyre* series on the BBC that you loved so much. You went to the wedding and had to wear a posh suit, remember?'

But she may as well have been speaking Klingon for all the meaning her words held for Geoff. Much as she tried to prompt his memory, he really couldn't recall his own son's wedding.

'And then, Dad, you turned to the chief bridesmaid – that was Libby, Zoe's sister – and told her she was beautiful. You said "I used to like older women, angel, but they're all dead now".'

He roared with laughter. 'I like it! Who said that again?'

Charlotte's throat tightened. 'I do love you, Dad.'

'I love you too, Charlie Barley,' he said warmly, 'but I can't stand here chatting all day. I don't know what you were thinking of, phoning me so early in the day. Haven't you got work to do?'

'Tonnes,' she said. 'Talk soon, OK?' but Geoff had already rung off, ensconced back in his small world of Albert Square, Mrs Cook and big forgotten chunks of the last six decades.

Charlotte hung her head and hoped that her red hair hid her tears. Dementia exacerbated by alcoholism was how the consultant had explained it, but to Charlotte it was worse than that. It was like losing him all over again only this time to something that she couldn't help him fight. No one could because all the love and hope in the world wouldn't be able to fill the shadowy absences in her father's mind.

Love will come to you through hope alone.

Unbidden and oddly loud, the words of Angela's prediction echoed through her mind as loudly as though the psychic was standing right behind her. Charlotte jumped and spun around. But there was nobody there.

She laughed nervously. Love would come to her through hope alone, would it? What a load of old rubbish. Would hope alone help Geoff? Had hoping that Richard loved her enough to understand how fearful she was of having children stopped him sleeping with another woman?

No, of course it hadn't. If there was one thing Charlotte Sinclair didn't have, it was hope.

She was fresh out of that.

Charlotte didn't confide in anyone about her father but as the day went on she felt more and more worried about him. He was clearly deteriorating. She needed to talk to Steve. Much as she hated to give her brother any stress when he was so newly married, Charlotte knew that any decisions that were made about their father had to involve the whole family.

And, unfortunately, her family didn't include a fairy godmother with a magic wand.

As soon as it was lunchtime Charlotte tore out of the office and dashed into Starbucks. One double espresso later she was starting to feel slightly less keyed up, the drumbeat in her temples was slowing down and her stomach was untangling itself. She fished her BlackBerry out of her bag and called Steve. Maybe if he visited their dad it would jog Geoff's memory about the wedding? Surely it had to be worth a try?

When her brother didn't answer, Charlotte dialled his home number instead. Sometimes Steve worked out of the office room but not today because Zoe answered, sighing with affectionate exasperation as she explained that her husband had forgotten his mobile.

'I should superglue it to him! What is he like?'

'Useless. Like most men,' Charlotte said tartly. 'Never mind, it'll keep, I suppose.'

'I've got a better idea. Why don't you come over for dinner?' Zoe suggested. 'Steve's normally home by half six so you can catch him then.'

'You guys are just back from your honeymoon,' Charlotte protested. 'I'll catch my brother another time.'

'Don't be daft! We'd love to see you. And please don't worry about being a gooseberry. Libby's living with us at the moment so we're not exactly swinging naked from the chandeliers!'

'How come?' Charlotte asked, rather taken aback. She'd been worried about popping over for dinner but moving in with newlyweds was something else. What a nerve!

But Zoe was laughing. 'It's typical Libby, really. She never got around to renewing the lease on her flat and was then totally amazed not to be able to find another one instantly. My little sister never thinks things through, I'm afraid. But maybe that's part of being twenty-four?'

'Mmm,' said Charlotte. Actually, she couldn't ever recall being as carefree and impulsive as Libby. Probably the most spontaneous thing she'd done when she was the same age was to change from Tesco to Asda. Libby's world of extreme sports, foreign travel and wildly unsuitable men was another planet compared to her own experience.

'Please come,' Zoe pressed. 'We haven't seen you since we got back from Italy. Besides, I really need to go through the wedding pictures and it would be great to have your help. You know what Steve's like; he'll just pick the first twenty he sees so that he can get back on the Xbox as quickly as possible. Honestly, I could throttle Libby for introducing him to that.'

'He was just as bad when he had the Sega,' Charlotte recalled. Goodness, it had been hell trying to prise him away from Sonic and Tails to do his homework while she tried to master the mysteries of cooking. Everything she made was invariably charred or raw. Steve had spat most of it out and demanded his mum back while Geoff had just stayed in the pub until time was called. Mostly they'd lived on toast.

No wonder she hated cooking. Zoe, on the other hand, was amazing at it and spending the evening with her and Steve would make a pleasant change from a microwaved meal for one and a lame whodunnit. Agreeing to be in Richmond for seven o'clock, she flipped her phone shut and dashed back to the office. Her in-tray still induced vertigo and Richard and Suzie were still the emotional equivalent of salt in an open wound, but in spite of all this she felt much more cheerful.

It felt good having something to look forward to.

'That was delicious, but I can't eat another mouthful!'

Charlotte looked regretfully down at her plate, which was still loaded with lemon chicken and fragrant basmati rice. It was quite simply the nicest food she'd eaten in ages.

Maybe toast and Marmite wasn't all it was cracked up to be?

'I'll finish yours, then!' Steve reached across for her plate and scraped the leftovers on to his empty one.

'Oi! Share that, you greedy pig!' Libby demanded, elbowing her brother-in-law in the stomach and spooning some rice on to her plate. 'I'd like seconds. This food rocks!'

'You'll be the size of a house at this rate,' he teased, but Libby just laughed and clapped a hand against her washboard stomach.

'Two hours of kick boxing will soon burn it off. But what's going to stop your gut spreading?'

Steve waggled his sandy eyebrows suggestively. 'I'm a newlywed, remember? Lots and lots of red-hot sex will sort my fitness out!'

Zoe sloshed him with her napkin while Libby made puking gestures. Charlotte just rolled her eyes and took another sip of wine. The warmth and easy chatter was a million miles from the strained atmosphere at work and slowly she felt the tension start to slide away. There was something so comfortable about being with Zoe and Steve; she didn't know whether it was the welcoming atmosphere of the dining room with its crimson walls and French windows flung open to the small courtyard garden, or whether it was the sense of love and acceptance she felt. But it was a world away from her cold, empty flat.

'So Steve's fitness plan involves lots of steamy shagging, does it, sis?' Libby teased her sister whose cheeks were peony pink. 'Sounds like a fab diet!'

'The F-Plan?' Charlotte refilled her glass. 'My ex-husband tried that one. Just not with me.'

There was a pause before everyone burst out laughing.

'You are so naughty,' Zoe said, shaking her blonde head. 'Poor Richard's ears must be burning worse than the fire of London.'

Poor Richard, indeed!

The next hour passed pleasantly as the four of them poured over the proofs that had recently been delivered by the photographer. There was that perfect day, forever frozen in time: Steve looking so handsome in his morning suit, Zoe looking picture-book perfect in her long dress with white roses woven into her hair, and Libby looking quite unlike herself in a cerise prom dress that showed off her tall, slim figure. Charlotte flicked through the pictures, pausing at one of Geoff looking dapper, if rather bemused, in his suit, a white rose in his button hole and a hand resting proudly on his son's shoulder. The photos of herself weren't very flattering, though, Charlotte thought critically. Maybe the black shift dress had been a mistake? She was frowning in most of the pictures and noticeably alone. The rest of the party made Noah's ark look like singles' night.

Damn. That lump was back in her throat again.

Taking a swig of coffee she gulped it away and turned

her attention back to the conversation that was now about the hen night and the huge amount of alcohol Priya and Libby had consumed.

'I seem to recall that you had a pretty major hangover too,' Steve reminded his wife. 'And there was I being read the riot act about how I should behave on my stag night. Oh the irony!'

'We were all very well behaved,' Zoe assured him, moving a picture of herself and Fern on to the 'keep' pile.

'And there wasn't a stripper in sight,' sighed Libby. 'I know I booked the psychic and everything, but I'd much rather have been running my hands over some bronzed love god's rock-hard pecs!'

'Rock-hard *what*?' repeated Charlotte, pulling a mock shocked face. 'Oh pecs! Sorry, Libby. I misheard you.'

'And they say *I'm* obsessed with sex,' giggled the younger girl.

'Just wait until the only place you have any hope of getting poked is on Facebook,' Charlotte laughed. 'Then you'll understand!'

'I've just eaten!' interrupted Steve. 'Please can I be spared the sordid details of your sex life, sis? Besides, what's this about a psychic at your hen night, Zo?'

'Nothing really,' Zoe said quickly – rather too quickly, Charlotte thought. 'Just another of Libby's zany ideas. It was a load of old nonsense.'

'It was not!' Libby disagreed with a toss of her white-blond mane. 'Angela was spot on with everything she told me.'

'It was all generic stuff designed to suck you in,' Charlotte scoffed.

Libby shook her head. 'You're wrong, Charlie. She's the real deal.'

'You kept this quiet,' Steve said to Zoe. 'I had no idea Mystic Meg was one of your hens. What did she tell you? No, wait! Let me guess. She said that you would marry a tall, handsome man?'

'If she did, she got that wrong,' dead-panned Charlotte.

'Thanks for that, sis.' Steve chucked a napkin at Charlotte then turned back to his wife. 'Come on, I'm really intrigued. What did she say? Anything exciting? Lottery wins? Kids? Is Elvis really alive somewhere?'

Zoe shrugged her slim shoulders. 'I really can't remember, babe. Nothing very important.'

After living with Richard for so long Charlotte had a finely tuned bullshit-ometer and right now it was on red alert. There was no way Zoe wouldn't be able to remember her reading. After all, Charlotte remembered every word of hers and definitely thought it was a big load of garbage.

'Mine was wicked!' Unlike her elder sister, Libby was bursting to share every detail. 'She told me that I'm a danger to men!'

'She was spot on there; you're a right maneater,' agreed Steve. 'I'm losing count of all the lovelorn messages on the answerphone.'

'And love will come to me through hope alone, apparently,' Charlotte recalled.

'That's good though, isn't it?' Libby asked.

Charlotte shrugged. Love was coming? Yeah right. She decided not to hold her breath.

Later, when Libby was blasting aliens on her Xbox and Zoe was embroiled in a phone call to Priya, Charlotte helped Steve load the dishwasher. They worked together with a speed and efficiency born of years of shared chores as she told him about Geoff's phone call.

'He's getting worse,' she finished bleakly. 'He's got absolutely no recollection of the wedding and he's so confused. I'm not sure how much longer he'll be able to cope alone.'

Steve pulled her into a bear hug, resting his chin on the top of her head. For a minute or two she let him, marvelling that her annoying kid brother had turned into this capable man.

'I'll pop in to Dad's tomorrow,' Steve promised, stepping back and leaning against the Aga. 'I'm more than happy to do my fair share of taking care of him. You've done more than enough already.'

Charlotte swallowed back the protests. Much as it went against the grain to admit that she needed support, she knew she couldn't handle this alone. 'Thanks.'

'Good. That's settled. What about you? How are you coping?'

'Me? I'm fine,' laughed Charlotte.

'Cut the crap; it's me you're talking to.' Clearly Steve saw through Charlotte as easily as he could see through the conservatory into the purple dusk. 'It can't be easy working with Richard and his new girlfriend.'

'It's fine,' she fibbed. 'Apart from the fact that they're practically having sex on the office carpet most days, you wouldn't even know they were together.'

'No hope of a reconciliation, then?'

Charlotte wasn't quite sure how to answer this. Part of her longed to turn the clock back and be with Richard again but surely things had gone too far for that to ever be a possibility? She was saved from having to try by her mobile ringing.

'Talk of the devil,' she said, holding the handset up so that her brother could see it was Richard calling. With a grimace she took the call.

'Isn't a booty call to your ex-wife in rather bad taste?'

Richard sighed wearily. 'I'm sorry for ringing so late in the evening. I hope I haven't interrupted anything?'

'Only a hot date with my toy-boy lover,' she told him airily.

'Ha ha,' said her ex-husband. 'Anyway, this isn't a social call; it's purely work. Suzie's been asked to take Dave's place on a three-day diversity conference so that means you'll have to join me on the trip up to Yorkshire.'

'Why me?' asked Charlotte. 'Why not someone young and silly like Cally? She's got a brain like an Aero, which makes her perfect for you.'

'I'll ignore that and remind you that you know those projects better than anyone else,' said Richard, and she could just picture perfectly the little crinkle of annoy-ance wrinkling his brow and the way he'd be tugging the curl above his left ear like he always did when he was frustrated. 'You're the senior communications officer so it has to be you. And just for the record, I'd much prefer to go with Cally – easier on the eardrums.'

'At least we both know where we stand, then,' she said calmly. Work was work after all. 'Fine. I think we can both manage to be adult about this and professional enough to make it up to Yorkshire without killing one another. Although', she added thoughtfully, 'they do say that arsenic doesn't have any flavour slipped into coffee.'

'I don't drink coffee any more. Suzie and I have gone organic and cut out toxins,' he informed her pompously.

Wow. Life in their household sounded a right barrel of laughs. Richard had always loved coffee. When he left the only thing he'd fought for was the Gaggia machine.

'Oh well, I'll just have to shoot you, then,' she said mildly.

Richard arranged to pick her up from her flat – which was still in both their names – horrendously early the next morning. Then he rang off leaving Charlotte about as relaxed as a coiled spring.

Fan-flipping-tastic. Several hours trapped in a car with her ex. A bikini wax would be less painful.

'At least you get to wrap those projects up yourself,' Steve pointed out after she filled him in on these latest and most frustrating developments. 'You were furious when Suzie took them over. What were they again?'

Charlotte opened her mouth to tell him but then started to laugh.

'What's so funny?' her brother said, looking confused.

'One of the charities is called the Hope Foundation.' She hummed the theme from *The Twilight Zone*. 'Maybe my prophecy is coming true after all.'

Steve's eyes widened. 'That's right! The psychic said love would come to you through hope! Maybe you'll find love at the Hope Foundation?'

Charlotte shook her head despairingly. 'Not you, too. Surely you don't believe that.'

He flicked her with a tea towel. 'Of course not. I'm just teasing, although there's nothing wrong with living in hope! In my book, there's always hope.'

Charlotte snorted. 'Spoken like a true romantic. I knew letting you read my teenage *Sweet Dreams* collection was a mistake.'

But Steve wouldn't give in and as they continued to clear up he went on and on about love and hope being more important than anything else until she tuned him out. Experience had taught Charlotte that there was no point putting your trust and hope in anything or anyone so hope wasn't an emotion she'd ever had much to do with.

Despair though – despair was quite another matter entirely.

Charlotte took her time checking and rechecking that the gas was off, the windows fastened securely and that she'd double locked the front door. Part of this was because she was thorough by nature, but the bigger part was because Richard was waiting outside in his silly little car, honking the horn and getting agitated. It was petty, but annoying Richard made Charlotte feel better.

When she'd satisfied herself that her flat could teach Fort Knox a thing or two about security, Charlotte made her way down the stairs, through the narrow communal hall with its skeletal spider plant and outside into the honeyed sunshine of an early September morning.

'About time too,' grumbled Richard as she stowed her luggage in the minuscule boot and slid into the passenger seat of the low-slung MX-5. 'I'd better put my foot down if we're going to make it to Yorkshire in time.'

Charlotte didn't know a lot about Yorkshire. Puddings, strong tea and *Emmerdale* were about the size of it, and, of course, *Wuthering Heights*, which she'd studied for A-level. Unlike most of the girls who'd swooned over Heathcliff, Charlotte hadn't really got the whole romantic hero thing. Hanging dogs and digging up corpses didn't really do it for her.

Yes, Heathcliff. Yet another man who'd treated his wife like crap. There seemed to be quite a few of them about.

The car was very small and every time Richard changed gear, his knuckles grazed her knee. Surreptitiously shifting as far away from him as possible she asked, 'How long will it take?'

'Five to six hours with me at the wheel.' Richard grinned. 'If you were driving, then about six weeks.'

If pushing buttons was what he wanted, two could play at that game. Leaning forward, she swapped radio stations from the blaring pop of Radio 1 to Radio 4 and the deceptively gentle tones of John Humphrys bullying some unfortunate politician.

'Hey, I was listening to that! Turn it back!' protested Richard.

Charlotte settled back into her seat. 'Aren't you a bit old for Chris Moyles? He's more for the twenty-somethings than the forty-somethings.'

He bristled, just as she knew he would. 'Radio four is hardly hip and happening, Lottie.'

'Should suit you down to the ground, then! Why don't you try and listen to it for a little bit? The current situation in Afghanistan is *slightly* more important than Comedy Dave's take on Jordan and Peter, wouldn't you say?'

Richard said nothing but his jaw clenched and he gripped the steering wheel so hard that she could see the knuckle bones through his skin. One, two, three . . .

'It's my car,' he snapped, flipping the station back to Radio 1, 'so I should be allowed to listen to whatever *I* choose.'

'That's mature,' Charlotte said. 'If you've paid for stuff or make more money then you call the shots, right?'

'That's rich coming from the world's greatest control freak!' Richard shot back. In a fit of rage he stamped on the gas and the car zoomed forward on to the Westway, slicing through the early morning traffic like a red bullet. 'No wonder you didn't want to have kids.'

That one stung. 'You were enough of a child for any woman! And I was right not to trust you to be there for me, wasn't I?'

His response to this was to put his foot down again, cutting up a white van and nearly causing them to crash into a BMW. Horns blared, hand signals abounded and for a second Charlotte's life flashed in front of her eyes.

Blimey. It didn't make for the most exciting viewing.

'I *would* have been there for you,' Richard was saying through gritted teeth, 'if you'd have let me. But you don't need anyone, do you, Charlotte? No one could ever match up to your exacting standards.'

'So I do have high standards, then? That's interesting. As I recall, you once said I was destined to be a terrible mother.'

That barbed comment, flung at her during a particularly heated row, stayed with her. After all, who was to say that being a useless parent wasn't genetic?

Her parents weren't exactly candidates for Mum and Dad of the year, were they?

Richard exhaled. 'I've apologised a thousand times for saying that. I didn't mean it. I was just pissed off at the time. You'd be a fantastic mum. Just look at Steve, if you need proof; you practically brought him up when you were a teenager, and he's turned out pretty well.'

Charlotte said nothing, pretending to be fascinated by the Art Deco splendour of the Hoover Building.

'You're never going to forgive me, are you?' said Richard sadly.

'I might think about it if you put Radio four back on,' she quipped.

With a martyred sigh her ex-husband changed the station back. 'Suzie always lets me choose,' he muttered.

Well, she's obviously as weak as you then, Charlotte thought to herself. Richard rarely saw anything through and could always be relied upon to change his mind. Today's little spat just showed that he was still the same. Why couldn't he stick to his guns, be it his choice of radio station or marriage vows? It was hardly the most attractive quality in a husband. Maybe she was to blame for choosing such a weak man in the first place? *Don't go there!* she told herself furiously. Blaming herself was toxic and she refused to do it. The truth of the matter was that he was a faithless git and Suzie – well, she was welcome to him. In the good-husband stakes Richard Sinclair had proven himself as much use as hot lettuce.

She closed her eyes wearily. It was going to be a long journey.

*

By the time Richard finally drew up outside a small hotel in the centre of York the sun was starting to slide from the sky and the city was bathed in light the exact hue of rosé wine.

Opening the car door, Charlotte almost fell out, grateful to be able to stretch her cramped legs at long last. It was also a relief to escape from an atmosphere that made the North Pole seem tropical. Since their argument they'd hardly spoken for the entire journey. Even when they'd stopped at the services they'd gone in separate directions. Richard had stomped off to the Burger King since Suzie wasn't there to lecture him, while Charlotte had plumped for a Marks and Spencer salad. If there were a sulking Olympics, Richard would definitely win gold. She'd thought she was off to York, not Coventry!

In any case, it was hard work being ignored, so when they were greeted by Cassandra, the Yorkshire District Arts Council's supervisor, her cheery smile and endless stream of chatter was a necessary tonic.

'Hello!' Cassandra beamed, pumping each of their hands with great enthusiasm. 'You must be Richard and Charlotte. Welcome to York!'

Cassandra's welcome was like basking in the Caribbean sun. She was a curvy brunette with skin like clotted cream and sparkling hazel eyes. Charlotte couldn't help smiling back. Before long even Richard had thawed.

'York's such a beautiful city,' gushed Cassandra,

escorting them up a flight of lichen-smothered steps and into the foyer of their hotel. 'Have you been before?'

'I'm afraid not,' Charlotte admitted, 'but what I've seen so far looks fabulous. The Minster is amazing.'

'Oh it is, it is!' Cassandra nodded, her wavy hair bouncing in agreement. 'You and your husband must have a look around when you get a spare minute.'

Charlotte opened her mouth to tell Cassandra that she and Richard only shared a surname these days – she'd never got round to taking back her maiden name – but before she could get a word in he took her arm and said smoothly, 'That would be great; wouldn't it, Lottie?'

What the hell was he playing at? Charlotte shot him a look that in a just world would have laid him out at her feet but Richard just smiled.

'Don't let's embarrass her,' he whispered. 'We can set her straight later.' To Cassandra he added, 'We can't wait to explore the city.'

'You'll certainly see a lot of it over the next few days,' Cassandra told him with great enthusiasm. 'The Hope Foundation's based in Picton; that's such a pretty village and I know you'll both love it. The Young Offenders Reform Company, YORC, is based in the city and they regularly put productions on at the Playhouse. That will give you lots of opportunities for some romantic exploration!'

'Great,' Charlotte muttered, glowering at Richard. 'We'll look forward to that, won't we, *dear*?'

'Heath – he's the man who runs YORC – is so inspirational,' Cassandra continued breathlessly. At just the mention of this name her eyes took on the zeal of a religious convert and her cheeks flushed prettily. Major crush alert!

'You'll love Heath, everyone does,' Cassandra was saying. 'The things he's managed to do with those young offenders are just awesome. Seriously, it's incredible! Heath transforms lives!'

'Wow. He sounds great,' Richard said. Catching Charlotte's eye he winked and, in spite of being annoyed with him, her lips twitched. Cassandra fancied this Heath rotten; it was obvious from the way his name peppered all aspects of the conversation. Even as they waited at the reception desk it was Heath this and Heath that. He was quite a paragon and by the time Cassandra paused for breath Charlotte had built up a vivid mental image of someone only slightly less holy than Jesus, bathed in pearly light and surrounded by hordes of adoring teenagers. Quite possibly a heavenly host were singing too. They certainly were for Cassandra, because after arranging to meet them both early the next morning she practically floated out of the hotel.

'Ain't love grand?' commented Richard.

'I wouldn't know,' Charlotte said crisply. 'But this Heath character must be something else!'

'Probably another bearded, socks-and-sandals wearing, next-to-perfect guy' said her ex-husband. 'I hate him already.'

'Now, now,' she scolded, 'we can't all be horrid cheaters like you.' She peered across the reception area and into the lounge bar beyond. For goodness' sake! Was anyone ever going to check them in? 'Hey, excuse me! Can we have some service please?'

A lumpen-looking figure with his back to them while he propped up the bar turned round slowly. He was nursing what looked like a whiskey and coke and Charlotte saw instantly that he had the high colour and bulbous nose that characterise the hardened drinker. In fact, stick her father in a tweed jacket and flat cap and he'd be a dead ringer for this character.

'Aye, just coming!' he called, giving them a cheery and totally unapologetic wave before weaving his way through the customers. After what felt like an age he arrived behind the reception desk and treated her to a Stonehenge-esque smile.

'I didn't see you two come in; just give me a minute and I'll fetch your key,' he said, diving under the desk and rattling about.

Charlotte felt her blood pressure start to rise. She was tired, desperate for a shower and couldn't wait to get away from Richard. Just her luck to be staying in York's answer to Fawlty Towers!

'I'm Archie Harries, the hotel owner,' continued a disembodied voice, followed by much rustling and clanking. 'Now where's that bloody booking sheet gone? Aha! Got it!' His head bobbed back up again and, squinting at a very screwed-up fax, he said, 'You must be Suzie Evans? We've spoken on the phone but it's right good to meet you in the flesh. And you're Richard Sinclair. I've given you room ten, the Honeymoon Suite, just as you requested.'

What! Charlotte was still reeling from the insult of being mistaken for her ex-husband's floozy when the words 'honeymoon suite' hit her like a bullet between the eyes. Richard and Suzie had booked the *honeymoon suite* for a work trip?

The bloody cheek!

'Nothing like dipping the pen in the company ink,' chortled Archie as he plucked a big brass key from a hook and held it out proudly. 'Still, I won't tell if you don't!'

Charlotte snatched the key from his meaty paw and scowled at Richard, who was so sheepish that all he needed was a fleece to complete the look.

'I'm really sorry, Lottie,' he said, totally unable to look her in the eye. 'I totally forgot to change the booking.'

'Oh!' Archie's bloodshot eyes were two big circles as he realised what was going on. 'She isn't . . . you aren't . . . well bugger me!'

'That's right,' Charlotte said grimly. 'I'm not. And we most certainly aren't. I'd like separate rooms please.'

'Oh dear, oh dear.' He shook his head sadly. 'I can't do that, I'm afraid, lass. All my other rooms are full. It's the music festival, you see. I'd be right surprised if there's a free room in the entire city this weekend.'

Charlotte's fingers curled around the key. It seemed that there were only two options left. One was to beat Richard to a pulp with the key – almost worth doing time for – the other was less satisfying but probably far less messy.

'In that case,' she said, fixing both men with a glare that should have turned them to stone, 'I'll be taking the Honeymoon Suite after all, and you, Richard Sinclair, can sleep on the floor!'

And with that she stormed out of the lobby leaving Richard open mouthed behind her.

5

B y the time she'd lugged her case up three flights of
stairs, each narrower and steeper than the one
before, Charlotte's face was as red as her hair and her
temper was simmering. How dare Richard book the
bridal suite for Suzie! In seven years of marriage he'd
never done anything like that for her.

If her temper had been simmering outside the room,
when she turned the key and flung open the door, it
practically boiled over; the room was absolutely
gorgeous. Nestled high in the eaves with the last rays of
the dying sun streaming through the windows like
crimson and orange ribbons, was an enormous,
fairytale-style, four-poster bed. Swathed with muslin
drapes drifting gently in the soft breeze and piled high
with pillows and duvets like snowdrifts, it was the most
romantic setting she'd ever laid eyes upon, and just
crying out for some Hollywood-style love scene. At the
far end of the room an oval window afforded a
breathtaking view of the city with the mighty spires of
the Minster peeking out over the haphazard rooftops,
and just beyond that was a smudge of green which had

to be the same moors where the Brontës' fevered imaginations had run riot. In front of this window, making the most of the incredible views, was an enormous roll-top bath complete with clawed feet, gold-plated taps and gallons of Jo Malone bath oils just begging to be used.

Richard could sleep in the bath, Charlotte decided, but she was having the products!

She padded to the bed, her shoes tapping across ancient floorboards that glowed warmly with beeswax, and threw herself on to it, nearly getting swallowed up in the process. Oh wow! *Call me Goldilocks, because this bed is just right*, she thought. In fact, she was going to spend the rest of her life all snuggled up in the soft marshmallowy duvet with the warmth of the September sun kissing her face. The rest of the world could just push off.

'Lottie?' Richard tapped on the door before peeking his head around. 'Are you decent? Can I come in?'

'If you're wondering whether I'm lying here naked and waiting for you, then the answer's no,' she snapped. 'Wrong woman, I'm afraid. I was once booked into a bridal suite with you, but not this time.'

'I feel terrible about this.' Richard massaged his temples with the heels of his palms and sank on to the bed beside her. 'I'm really sorry.'

'Sorry you booked it or sorry that I found out?'

'Sorry that I hurt you so much in the first place?' Richard's eyes were wide and pleading.

The comment made Charlotte's heart lurch. Was he

really sorry? Or perhaps he was just hoping that she wouldn't grass him and Suzie up to Dave. Their manager would not be impressed if he knew the Arts Council was funding Richard and Suzie's romantic break. If she was feeling really nasty Charlotte knew she could cause a whole lot of trouble for both of them. But what would be the point? It wouldn't undo the events of the past eighteen months, would it? And she was sick of being more bitter than the Jiff lemon factory. She might as well just enjoy making him sweat for a minute and then make the most of this beautiful room.

But maybe she'd make Richard take her out for a very expensive meal first. It was the least he could do under the circumstances. Besides, it had been hours since she'd eaten that feeble salad at the service station and her stomach was starting to rumble.

'Let's not start going over all that again,' she said wearily. 'How about if you take me out to dinner and we bury the hatchet?'

'You promise not to bury it in my head?' Richard asked warily.

'Hmm, tempting – but I'd rather eat!'

He jumped to his feet and held out his hand, his fingers closing around hers warm and strong and familiar as he hauled her off the bed. 'Well, come on, then. Let's go!'

A few hours later, with a very full stomach and pleasantly woozy from sharing a lovely bottle of white Burgundy – Richard always had had great taste in wine

– Charlotte was back in the room unpacking her suitcase.

In the end they'd ended up eating in the hotel because the menu looked superb. The meal had been exquisite, the rack of lamb so tender that the meat practically fell off the bone and the gratin dauphinois so swimming in cream and cheese that she'd blown her diet just looking at it. They chatted as they ate and Charlotte remembered with a pang just what good company Richard was. He was funny, he was good-looking and he had a witty anecdote about most things. But then enjoying his company had never been a problem, had it? She'd not ended it with him because he was boring.

To finish off the lovely meal, Archie insisted that the drinks were on the house to make up for the room fiasco. It was kind of him, but Charlotte had decided as she sipped her amaretto that if he made one more nudge, nudge, wink, wink, comment about her and Richard sharing the Honeymoon Suite, she'd rip his head off and beat him to death with the soggy end. She didn't find it easy being around Archie anyway; alcoholics always reminded her of her father and made her nervous. By the time she left the bar, Charlotte was feeling decidedly tetchy.

'Sorry about him,' Richard said eventually, breaking the silence as they got ready for bed.

'Who?'

'Archie. Honestly, I could have brained him for making all those silly comments about our room.'

She shrugged. 'It doesn't matter. He's not to know about our history.'

'I suppose not, but I know how hard you find it being around people who drink heavily.' He placed his arm around her shoulder and drew her against him. For a moment she stayed there, enjoying the familiar feeling of his body close to hers, but then he said, well and truly breaking the spell, 'Do you want to talk about it? It might help.'

Charlotte stepped back and goggled at him. 'Who do you think you are? Oprah bloody Winfrey? Of course I don't want to talk about it. I never did when we were married so what makes you think I'd want to now?'

He shrugged. 'I just thought it might be easier now that there's more of a distance between us. I know you don't like letting people get too close in case they let you down.'

Charlotte laughed. 'Nice try, Freud, but I'm really not that complicated! I just like to keep things private.'

'Yeah, I know that,' he said sadly. 'After all, you never did share anything with me.'

'I don't like talking about Dad. It's too upsetting.'

'But I wanted to support you!' Richard shook his head in frustration. 'I was your husband, Lottie! That was what I was there for. I worry about you. Keeping everything bottled up can't be healthy. There're so many of us who want to be there for you; Steve, Zoe and even me. Don't shut us out. Let us help.' He stepped closer and put his arm around her trembling shoulders once more. His touch was so comforting that her vision blurred dangerously.

'Don't cry,' he murmured into her hair. 'I didn't mean to upset you.'

'You haven't; I'm just tired,' she said, stepping out of his embrace and pretending to be totally absorbed in sorting out her washbag. She hoped that ignoring him showed that the conversation was closed. Richard sighed heavily but didn't argue. Instead he busied himself making up a bed on the floor, looking pained from time to time, but never once daring to suggest that they shared the four-poster. Charlotte couldn't help feeling pleased Richard knew her well enough to realise that when she made her mind up there was no point in trying to change it.

He had the divorce papers to prove it.

Still, later on that evening as she lay marooned in the middle of the enormous bed and her ex-husband snored softly from the floor, silent tears slipped down her cheeks and soaked into the feather pillows. Worry about her dad, deep sadness about the failure of her marriage and a horrible creeping fear that all these things were her fault, broke over Charlotte like waves. A tiny voice inside her said it wished so much things could have been different and that Richard was sleeping beside her, his arms holding her so close that she could feel her heart beating and his soft breath fluting against her cheek.

La, la, la! Her fingers were in her ears and she couldn't hear anything about regrets and sadness. Much as she might miss Richard, he was with Suzie now and everything had changed beyond recognition.

And there was no way she could forget that.

No way at all.

'Welcome! Welcome!' gushed Cassandra, who was waiting to greet them inside. 'Isn't Picton beautiful?'

'Stunning,' agreed Richard. 'We admired the scenery on the way up, didn't we?'

The only view Charlotte had enjoyed was of the inside of her eyelids as Richard drove like Michael Schumacher in a hurry, but she nodded anyway. Picton was set on rising ground north of York and consisted of a cluster of pretty cottages, a church and a pub. Personally, Charlotte got twitchy if she was less than two minutes from a Starbucks, but, as villages went, she had to admit it was very picturesque.

'We're really busy here today,' Cassandra was saying, gesturing towards a trestle table where a group of children and several adults were busily splashing paint around. 'As you know, the Hope Foundation's volunteers bring the arts to children in rural communities and at the moment we're gearing up for the Valhalla Festival. We're making banners and costumes today. Why don't you have a look and meet some of the children? Heath was only saying earlier how well they're doing when he popped in to drop off some paint for scenery making. Imagine! He drove all the way over just for that! But then, that's Heath for you. He always thinks of everyone else.'

Heath again eh?

'But anyway,' Cassandra said, blushing, 'I'm rambling. I expect you're dying to get chatting to the children.'

Actually, Charlotte would rather eat her toenail clippings. Children were an anathema as far as she was concerned. She never knew quite how to act with them, hating the idea of talking down to them, but never quite sure exactly what to say.

'Charlotte doesn't do children,' said Richard, and the edge to his voice was Sabatier sharp. 'They're not her cup of tea.'

From the look on Cassandra's face you'd have thought Richard had said Charlotte killed kittens in her spare time. It was a reaction Charlotte was getting more and more used to as she crept through her thirties.

'You don't like children?' asked Cassandra, amazed and horrified in equal measure.

'It's hard to like people who eat sweets all day and don't get fat!' Charlotte quipped swiftly, and luckily Cassandra laughed.

'You had me going there for a while! Why don't you have a chat with the group making Viking helmets?' she suggested. 'They're getting ready for a reenactment of the invasion of York in 975.'

Leaving Richard and Cassandra to discuss funding issues, Charlotte wandered towards the lively group of children wielding paintbrushes. They were laughing and chatting as they worked and the plastic mats around them were splattered with bright paint. Taking a deep breath, and wishing she'd chosen to wear her plain black Marks and Spencer trousers rather than her Donna Karan suit, she joined them.

She'd show Richard she wasn't useless with children!

'Hello, everybody,' she said brightly. 'Are you all having lovely fun?'

Abruptly the laughter died and ten pairs of eyes fixed themselves on her face. Charlotte wished she could sink through the scuffed floorboards. Hello everybody, are you all having lovely fun? What did she think she was? A 1950s BBC announcer?

'Why have you got those big lines by your mouth?' piped up a small girl with bright boot-button eyes. She pointed her paintbrush at Charlotte, oblivious to the gloopy brown paint dripping down her hands. 'Is it because you're sad?'

'Isla, don't be so rude! Say sorry to the lady,' gasped one of the adult helpers in horror, while the other children started to giggle. Fighting the urge to check her wrinkles in her compact, Charlotte pasted a bright smile on to her face and said that it didn't matter at all.

'Say sorry, Isla,' insisted the helper, but the little girl just looked confused.

'Is the lady very sad, even though she's smiling?'

Blimey, thought Charlotte. *Talk about out of the mouths of babes!*

'Of course she isn't!' Red-faced, the helper could hardly look at Charlotte.

'But she *has* got sad lines there! Like this!' Raising her paintbrush the child painted two big streaks round her mouth and, in spite of herself, Charlotte started to laugh. Soon all the children were laughing and slopping paint on to their faces until they resembled a tribe of braves. Their helper rolled her eyes.

'Now they're off! We'll never get these costumes finished now.'

Charlotte sat down at the table, picked up a paintbrush and waved it in the air. 'I'll be an extra painter. What do I do?'

'I'll show you,' Isla offered, slipping from her seat and, to Charlotte's great surprise, wiggling up on to her lap. 'It's easy. All you have to do is colour. But inside the lines, OK?'

'OK.' She nodded. 'I'll give it a go.'

Isla painted, her small pink tongue poking out between her lips as she concentrated. Richard joined them.

'What's been going on?' he asked with a grin. 'It looks like you've been teaching them how to put on make-up, Charlotte. They all look just like you!'

'Very funny!'

'Who said I was joking?' He pulled a face, waggled his eyebrows, sending the kids into peals of mirth. 'Now are you guys able to look after Charlotte for me while I do some paper work with Cassandra? Just call me if she misbehaves, OK?'

The children nodded and Richard winked at her. 'Try not to drown them in the paint, Lottie! We know what you're like with children.'

He was such a natural with kids and this had always

made Charlotte feel worse. Maybe she would have been a hopeless mother? Maybe not. The point was he'd been pretty quick to give up on her.

And that really hurt.

Well, she'd show him just how good she was with kids. These guys were having lots of fun, weren't they? And little Isla seemed very happy sitting on her lap so she couldn't be all bad.

Before long the children had finished painting all their banners and the helper was busily pegging them on to a makeshift washing line so that they could dry. *I actually enjoyed that!* Charlotte was surprised to find herself thinking. Buoyed up by this success she started playing an imaginary game with Isla and some of the smaller children. It involved imagining that the table was a kitchen and the red paint a big bowl of tomato soup. The kids were giggling away and having a lovely time until one small boy decided he wanted to eat some.

'Oh no, Harry! Don't really drink it! It's pretend soup!' Charlotte cried, reaching across the table to stop him. Unfortunately, she didn't have arms the length of Mr Tickle's. Seconds later, the little boy had downed the lot.

Charlotte's hands flew to her mouth in horror. He'd drunk half a pint of paint! *Oh my God! I've poisoned a child!*

'Harry!' She leapt to her feet, not caring that she'd knocked canary yellow paint all over her expensive trousers, and flew to the other side of the table. 'Harry! What have you done?'

Harry's bottom lip quivered. 'You said it was soup!'

'Pretend soup!' Charlotte said in despair. 'It was a pretending game, wasn't it? You weren't supposed to drink it.'

Oh God, what did she do now? Pour him some water? Rush him to hospital? For a split second she was frozen with indecision – not a sensation she was accustomed to – before Harry solved the problem by being sick all over the table.

'Yuck!' squealed Isla, jumping away in disgust and knocking more paint over. The other children joined in, voicing their disgust loudly and flicking paint at one another. Harry started to wail, some of the smaller ones joined in the sobbing and, try as she might, nothing Charlotte said could comfort them or stop the bigger ones from splattering each other.

She'd totally lost control. How had that happened? Charlotte Sinclair was *always* in control.

'What on earth's going on?' Storming in like a paratrooper Cassandra took in the chaotic scene with wide and horrified eyes.

'That lady told Harry to drink paint!' said Isla, pointing at Charlotte. 'And he's been sick!'

'I didn't tell him to drink the paint,' Charlotte said quickly. 'We were playing an imaginary game and—'

But Cassandra wasn't listening, she was too busy clapping her hands and restoring order to the room. The helpers – who'd been outside on a cigarette break – were quickly set to work clearing the mess and mopping up the children, while Cassandra wiped Harry's face and quietened him.

'I'm really sorry,' Charlotte said. 'I had no idea he'd take the game literally.'

'Harry's got Aspergers,' Cassandra said wearily. 'It's a form of autism that means he takes everything literally. He doesn't understand the idea of pretending.'

Charlotte felt terrible. 'I'm so sorry! I just assumed they'd all be able to tell imaginary things from real ones.'

'That's why you should never assume anything when working with children,' Cassandra snapped. Even her corkscrew curls seemed to bob in outrage and Charlotte felt even worse. 'Luckily the paint's water based, but I think I'd better nip down with him to the doctor's for a check over, just in case. When it comes to safeguarding children we can't be too careful.'

Charlotte hung her head. There wasn't anything she could say, was there? In the space of twenty minutes she'd practically poisoned one child, made four others cry, and allowed the rest of them to behave like something from *Lord of the Flies*.

Richard was right all along. She would have been a hopeless mother.

The afternoon's activity didn't involve paint – thank goodness – but making balsa-wood Viking ships instead. No accidents had occurred, to Charlotte's great relief, and now the excited children were going to race their boats down the small stream known as the Picton Stell. Competition to win was fierce and as Charlotte walked down to the river, the warm September air was filled with excited voices piping even more loudly than the larks and swallows guzzling the midges by the river bank.

The boat-making activity had been organised by Isla's father Paul, a broad-shouldered and open-faced man who clearly adored his daughter. The children all sensed his apparent kindness and flocked around him, hanging on his every word and really keen to impress him with their boats. The afternoon had flown by.

'Have you enjoyed today?' Paul asked her as they walked along the river bank.

'Actually I have!' Charlotte replied, pretty astonished. The day – paint-drinking disaster aside – had actually been a lot of fun.

Paul gave her a cheeky wink. 'Does that mean we'll get another year's funding?'

'Now that would be telling! Although after what happened to poor Harry, another year's funding is probably the least I can do.'

'You really should stop beating yourself up about that. You weren't to know Harry's autistic,' he said sternly. 'These things happen. I know the others are teasing you, but try not to take it to heart. It could have happened to anyone.'

'Could it?' Somehow Charlotte doubted this. After all it hadn't happened to anyone, had it? It had happened to *her*.

Once it had become clear Harry was none the worse for his misadventure, the paint saga had been a source of much mirth and although Charlotte had taken it in good humour a part of her was still really upset. Richard, who had about as much sensitivity as Simon Cowell, cracked jokes endlessly, but Paul had sensed she was upset and steered the conversation round. Charlotte could have kissed him for that. Actually, maybe she could have kissed him anyway. He wasn't her usual type, being sandy haired and stocky with a freckle sprinkled snub nose, but she couldn't help finding his sweet personality attractive.

'I shouldn't have assumed they knew the difference between pretending and reality,' Charlotte said sadly. 'I'm not much use with children.'

Paul shook his head. 'Are you kidding? You're *great* with them. Isla thinks you're brilliant.'

She shot him a sceptical look. 'Because I let her paint her face and throw paint around?'

'No, you're wrong. She likes you because you take the time to talk to her. Not everyone can be bothered to do that. You must admit, Isla does ask a lot of questions.'

Charlotte laughed. That was an understatement. While they'd built their boats, Isla had interrogated her thoroughly, on everything from why she was sad to why was her hair such a funny colour?

'I like talking to her; she's a great kid,' she told him.

'I'm biased, but I certainly think so!' Paul smiled and Charlotte found herself thinking how much she liked the way his eyes twinkled. 'I don't know what I'd do without her. Kids give you a reason to keep going. When things went wrong with Elise, it was only because of Isla that I was able to get up in the mornings.'

'Elise? Is she Isla's mum?' Almost of their own accord Charlotte's eyes slid to the third finger of his left hand which was circled by a plain wedding ring. Glancing up she realised that Paul had seen her checking his ring finger out and her cheeks flamed.

'Sorry, that was really nosey. It's none of my business.'

Paul sighed. 'It's no big secret that we're separated. Elise is my wife and Isla's mum. We're not together at the moment and I'm not sure if we ever will be again. It's all down to Elise, really.'

Paul looked upset so Charlotte didn't press the matter. She supposed, like Richard, he'd cheated. Men! Why couldn't they be satisfied with what they had, appreciate how good it really was? Was there a man alive who wasn't a total disappointment?

For a few minutes they walked along in thoughtful silence, warm in the hazy September sunshine and soothed by the merry babbling of the river. A tractor was ploughing the field on the other side of the river, a flock of greedy birds following the tracks scored into the rich red earth just as the children were following her and Paul by the water's edge.

'How long are you staying in Yorkshire?' Paul asked eventually. 'Will you be around for the Valhalla Festival? I've been working on a life-sized replica of a Viking longship for the opening ceremony; we're going to sail it down the Ouse. It should be quite a spectacle.'

The subject of Isla's mum was closed. Well, that was fine. She knew how hard it was to talk about personal things; hadn't she evaded all his questions about her personal life?

'I'm only here for a few days, unfortunately. The festival sounds like a lot of fun, though. I'd have loved to have seen it.'

'Maybe you could come back?' Paul suggested softly. 'I'd be happy to show you around, if you'd like? No pressure, it might be fun.'

She looked up into his open, honest face. 'Do you know, I think I could use some fun! Maybe I'll take you up on that offer.'

'You make sure you do,' he said and they smiled at each other for what felt like ages until Richard broke the spell by jogging over and interrupting.

'There you are, Lottie,' he said, a frown creasing his brow when he saw how close she was standing to Paul. 'Listen, I don't want to be a party pooper, but can we get a move on? There really isn't time to play with boats, I'm afraid. I've got serious amounts of work to do and I really need an Internet connection.'

'Really?' Charlotte was surprised at his sudden keenness to leave. Richard normally put work off for as long as possible. Then she saw the suspicious expression flitting across his face and the penny dropped. He was jealous! The irony! He, of all people, had no right to be possessive. Oh, this was far too good to waste!

'Don't worry about the boats,' Paul said quickly. 'You guys go if you need to. I can handle the balsa boat racing. It's nothing compared to the big ones, believe me.'

'Oh?' Tilting her chin flirtatiously Charlotte widened her eyes at him. 'I thought size wasn't important?'

Paul laughed. 'No comment! But pop in to the workshop and see for yourself!'

'She will not!' spluttered Richard. He looked so indignant on her behalf that Charlotte started to laugh.

'He means the boat he's building,' she reassured him. 'At least,' she added cheekily to Paul, 'I think that's what you mean?'

'What else?' He dead-panned.

'Well, maybe I'll find out if I pop over and see your etchings – I mean carvings,' Charlotte said. 'I'd love to know more about the festival too.'

'Maybe over lunch,' Paul promised her. 'Now I'd

better go and race those boats or I'll have a mutiny on my hands!' And he waved as he walked back towards the children.

'Can you believe that? He was chatting you up!' Richard exclaimed.

'Don't sound so surprised. It does happen,' Charlotte said tartly.

'I didn't mean it like that. You're not going to meet up with him, surely?'

'Why not? He seems really nice.'

Actually Charlotte hadn't really got any intention of meeting up with Paul. One unfaithful man was enough for any lifetime, thanks, but there was no way she was going to tell Richard that. Firstly, it was none of his business and, secondly, seeing him so annoyed was very satisfying.

'I don't trust him,' Richard huffed. 'And neither should you. A single dad playing the sympathy card is only after one thing.'

Charlotte flicked her hair back from her cheeks and gave her ex-husband a dazzling smile.

'In that case,' she said airily, 'I'm *definitely* going to meet him!'

7

Charlotte decided that she was feeling really excited about the day. She was looking forward to seeing how YORC had developed over the past twelve months and to meeting the mysterious Heath, of course. She just hoped that Richard would be in a better mood. What must Paul have thought? She'd never actually got around to explaining her situation but he must have guessed that she and Richard had more history than David Starkey. It couldn't carry on. She'd have to lay it on the line with Richard or they'd never manage to work together.

Just as she was thinking this, her mobile rang. Sure enough it was Richard.

'There's no one here with me, if that was what you were about to ask,' she said wearily.

Richard sighed. 'I'm sorry about yesterday. I behaved like a bit of an idiot, didn't I?'

Charlotte remained silent.

'OK! I behaved like a complete tosser,' he admitted. 'Of course you can date whomever you like; it's none of my business any more. I've forfeited the right to be possessive.'

'About the same time you decided to sleep with Suzie,' she replied.

'I asked for that. But you're right. I'm the last person who has any right to behave that way. Can you forgive me for being a dick?'

'Provided you don't pull that Neanderthal act again. It's YORC today and the only people behaving like adolescents should be the adolescents!'

'I totally agree,' said Richard swiftly. 'And talking of YORC, I've just had a message from Heath. He's going to pick us up from the hotel at half eight. Apparently parking's a real pain in the city centre and it will save us trying to find a space if we go with him.'

Charlotte checked her watch. Goodness, that was less than an hour away! Telling Richard that she wasn't going down to breakfast and would see him outside the hotel, she leapt out of bed and started to run a bath. Sloshing in a gallon of Jo Malone's Grapefruit and Basil and slapping on a face pack, she soaked for ten minutes before calling room service and ordering strong coffee and toast. While munching her breakfast she applied her make-up and selected her outfit for the day. What a shame that the Donna Karan suit was out of the question. Its figure-skimming lines always made her feel confident and professional, two qualities that she really wanted to convey to the infamous Heath when she finally met him. Her only other suit had a very short skirt and there was no way she was going to meet him showing that much leg. She might as well write *come and get it* on her forehead! There was nothing for it but her black boot-leg jeans, scoop-neck grey sweater and spike-heeled ankle boots. It was a casual outfit but still smart and at least it didn't look as though she'd tried too hard.

Not that she was even thinking about trying hard. Why on earth should she?

Still, as she left the room Charlotte couldn't resist giving herself a quick once-over in the full-length mirror. She looked smart but the boots gave her outfit an edgy twist. She was still wearing her trademark subdued colours but at least her red hair was nice and cheerful and her skin rosy from the bath.

She'd do.

Outside it was a beautiful September morning with sunshine drizzled over the old buildings like honey and a faint nip in the air. The Virginia creeper that smothered the hotel was deepening to a russet hue and the petrol-blue sky arching above was clear and cloudless. After staying up late reading *Wuthering Heights* to get her in the spirit Charlotte couldn't help feeling the day was better suited for a stomp on the moors than being stuck inside a theatre. Yorkshire was starting to get to her. Maybe she wasn't such a townie after all?

There was no sign of Richard – he was probably still wolfing down bacon and eggs – and neither was there any sign of Heath. He was probably too busy saving the world.

She raised her face to the sun, closing her eyes and

revelling in the warmth. When she opened them again a muddy Defender had parked defiantly on a yellow line outside the hotel. The driver's door creaked open and a pair of long denim-clad legs swung out, followed by a muscular torso in a holey sweater, and then a big bouncy dog the exact colour of autumn leaves.

Charlotte checked her watch. When she looked up the driver was striding towards her, his powerful legs eating up the distance between them in just a few easy strides. She couldn't help staring because he had to be one of the most attractive men she'd ever seen. Beneath a mane of thick corn-coloured hair was a tanned and rugged face, the jawline of which was sprinkled with golden stubble. He had sparkling emerald eyes and a wide, generous mouth which curled into a welcoming smile as he held out a hand to her.

'Hi! You must be Charlotte? I'm Heath Fulford, from YORC. It's great to meet you!'

It wasn't often that Charlotte was lost for words but as Heath encased her slender, freckled hand in his large strong one she was rendered totally speechless. This was no bearded, caring, sharing, eco-type in Birkenstock's. Far from it! Heath Fulford looked more like a Botticelli angel, albeit a rather dissolute and sexy one, than a grungy do-gooder. Cassandra's obsession was starting to make a whole lot of sense!

'I'm sorry about the tatty Land Rover,' he was saying in a clipped public school accent that only contained the faintest trace of a Yorkshire burr. 'It's a real boneshaker, I'm afraid, but I live up on the moors and when the weather's bad it's a godsend. Oh, and I hope you don't mind Tilly being with us,' he added, nodding at the dog. 'She loves to come out for a drive and when she gives me her pleading look I just can't say no!'

The conker-bright Irish setter, all floppy ears and shiny ginger coat, was gazing adoringly up at her master with big brown eyes, a look that Charlotte would bet was repeated in the eyes of every other female the man came across.

'It's good to meet you too. And you too, Tilly,' she replied, relieved that she sounded calm and collected. Heath's good looks aside she was also taken aback by his height because he seemed to tower over her. At five feet ten she was not exactly vertically challenged and so feeling tiny and fragile was an alien sensation. She felt awkward but Heath was totally at ease, chatting away about YORC and how busy they were with the Valhalla Festival approaching. His manner was so open and friendly that in spite of herself she began to relax.

'I'm really looking forward to showing you guys around today,' Heath was saying, his hand idly smoothing Tilly's head as he smiled down at Charlotte. 'The kids I've been working with have so much acting talent. I think you'll be amazed how good they are.'

'I'm looking forward to meeting them too,' Charlotte said, smiling back. 'And it's nice to put a face to your name. I've heard an awful lot about you.'

Heath raised a quizzical eyebrow. 'Oh dear! That sounds ominous! I suspect *awful* is the operative word! Can I assure you that only the good bits are true?'

'I didn't hear any good bits, I'm afraid,' Charlotte dead-panned, and Heath laughed.

'Are the bad bits interesting? Maybe I should say they *are* true?' His eyes locked with hers and Charlotte felt her cheeks grow warm under the intensity of his gaze.

'You're looking a tad pink, Ms Sinclair! What on earth has Archie been telling you?' Heath grinned, a dimple playing hide and seek in his cheek when he saw her horrified face.

'What do you think he's told me?' Really, she wanted to hear more from the horse's mouth.

'Let me guess,' said Heath slowly, running a hand through his hair. 'How about: I have more baggage than Louis Vuitton and a reputation that makes Casanova look like a monk? Am I right?'

'Something like that,' she said, and wondered what on earth this baggage might be. A tragic tale? A broken heart? A yarn worthy of Brontë and Shakespeare put together? For goodness' sake, now she was at it! How did Heath Fulford inspire such romantic notions in women?

Heath laughed. 'That sounds way more exciting than the truth! Widower who lives in the middle of nowhere with three adorable stepchildren and a very demanding dog is far closer to the truth, but not nearly half as exotic. As for having an exciting love life . . .' He shrugged ruefully. 'Believe me, nothing wrecks your love life more thoroughly than having kids around.'

'I find having colleagues in tow wrecks mine,' said

Charlotte dryly as Richard came haring out of the hotel towards them, clutching a bacon buttie.

They were still laughing at this when Richard joined them, looking a bit put out not to be in on the joke. Introductions made, Heath ushered them into the Defender, apologising for the dog hair, sweet wrappers and empty fast-food packaging that covered practically every surface, and they got on their way.

'Tell us a bit more about YORC,' Charlotte said to pass the time on the journey and to cool her rising temperature.

'As you know, our goal is to try and channel juvenile criminals into the dramatic arts to give them some focus and outlet for their energy,' Heath said, his green eyes meeting hers warmly. 'Twice a year we approach fourteen- to eighteen-year-olds with the chance to audition for a play which we put on at the Playhouse. It's a big deal; sometimes we even get talent scouts and agents coming to watch which really gives the kids a buzz. Some of them have had no hope since birth and to see them blossom on the stage is just amazing!'

Heath's voice was brimming with emotion. *He really loves what he does*, Charlotte realised. It was more than just a job; working with these young people was his passion.

'What's the play this year?' Richard asked.

'*Wuthering Heights*,' Heath said. 'No jokes about my name please!' he added when Richard started humming the Kate Bush song. 'Blame my mother; she was a big Brontë fan!'

'Mine too!' Charlotte said, delighted at this common ground. 'I was named after Charlotte Brontë, her favourite author.'

'Parents eh? Didn't Philip Larkin have a good point about them fucking you up?'

She had to agree. Her mother and Geoff had done a sterling job on her.

'It's a bit of a cliché, but it certainly applies to some of the kids you'll meet today, that's for sure. That's why it's so important to give them other opportunities and boost their self-esteem. Drama's fantastic for that. It really transforms them.'

Despite her reservations, she couldn't help liking Heath. His devotion to the kids was really impressive.

They pulled up outside a square concrete building and Heath switched off the engine. The sign on the door said YORC in big letters, and underneath were some choice words written in scrawled graffiti. Charlotte guessed they had arrived.

'Before we go in there're just a few things to bear in mind.' Heath paused, his fingers on the handle of the driver's door. 'Some of these kids won't be easy – in fact, they'll be bloody hard work, and they might be a little antagonistic to start with. Just bear in mind that all they really need is consistency and someone they can trust, someone who won't rise to the bait. And, believe me, surly teenagers really know how to bait you.'

'They sound just like you, Lottie,' Richard said, grinning.

Heath's mouth set in a determined line. 'I'm serious.

Don't rise to anything they say and don't take it personally if they're not particularly welcoming. It takes these guys a while to trust anyone so they'll be pretty suspicious of you at first.'

Charlotte swallowed. Small children were one thing, but great hulking teens quite another. Still, it wouldn't do to let Heath see that she was feeling nervous.

'I can't wait to meet them,' she said brightly.

But as they walked into the youth centre Charlotte felt quite intimidated by the hard, challenging stares of some of the teenagers. Chewing gum and looking as though they had PhDs in boredom, they were certainly less than welcoming towards her and Richard. Two skinny girls curled their lips and sneered openly while a couple of lads sniggered. Charlotte gulped.

Their reaction towards Heath, though, was another matter entirely. As he guided his guests past posters of a glowering Eminem and into a room crammed with bean bags and battered sofas, lots of the kids called out to him, their sullen faces lighting up as though someone had switched on the electric.

The difference in them was staggering and Charlotte was filled with admiration. It was clear that these kids absolutely adored Heath and she could hardly wait to see what magic he worked to make such a transformation.

'Heath, my man! Good to see you, bro!' called a lanky black lad, high-fiving Heath who returned the greeting enthusiastically.

'Damien! Good to see you too! How's it going?'

'Safe,' Damien told him. 'I got a job at Morrison's. I start next week. Result!'

'That's great!' Heath was clearly delighted with this news. 'Well done, Damo! That's fantastic.'

'Yeah,' Damien agreed. 'But it means I can't be in your play, man.'

Heath slung an arm around Damien's wiry shoulders. 'Damien's one of YORC's star actors. He was the most amazing Tybalt in our *Romeo and Juliet*. He got a standing ovation and a local agent signed him.'

'Wow, well done,' said Charlotte. 'You like acting, then?'

'Yeah! It's pretty all right, as it goes.'

Once Damien had high-fived Heath again and gone on his way, Heath explained his situation.

'Damien did time for dealing,' said Heath. 'His background's bloody awful and it's a miracle he's actually made it to seventeen. Anyway, to cut a very long and very bleak story short, he got involved with YORC last year and he's a seriously talented actor. Finding something he's good at made a huge difference to his self-esteem and I'd be very surprised if he reoffended now.'

'That's some success story,' Richard said, looking impressed.

Heath nodded. 'Damien's worked really hard. He's even helped to write the play we're putting on now. Not bad for a kid who left school without a single qualification.'

'Not bad at all,' Charlotte agreed. 'In fact, that's amazing.'

Before long the room was crammed with teenagers.

Some were really shy and just listened as he explained what the play would involve, some were really excited and asked lots of questions and some were just plain difficult and mocked the whole idea. Heath didn't seem bothered by this; he just shrugged and suggested that they give it a try – it might be more fun than sitting around doing nothing. Before long, scripts were being circulated and groups of teenagers were reading the lines aloud to one another. Listening in, Charlotte realised with a shock that some of them were really struggling to read.

'A high percentage of young offenders have really poor literacy skills,' Heath explained when she expressed her surprise. 'They fail at school, aren't supported at home and are truant for most of their school career. Then they end up getting into trouble and the whole cycle of criminality begins. Damien's kept the language in the script quite straightforward but some of the kids will still struggle to read it. That's not good for their self-esteem so I've tried to make sure there's one fairly reasonable reader in each group to help out and I've also let them improvise.'

'You know them all really well.' Charlotte was impressed. There had to be at least thirty teenagers in the room.

Heath smiled. 'I guess I do now. They're great kids and they all have something to offer, even that lot.' He gestured to three boys who'd scrunched their scripts up into balls and were kicking them about. 'Isn't that angry, insecure attitude pure Heathcliff? Let's start the auditions, shall we, and see what they can do! That lad there, Justin, is a good sport. He's been in trouble for graffiti – his tags are everywhere in York, I'm afraid – but his heart's in the right place.'

Pushing his thick golden hair back from his face, Heath strode over to the lads, beckoning to one with a mane of curly brown hair and eyes as dark as molasses. 'Hey, Justin! Do us a favour and read a bit of Heathcliff's part for us, would you?'

Justin pulled a face but unscrewed his script good naturedly and sauntered into the centre of the room. Within seconds a hush had fallen as the kids formed a semicircle and waited for him to perform. He didn't disappoint, hamming up the part by reading it in a really camp voice and playing it for laughs, which he certainly got.

'Cathy! Cathy!' he lisped, mincing across the stage like a young Alan Carr. 'Ooh! I love you so much!'

Then Justin gave the audience an exaggerated bow and turned to Heath.

'Have I got it?' he said cheekily.

'You can't act, you can't sing, you can't dance,' said Heath in a scarily good Simon Cowell impersonation, steepling his fingers under his chin and narrowing his eyes thoughtfully. 'That was quite simply the worst audition I have ever seen.' He turned to Charlotte. 'What do you think, Cheryl?'

'I loved him!' Charlotte said enthusiastically, trying, and failing, to do Cheryl Cole's Newcastle accent. 'One million per cent yes!'

The other kids cheered and she felt ridiculously chuffed. They were coming round, just as Heath had promised. Richard had relaxed too and was chatting to a group of lads about the parts they wanted. Heath had been right; trust was the key to helping these damaged youngsters.

'OK, Justin.' Heath nodded. 'You can have the part, but only if you do it in that *exact* voice and dressed up like Lily Savage!'

'No thanks,' Justin said quickly. 'Couldn't I work behind the scenes?'

'Why don't you take charge of the scenery?' Charlotte suggested, struck by a sudden bolt of inspiration. 'I've heard you're quite an artist!'

'A piss artist!' yelled one of the boys and Justin flipped him the finger.

'I've never been called an artist before,' he said to her with a wide grin. 'I'm not Van Gogh, Miss. I spray paint bridges and walls. I don't paint pictures.'

'If you can spray paint bridges, I'm sure you could design sets,' Charlotte said, instinctively knowing this was something that really mattered to Justin. 'I bet you'd be brilliant! Just think of all those blank walls that you'd be able to paint *without* getting into trouble.'

'Wicked! Can I do it, Heath?' cried Justin.

'Of course, if you'd like.' Heath gave Charlotte an appreciative smile.

'Cool!' More bouncy than Tigger, Justin bounded across the room, bubbling over with ideas of how he could bring an urban hip hop vibe to the Brontës.

'That was inspired,' Heath said warmly. 'He *is* a really talented artist, even if he doesn't have any faith in himself, and this'll keep him off the streets for weeks. I think I need to poach you from the Arts Council.'

Under the gaze of his emerald eyes, so thickly fringed with dark lashes and so undeniably sexy, Charlotte's cheeks became hotter than the nuclear core of Sellafield and she looked away hastily. 'I don't think so; I'm hopeless with kids.'

'That's rubbish. See that sulky pair, Shannon and Kylie?' He nodded towards two skinny gum-chewing girls with big hooped earrings, hair plastered into high ponytails and their faces caked in so much make-up that they made Jordan look natural. 'I overheard them saying how your boots look mint.'

Charlotte was confused. 'What have my boots got to do with anything?'

Heath laughed. 'Getting a compliment from those two means you are in!'

'Really?'

His appraising eyes never left Charlotte's. 'Yes, really. Why do you find that so unbelievable?'

How long had he got?

'The kids like you,' he went on. 'Believe me, you'd soon know if they didn't!'

Digesting all this, Charlotte felt ridiculously pleased. Nobody had ever said she was cool before. Cold yes, but cool? Never.

After Justin's star turn the auditions carried on for another hour. Just when it seemed that everyone who wanted to had read for a part, a plump girl who'd been scrunched up on a bean bag and hiding behind a curtain of limp brown hair asked if she could audition for Cathy's role. When she said this Kylie and Shannon sniggered nastily and even Heath looked surprised.

'Are you sure, Ruby?' he asked.

Ruby nodded. 'I've learned the words,' she whispered.

'Of course you can.' Heath still looked taken aback but he gave her an encouraging smile. 'Start whenever you're ready.'

Ruby clomped into the centre of the room, heavy and awkward in her oversized top and clumpy boots. Instantly there were more sneers and nasty comments about her weight and baggy clothes. Flushed with mortification but determined to do her audition, she acted out the part with real feeling and intensity.

'I am Heathcliff, Nelly!' she cried, her hand on her heart and her eyes bright with passion. 'He's more myself than I am!'

'Poor Heathcliff,' sniggered Kylie. 'She'd squash him flat, the fat cow!'

Ruby stopped mid-line and her plump cheeks grew red.

'Yeah, it's a play not a wrestling match, fatso!' added Shannon nastily, and all the others joined in laughing while poor Ruby's eyes filled.

What a nasty piece of work! Charlotte hated bullies – they'd made her school days pretty damn miserable and even now the taunts of *gingernut* and *Duracell* still rang in her ears – and she couldn't stand seeing anyone picked on. There was only one remedy for girls like them – a large dose of their own medicine!

'OK girls,' she said sweetly, 'you obviously think you can do better, so let's prove it, shall we? How about you, Kylie? Do you fancy going next?'

Kylie paled at the thought. 'No miss, please don't make me. I don't like doing stuff in front of people. It's embarrassing.'

'Really? That's odd, from what you said to Ruby I assumed you must be a really good actress. Well, what about you, then, Shannon?'

Suddenly Shannon found the tips of her scuffed ballet pumps absolutely fascinating and her bitchy comments withered on her bright scarlet lips.

'What, neither of you are going to audition?' Charlotte asked in mock amazement. 'It's just as well other people are brave enough to have a go, isn't it?'

'Yeah, like Ruby just did,' chipped in Justin as the two girls slunk away. 'Respect, Rubes!'

Ruby flushed and looked as though she wanted to sink into the floor. *Poor kid*, thought Charlotte. Any attention, even the positive kind, was unwelcome when you were that self-conscious.

Auditions over, Charlotte helped Heath gather the scripts together.

'Why's Ruby here?' she asked. 'She doesn't seem the type to be on a young offenders' programme.'

Heath's eyebrows shot up into his thick blond fringe. 'And what *type*'s that, exactly? A girl with a cheap pink tracksuit and big hooped earrings? Or maybe someone who can't read and who doesn't speak properly?'

Oops. She'd really dropped herself in it. That was *exactly* the kind of kid she'd pictured.

'That's the kind of prejudice these teenagers face every day,' Heath continued, his deep voice laced with irritation. 'That's why it's so difficult for ex-offenders to move on even when they want to make a fresh start. People make assumptions about them and before long those assumptions become self-fulfilling prophecies.'

'I'm so sorry. I didn't mean to be insensitive. I just wondered why she was here,' Charlotte apologised. Heath looked really annoyed; those eyes were the dark stormy green of an angry sea now. She'd only asked a question, surely this was a bit of an overreaction?

'If you want to know, why don't you ask her?' he suggested quietly.

Yet again she'd messed up. How many signs did she need to have before the truth finally sank in? She really wasn't cut out to work with kids. Teen or tot, it didn't matter.

She was equally hopeless with both.

With a heart heavier than concrete, Charlotte gathered up her notes and joined Richard who was shooting pool with a couple of teenagers.

'Hey, Lottie, fancy a game? Us against them?' He grinned, looking up from the shot he was lining up. 'Zak and Nick here have been thrashing me and it's not good for my ego . . .'

'Nick's well good; don't feel too bad, man,' said a tall, skinny lad with a shock of carroty hair, Zak she presumed, who was lolling against the pool table and chewing gum with a loud smacking sound. 'He beats Heath every time.'

'Heath is crap,' said Nick.

'Where is St Heath anyway?' Richard asked. 'Don't say he's abandoned us to this lot of savages? We'll never get out alive.' As he said this he winked at the boys who laughed and gave him the finger. They were really at ease with Richard, Charlotte thought with a twinge of jealousy. What was wrong with her that everyone she came into contact with ended up feeling awkward or upset?

She sighed. 'I think I've annoyed Heath by being tactless.'

'That doesn't sound like Heath.' Nick looked surprised. 'He's normally well chilled. Remember when you hit him with that table?' he added to Zak. 'Most olds would have been well pissed off, but he was OK.'

Charlotte gulped. Big sixteen-year-old lads chucking furniture about wasn't her idea of fun. She felt a surge of respect for Heath because he could work with these difficult kids and literally handle everything they threw at him. And more than that, he really cared about them too. YORC was one of the most challenging projects she'd ever come across and after spending the morning with the kids she was starting to see how working with drama was pivotal in rebuilding their damaged lives. Zak had tried out for the part of Hindley Earnshaw and, with his smouldering temper, he'd be a natural for the role, something she now realised that Heath had known all along. Far better to be working through his anger issues on the stage than by chucking things at people.

Suddenly Charlotte really wanted him to know that she understood what he'd been saying, needed him to know that she *got* YORC.

'Finish your game. I need to find Heath,' she said to Richard.

'Richard won't be long! He's no match for me!' Nick boasted, and unable to resist the challenge, Richard brandished his cue and broke. Leaving him to it, she turned on her spiked heel and strode from the room, only to cannon straight into Heath.

'Easy, tiger!' he said as he caught her shoulders and steadied her. 'Not running away, I hope? Although I wouldn't blame you after the way I just lectured you.'

'I was on my way to find you,' she replied. Goodness, it was a weird experience to have to crane her neck upwards to look at a man. 'Heath, I'm so sorry I wasn't more sensitive about Ruby. It was really crass of me to make assumptions. Her past's absolutely none of my business.'

Heath shook his head, the lion's mane falling into his eyes. 'You've got nothing to apologise for. In fact, I was just on my way back to apologise to *you*. I had absolutely no right to preach at you like that. I'm afraid I'm a tad oversensitive sometimes when it comes to the kids.'

'Just a tad?'

'Well, maybe more than a tad!' Releasing her shoulders he held out a hand. 'Friends?'

'Friends,' Charlotte agreed, letting him take her hand. His fingers were strong and calloused with the nails cut short. Working hands, she found herself thinking, and totally unlike Richard's which were more manicured than any WAG's.

'I'm forgiven? You won't pull the plug because I was an idiot?'

'Of course not,' she assured him.

'Phew!' Heath looked relieved. 'I thought I'd blown it! Seriously, though, I really am sorry for going off at the deep end. How about if, to make up for it, I take you out for dinner tonight?'

'Dinner?'

'Dinner.' Heath nodded, his green eyes twinkling down at her in amusement. 'It's when people sit down and eat food? I don't know what you lot do down south but we northerners really enjoy it!'

Charlotte hesitated. Heath seemed genuinely contrite and for most of the day he'd been great company. But dinner? She didn't usually socialise with her clients, unless sandwiches with Cassandra and the kids counted! Instinctively, she felt herself stepping back and her fingers slid away from his firm handshake.

'That's a very kind offer but you really don't need to.'

'No, I'd like to. Richard's invited too, of course. You've both been such a great help and I'd like to thank you. I know a great Italian. Their Carbonara's to die for.'

'I don't think it's a good idea, people might misconstrue—'

'People? Do you mean the Arts Council's spies in York?' he teased. 'Now I'm really scared. Seriously, though, if it helps, I'll ring your boss and clear it with her.'

Charlotte thought that the last thing Suzie probably wanted to hear was that her boyfriend and his ex-wife were gadding about all over York together and living it up in Italian restaurants. She'd flip, summon them back and probably make Richard drink nothing but green tea for a week.

'That really isn't necessary,' she said quickly.

'So come to dinner, then,' insisted Heath. 'Try and convince her!' he begged Richard who had just joined them.

'Convincing Charlotte to do anything she doesn't want to do is nigh on impossible,' Richard sighed theatrically, 'as I know, to my cost. What are you trying to persuade her to do?'

'I'd like to take you guys out for dinner as a thank-you for all your help today,' Heath explained but, although the words were addressed to Richard, that intense green gaze never left her face. 'Charlotte's worried it will compromise your integrity as assessors.'

'Rubbish!' snorted Richard. 'Course it won't, unless the food's terrible, in which case it might seriously jeopardise your chances. Where are you taking us? Not McDonald's, I hope!'

'I had thought Burger King, but maybe you'd prefer this Italian I know? It's small but the real deal, run by a family from Naples. And if that doesn't convince you, they have a great Prosciutto.'

Richard's eyes lit up. 'After being thrashed by Nick, I need a drink!'

'How can we be impartial chattering over wine?' Charlotte protested but she may as well have been talking to herself because Richard was accepting Heath's invitation on her behalf and punching the restaurant's details into his BlackBerry. Charlotte supposed she could stay at the hotel but the thought of spending an evening propping up the bar with Archie didn't appeal. Besides, she couldn't trust Richard to not say anything embarrassing if she didn't accompany him. Once he had a few drinks he tended to become the life and soul of the party and what little discretion he did have went right out of the window.

She took a deep breath. 'Fine, I'll come. But it can't be a late night.'

Heath gave her that stomach-flipping smile. 'Don't worry, it won't be. My stepchildren and animals get me up at the crack of dawn so I need my beauty sleep! We'll talk about everything except work and I promise one hundred per cent not to bring my high horse with me, let alone mount him!'

And with that, Charlotte supposed, she had to be content.

A few hours later Charlotte was seated in a snug red booth, squeezed far too close to Richard for comfort, and sipping at white wine so deliciously chilled that the glass streamed with condensation. The restaurant was dimly lit and at each table a candle shoved into the neck of a Chianti bottle dribbled stalactites of wax over smudged green glass. The walls were smothered in bright murals of the Amalfi coast, ice cream-coloured houses clinging precariously to sheer brick-red cliffs while a bright blue sea churned below the dizzy heights. She and Richard had always loved Sorrento, spending many holidays there, and she looked away quickly. Why did it still hurt even after all these months? She glanced down at her menu but it wasn't really much of an escape, seeing as it was all written in Italian. Just as well she'd visited so many times with Richard; she could probably just about manage to translate.

Delicious smells of wine and garlic drifted in from the kitchens every time the waiters charged through the swing doors, and her mouth watered. Maybe this evening wasn't such a bad idea after all?

As though reading her mind Heath said, 'It's a great restaurant, isn't it? Are you glad you came now?'

'Certainly am, it's fantastic,' Richard agreed, sloshing more wine into a glass the size of a bucket. 'I love the fact they haven't even bothered to translate the menu!'

'They're fiercely proud of being Neapolitans,' Heath explained. 'Giuseppe wouldn't countenance polluting his precious menu with English.'

'We'll get by,' Richard said, running his finger down the menu and hovering it over *Pescatore*. 'Lottie and I've spent a lot of time in Italy. It's one of our favourite holiday destinations. We love Capri, don't we?'

'Hmm,' Charlotte muttered. Great, now Richard was wittering on about all the places they'd visited. She hoped he wasn't going to spend more time wandering down memory lane than eating his dinner. He'd only had half a glass of wine and already he was getting pink-cheeked and nostalgic. She took a big slug of her own drink. She really didn't want to get into another relationship autopsy in front of a client.

Heath dashed his palm against his forehead. 'The penny's just dropped. You guys are married, aren't you? You have the same names. Like *duh*, as my stepdaughter would say!'

Damn! Charlotte knew she should have got a new business card with her maiden name blazoned across it in glorious Technicolor. Luckily she was saved from the awkwardness of having to explain their situation when the waiter arrived and they were totally occupied with translating the menu.

'Do you two have children?' Heath asked her later when Richard had nipped to the bathroom.

Charlotte's stomach went into freefall. She hated it when people asked that question and normally snapped back to keep their nose out, but something about the openness and sincerity in his green eyes stopped her in her tracks. As far as Heath Fulford knew she was a happily married woman in her mid-thirties. What could possibly be more normal and more natural than having children?

'No,' she replied quietly. 'We don't. It's a long story. Let's not go into it right now.'

Heath looked mortified. 'I'm so sorry, Charlotte. That was a bloody tactless thing to ask. I ought to know better – I used to hate it when people asked me and Rachel that. It's just that the kids loved you today. I couldn't help thinking you'd be great parents.'

Charlotte looked down at her wine glass and tried her hardest to swallow the lump that had suddenly materialised in her throat.

'Things aren't always the way they seem,' she said eventually.

There was a pause and when she looked up those appraising green eyes were smoky with sadness. 'Oh, I know all about that,' he said softly. 'I really do.'

Charlotte took a deep breath. Something about

Heath inspired confidence. He was such a soothing presence and a careful listener. Just as she was about to tell him the truth, that Richard had left her because she was too afraid to have children, her ex bounded through the restaurant with the speed of a pinball, cannoning off tables and apologising loudly to the other diners.

Heath said kindly, 'That wine must be stronger than it looks! I'd better be careful. If I roll in drunk tonight, I'll never hear the end of it. I'll be grounded for setting a bad example!'

Taking his cue she asked, 'How many stepchildren have you got?'

'Three,' Heath replied, topping up their glasses with the dregs of the wine before Richard could pinch it. 'Rachel and I would have had our own but the cancer put paid to that idea. I'm so lucky to have the stepkids, though; they really kept me going when we lost her.'

Heath really was a nice man, Charlotte decided, blinking back the tears that suddenly blurred her eyes.

'I'm so sorry,' she told him.

Briefly, so briefly it was almost as though she'd imagined it, he put his hand over hers. 'Thanks,' he said softly.

Then Richard was plonking himself down at the table, dropping a kiss on to Charlotte's cheek, pulling her tightly against him as though the past eighteen months had never happened, and her moment of intimacy with Heath vanished like mist in the sunshine.

'A guy nips to the loo and all the wine gets guzzled!'

Richard grumbled, holding the bottle up to the light and squinting at it. 'I'll order us another bottle, shall I?'

Catching her eye, Heath raised an amused eyebrow. 'Looks like I'll be getting that lecture after all!'

'You could hire your stepchildren out,' Charlotte suggested. And they could start with Richard.

Richard knew how much Charlotte hated people getting really drunk around her. A few drinks and a good time were fine, but being properly drunk was something else entirely. She just hoped he'd not choose tonight to get totally plastered. That really wouldn't look professional.

Over dinner – which was every bit as delicious as Heath had promised – they chatted easily about everything from the Valhalla Festival to Heath's passion for drama. Richard told a few terrible jokes but Heath seemed to think them amusing and even Charlotte found herself laughing at his stories. Richard had always been a brilliant raconteur, leaping from topic to topic like a verbal gymnast, and he was never afraid to make fun of himself. She was laughing so much over a tale about how he'd managed to lock himself out of the house naked that she'd hardly noticed his hand slipping from her shoulder to her knee, so that his smooth fingers were now caressing the top of her jeaned thigh. He might be tipsy but this was really pushing his luck, she thought as she shifted her leg away. Just because she didn't want to embarrass Heath by explaining the truth about their relationship didn't mean she was giving a green light to Richard.

Anyway, what the hell was he playing at? They were divorced, for heaven's sake! He was with Suzie now. If he tried anything else he'd be wearing the tiramisu as a hat, and bollocks to what impression she gave Heath!

Once the Amaretto coffees were drained and Heath had gone to settle the bill, she unpeeled Richard's arm and hissed, 'What are you doing?'

Richard peered at her, which must have been harder than it looked because his pupils kept sliding in different directions.

'I love you, Lottie,' he slurred, trying to take her hand but missing it. 'You know that, don't you? I should never have let you go.'

'Don't start,' she groaned. 'I'm really not in the mood to deal with you in this state.'

Richard pulled his sad puppy dog face. 'Don't be horrible; I'm not a drunk. I've had a few too many glasses of wine, but I'm not your father!'

'Don't bring Dad into this!'

'Why not? He's what all this is really about. You think men are all the same and that we're all going to let you down.'

She glared at him. 'I haven't exactly been proved wrong so far, have I?'

It was just as well Heath returned at that moment to say their taxi had arrived because she was ready to brain her ex-husband with an empty bottle. How dare he talk about her father? That was private family business.

And as her *ex*-husband he was no longer a part of her family.

'Are we going now? Oh shit! The floor's moving!' Richard clambered to his feet, swaying dangerously from side to side, and clutching Charlotte for support.

Heath looked alarmed. 'How's he managed to get himself into this state?'

'He isn't usually this bad!' Charlotte said.

Heath helped Richard up. 'Come on, lean on me. I'll help you to the taxi.'

Somehow between them they managed to guide Richard through the restaurant without wrecking the place, and bundled him into a cab. Promising to call the next day and arrange a return visit to YORC, Charlotte bade Heath goodbye and sank into the seat as the taxi pulled away. What a nightmare. She *knew* she should have stuck to her guns and said 'no' when Heath asked them to dinner. Now she'd have to get Richard back to the hotel, up three flights of stairs and into bed, which was above and beyond her duties as a colleague, never mind as an ex-wife.

'I'm really sorry,' Richard said in a small voice. 'Honestly, Lottie, I didn't mean to get pissed. You believe me, don't you, babe?'

Charlotte exhaled wearily. This was typical Richard; he never meant to do any of it. From bringing mud into the house to sleeping with their boss, he never *meant* it to happen. Things just happened to him.

'It's OK,' she said, resigned to having to drag him to his room and put him to bed, fully clothed obviously, because there was no way she was getting quite that up close and personal with her ex. 'When we get back to the hotel you're going to drink lots of water and then sleep it off. You'll be fine in the morning.'

In the darkness Richard reached for her hand and clasped it tightly.

'You're the best. You really are. I don't deserve to have you.'

'You don't have me,' she reminded him. 'You have Suzie, remember?'

'But I still love you,' he said sadly. 'Suzie was a big mistake. I only slept with her because I was angry. I love you, Charlotte. I always have. I really, really love you.'

'Be quiet, Richard; you're drunk,' she said, exasperated. 'You don't know what you're saying. Shut up now, or you'll feel even more of a prat tomorrow.'

'Yes, I'm drunk,' he slurred, 'but I'm not so drunk I don't know what I'm saying. I love you, Lottie. I love *you*. I've always loved you.'

Charlotte ignored him. Richard was an affectionate drunk, given to loving everyone when he'd had a few beers.

'I mean it,' he said. 'I want us to have babies and everything.'

'Oh do shut up,' said Charlotte wearily.

Richard sighed heavily. 'You don't believe me, but it's true. I love you.'

Once they were back at the hotel, with the help of the cabbie and Archie she managed to drag Richard up the stairs and to the Honeymoon Suite. Charlotte was relieved to finally be alone in her attic room. Pulling off her spike-heeled boots – what bliss to wiggle her toes –

she flopped on to the four-poster and closed her eyes. Although the room was peaceful, her noisy thoughts were whizzing around like Formula One drivers on the final lap of the Grand Prix.

He'd been drunk, that was certainly true, but he'd been pretty insistent that he meant what he was saying. Was there any truth in it? Did he really still love her as he claimed? Was there still hope for her and Richard?

That night, and for the first time in months, Charlotte fell asleep smiling.

Charlotte's good mood evaporated first thing in the morning when she wandered into reception only to be told by Archie that Richard had left for London. Taking his car with him!

'Apparently your boss needed him back urgently,' said Archie apologetically. 'He didn't look great.'

She bet he didn't after the state he'd been in last night. The idiot was probably still over the limit. Charlotte felt like screaming. When would Richard grow up? Yet again he'd run away to avoid a tricky situation.

'He asked me to tell you that all your travel costs will be reimbursed by the company,' Archie continued. Well, that was the least he could do. Charlotte had a good mind to call a limo company and hire herself a personal chauffeur.

'Let me get you some bacon and eggs,' said Archie, leaping up from his bar stool. 'A good hearty Yorkshire fry-up's what you need.'

Charlotte grimaced. No it wasn't. In fact, she couldn't stand the thought of breakfast; she'd much prefer her usual espresso but Archie seemed to have broken the machine so all that was on offer was tea the colour of varnish. Besides, even if she had felt hungry earlier, suddenly she didn't any more. Now she felt sick, sick with fury at herself for almost falling for what Richard had said last night. Never again!

So much for *in vino veritas*. It was off to the Hope Foundation on her own. She called a local cab, reasoning that although a limo might be nice, it wasn't the Arts Council's fault that her ex-husband was a coward, and the cab was rather comfy.

When she arrived in Picton the children were making swords and Viking helmets out of tinfoil and cardboard. Deciding not to get involved this time – cardboard or not, those swords looked lethal – she cast her eye around the hall. Isla was hard at work on her tinfoil helmet but there was no sign of Paul. What a shame, it would have been nice to have seen a friendly face. Waving at Isla and promising to admire her handiwork later on, Charlotte resigned herself to a gruelling morning of paperwork and number crunching with Cassandra.

'Morning!' Cassandra beamed, curls boinging merrily and cashmere-clad boobs jiggling as she scuttled across the hall to meet her. 'How are you this beautiful day?'

'Fine, thank you,' Charlotte replied, but she was thinking: *Crap, actually. I'm feeling like an idiot because I nearly gave my ex-husband a second chance.*

Dealing with the Hope Foundation without Richard turned out to be a godsend, Charlotte decided later as she queued for a much-needed coffee in the hall. Without having Richard there she could concentrate fully on her work. Last night her personal life had been in danger of overshadowing her professional one and this morning's sensation of losing control had been hideous. Maybe it was time she looked for another job? Working with Richard and Suzie was proving to be more and more difficult and it was hard to make a clean break when she saw him day in, day out.

But I love my job, she thought angrily. *Why should I have to lose it because of them?* She'd worked at the Arts Council first and, childish though it might sound, Charlotte felt this gave her the right to stay. She'd known it had been a bad idea for Richard to apply for a job in the same office, but he'd shrugged off her concerns and applied anyway, saying that working together would be fun.

No one was laughing now.

At least she'd managed to escape the morning's workshop and actually got quite a lot of red tape completed, not as easy as it sounded with Cassandra suffering from Heath Tourettes. At every opportunity she dropped his name into the conversation and couldn't resist boasting that she was meeting him for lunch. If she could have hung a sign on him that said: *Hands off, he's mine!* Charlotte suspected she would have done. They were dating, then. This rather surprised Charlotte. She'd only met Heath once but she would never have thought that Cassandra was his type. Then again, what did she know about relationships?

'Tea or coffee?' asked the pretty blonde who was manning the urn in the hall. Her wrists were so slender that it was a miracle lifting the mugs didn't snap them. 'Or would you rather have a fruit tea?'

'No, thanks. I need some caffeine!' Charlotte replied with feeling. In fact, after two hours in the company of Heath Fulford's number one fan, a stiff gin would have been more like it. 'Could I have two spoonfuls of coffee, please?'

The blonde girl laughed. 'Goodness! I take it you've had a heavy morning?'

'Paperwork mostly.' Charlotte pulled a face. 'The Arts Council's pretty big on pen pushing and box ticking and I'm the lucky girl who gets to have all the fun.'

'Sounds riveting! And Cass, bless her, isn't the most scintillating company at the moment, I don't suppose?'

Charlotte laughed. 'I am a bit *Heathed* out!'

'Oh dear, aren't we all?' The girl smiled, spooning two huge spoonfuls of Nescafé into a mug and adding water from the urn. 'Still, I suppose you can't blame her for being all starry eyed. Heath Fulford's sex on a stick, isn't he?'

'Hmm,' Charlotte replied noncommittally.

'Good for Cass, I say. When you get to our age, decent single men are a bit thin on the ground, aren't they? Rarer than the Dodo in these parts.'

'Too right,' agreed Charlotte, with feeling.

The girl sloshed milk into the mug and passed it to

Charlotte with a smile. Delicate lines fanned out from the corners of eyes, the same soft blue as her faded jeans. Looking at her more closely, Charlotte realised that she was older than she appeared, mid-thirties rather than early twenties, although she had the slim frame of a teenager and her bouncy blond ponytail continued the illusion.

'Oh dear. You've had an ex from hell, I take it?' She tipped a packet of chocolate digestives on to a plate and offered one to Charlotte. 'Sorry! Ignore me, if you like. I ask far too many questions. My daughter takes after me!'

She waved at a group of children who were still intent on tipping glitter on to their swords. Isla, the small blonde always asking questions, looked up and beamed at them.

'Come and see my shield, Mummy!' she called. 'And you, Mrs Charlotte!'

'Oh my goodness!' gasped Charlotte as the penny not so much dropped as walloped her on the head. 'You're Isla's mum! You're Elise!'

'Oh dear, who's been talking about me?' Elise grinned.

Charlotte's face burned with embarrassment. 'I'm so sorry! That sounded really rude! It's just that I spent a lot of time with Isla and Paul when I was here last.'

'I know.' Elise smiled. 'You're Mrs Charlotte and my daughter thinks you're the bee's knees. It's been Charlotte this and Charlotte that at home!'

'She talks about you non-stop too,' Charlotte told Elise. 'She thinks you're wonderful.'

Elise's eyes grew suspiciously bright. 'Believe me, the feeling's mutual!'

'No, you're spot on. She's very honest, but that's not necessarily a bad thing.'

'She gets that from her dad.' Elise laughed. 'Paul always says what he thinks, which sometimes drove me crazy. But never mind *my* ex, I think you were just about to spill the beans about yours? And being a nosey cow, I'm intrigued!'

Charlotte shrugged. 'It's not very exciting really. There's not that much to tell.'

Elise raised an eyebrow. 'Now I don't believe that for a minute!'

Charlotte laughed. 'Guilty as charged. Where do I start? It's such a cliché I'm almost embarrassed to tell you. We'd had a row and I asked him to give me some space, which he interpreted as my giving him permission to go and sleep with another woman. Apparently it was meaningless but I don't believe that. Sex is never meaningless, is it? Somebody always gets involved or hurt.'

Elise said nothing, and Charlotte went on, 'Richard isn't all bad, but how do you ever forgive somebody for betraying you like that? He threw our marriage vows back in my face and now every time I look at him all I can think about is him sleeping with Suzie. The trust has gone and it can't ever come back, can it? He probably did me a favour in the long run. Who wants to live with a cheat for the rest of their life?'

She paused. Elise's wide blue eyes shimmered with

tears. Immediately Charlotte could have kicked herself with her spiked heel. How could she have been so tactless? Elise was separated from Paul who, charming and sweet as he may have appeared, had more than likely cheated on her too.

'I'm so sorry,' she said quickly. 'That was really thoughtless. I know you and Paul aren't together any more.'

Elise dabbed her eyes with her sleeve. 'Did he tell you why?'

'No, but I can guess. Men are all the same.'

'No, they're not,' said Elise, taking her arm. She led her away from the coffee station to the back of the hall where it was quieter. Exhaling wearily she said, 'Paul didn't cheat, Charlotte. I did. I slept with someone else and I broke his heart.'

Charlotte's mouth swung open on its hinges.

'I'm not trying to justify what I did,' Elise continued, her voice clotted with regret, 'but things between us weren't good. Isla was tiny and I was rushed off my feet looking after her all day. I felt like I'd woken up in somebody else's life. Paul was working such long hours that we hardly saw each other. He'd come in from work, wolf down his dinner and then crash out on the sofa. We'd stopped seeing each other as people and I felt unloved. More than that, I think I felt unlovable.'

She paused and took a sip of coffee before shaking her head sadly. 'You can probably guess the rest. We had a row one night over something petty and I stormed out. I ended up in our local and before I knew it I was plastered. It was a stupid, meaningless one-night-stand and it ruined my marriage. Paul can't forgive me and I can't say I blame him. I really didn't mean to, though, and not a day goes by when I wish I hadn't!'

There was absolutely nothing Charlotte could say to this. She felt desperately sorry for Elise who was mopping her eyes again with her sleeve. She obviously loved Paul. Then again, if she'd truly loved him so much how could she have treated him so badly? Black and white made sense to Charlotte. Grey areas irritated her. But this situation made her stop and think.

'I'm sorry,' she said awkwardly. 'That's a very sad story.'

'Well, there you are,' Elise agreed miserably. 'The worst thing is it's Isla who suffers because she doesn't have her parents together.'

Charlotte glanced at Isla who was shrieking with laughter at Harry whose hat had dipped right over his face. 'She seems really well adjusted to me.'

'We've tried hard to keep things normal for her sake,' Elise explained. 'Paul and I mostly get on fine and we've never argued in front of her. I suppose I always hoped he'd come round one day and we could try again. But now I'm starting to wonder . . .' Her voice trailed off sadly.

Elise's head was drooping like a thirsty tulip and, although her sympathies were obviously with Paul, Charlotte couldn't help feeling desperately sorry for her. She also felt a prickle of guilt regarding her own attraction to Paul, especially now seeing as she'd really warmed to Elise.

'Sorry,' Elise sniffled, giving Charlotte a watery smile. 'I didn't mean to inflict my tale of woe on you. What, with a morning of Cass, and now me, I wouldn't blame you if you cancelled our funding altogether and hot-footed it back to London!'

'Don't be silly,' Charlotte said. 'Actually, I've been really impressed with what I've seen here.'

Elise nodded. 'Isla can't stop telling me all about the Vikings. Thor the Thunderer and all his Valhalla gang are like members of the family these days! And talking of Isla, she'll never forgive us if we don't go and see what she's been working on. I'm not really sure whether Vikings actually had pink glittery weapons. It's a bit too blinging for the dark ages, in my opinion!'

'Pink Vikings?' Charlotte grinned at the thought. 'This I must see!'

Leaving Elise to clear away the tea and coffee things she joined the glitter-smothered children at their craft table. She admired Isla's lipstick-pink sword and Harry's acid-green shield and it wasn't long before she was making one of her own, and thoroughly enjoying every minute. There was something really soothing about messing about with a Pritt stick and a tub of glitter, Charlotte decided as she put the finishing touches to her design, and chatting to the children was also good fun. They had such vivid imaginations and before long they were embroiled in a game which involved Vikings and Saxons having a fight. Minor skirmishes abounded as glue sticks, screwed-up paper and even balls of wool were lobbed across the table.

Moments later Harry was sobbing loudly because a glue stick had hit him on the head and Isla was wearing the entire contents of a tub of table confetti. It was a glue-and-glitter massacre!

Charlotte's stomach was churning like a washing machine on the spin cycle as she felt control slipping away. Not again! Why was it that as soon as she got involved the kids decided to flout every health and safety directive going? Seeing Harry's hand hovering over a pair of scissors, Charlotte knew she had to act fast. Spotting Paul arriving she saw her chance.

'There's the big, bad Viking King!' she cried, pointing to Paul who instantly cottoned on, picked up a tinfoil sword and roared loudly.

'Who dares to catch the Viking King?'

Brandishing her own sword Charlotte turned to the wide-eyed children. 'We can't fight each other now! We need to catch the Viking King! Come on warriors, after him!'

Their squabbles instantly forgotten, the children leapt up and charged towards Paul. Like the experienced father he was, he allowed them to chase him around. Tinfoil swords flashed, glitter dusted the floor and the children screamed with excitement.

'You'll never get me!' Paul shouted. 'I'm the Viking King!'

But the children just squealed all the louder and chased him some more as he pretended to run away, leaping behind tables, weaving in and out of chairs and finally ducking behind Charlotte.

'Save me,' he pleaded, cowering behind her as the children advanced, led by Isla and her bright pink sword. 'Don't let them get me!'

But it was too late. A sea of small people engulfed Charlotte and Paul, cardboard swords slicing the air and shields bumping against their calves. Pretending to fight them off and making some very convincing blood-curdling noises along the way, Paul fell to his knees.

'I surrender!' he gasped, slumping on to the floor with his arms and legs spreadeagled. 'Your army is too good! You win!'

'We got you! We got you!' squealed Isla, jumping on to his chest and screaming with excitement when her father bench pressed her into the air.

'You sure did,' Paul agreed. 'You guys were awesome. Those weapons really worked, didn't they?'

Harry looked at him pityingly. 'They're not real. They're cardboard.'

'And he's not really a Viking king. He's my daddy!'

She said this so proudly that Charlotte felt a pang of loss which almost took her breath away. Would she ever know how it felt to hug her own child tightly and love them right back, the way that Paul was hugging Isla now? Probably not, because Suzie hadn't only stolen Richard, had she? She'd also stolen any hope Charlotte had of having a family of her own.

'Hey, are you all right?' Paul asked, concerned. 'You looked really sad just then.'

'I'm fine,' Charlotte said quickly. This was no time for her biological clock to start ticking, not when she'd been hitting the snooze button for years! Taking a deep breath she added, 'I just need to get my breath back. We childless folk aren't used to so much fun.'

'You don't have any children?' gasped Isla, eyes wide with disbelief. 'Why not?'

'Isla!' Paul said sharply. 'You can't ask grown-ups things like that!'

Isla looked confused. 'Is it rude?'

'It's a very personal thing to ask,' floundered her father.

Isla's little face screwed up into a frown. 'But I think Charlotte would be a lovely mummy. She makes up really good games! Don't you like children?'

Paul looked mortified. 'Of course she does, sweetie. But not everyone has children.'

'Why not?' demanded Isla.

'Umm . . . Well . . .' Flustered, poor Paul couldn't think of the words to explain to a little girl all the social, economical and biological reasons that someone might not have a baby.

'Please don't worry,' Charlotte said. 'I'm not embarrassed Paul, I promise. Quite the opposite, actually!' Isla's comments about her being a lovely mummy had given her a warm glow. If Isla liked her, maybe she wasn't quite so useless with children after all.

'So why don't you have any children?' Isla asked.

That was the million-dollar question, wasn't it? Charlotte was starting to think that even if she spent a year in therapy, she'd never get to the bottom of this one, so explaining it to Isla wasn't going to be easy.

'I haven't had any children because it just never seemed the right time,' Charlotte told her finally. 'But I think people who have got them are very, very lucky. And your daddy is especially lucky to have you.'

'I won't argue with that,' Paul agreed, setting Isla down and ruffling her hair. 'But Isla's right; you're a natural with kids, Charlotte. They loved every minute of that game, although I need a lie-down now and an Anadin to get over it.'

The little girl nodded. 'It was brill! Charlotte made it up and it was much more fun than fighting with glue sticks and scissors.'

Paul's eyes met hers. 'Well done, you! That sounds like quick thinking.'

'Never quicker. After the other day's paint-drinking trauma I wasn't prepared to take any risks.'

His gaze locked with hers. 'So you don't like taking risks?'

Charlotte gulped. This time there was no mistaking the interest in his eyes. *I like you*, they seemed to say, *and I think you feel the same, don't you?*

The question was, did she?

'I guess it depends on what I'm risking,' she said slowly.

'Having a drink with somebody?' Paul suggested. 'Too risky?'

'I guess it depends on who was asking,' Charlotte replied. Oh God, was she flirting? And with his ex-wife only across the room? This was so not a good idea.

But the pitter-pattering of her heart seemed to say

quite the opposite. Maybe it was time to stop being sensible.

'What if it was me?' Paul said softly and her stomach flipped like a pancake.

'Daddy really likes you,' Isla piped up. 'He was talking about you loads yesterday!'

'Oh dear, there goes my cool!' Paul sighed. 'Aren't kids great? In my defence, I was saying some very nice things!'

'He was?' Charlotte asked Isla, aware of Paul's face turning into a beacon and thoroughly enjoying it. 'Like what exactly?'

'He thinks you're really nice and your hair is lovely too,' Isla said. 'What's wrong with your face, Daddy?'

Paul, his face the same colour as his crimson shirt, rested one large paw tenderly on his daughter's soft head and smiled at Charlotte, shaking his head ruefully. In fairness, her own cheeks were feeling pretty hot too.

'Charlotte's gone all red!' Isla giggled. 'She looks like a tomato!'

They stood, smiling and blushing until Harry charged over waving his tinfoil sword and challenging Paul to a fight. Charlotte busied herself with her BlackBerry. What was wrong with her? This wasn't typical Charlotte Sinclair behaviour. Normally she had a witty one-liner or cutting put-down for every occasion. She didn't usually stand beaming and blushing like an idiot.

Sensing Paul looking across, she fixed her eyes firmly

on her in-box, scrolling through junk mail as though she really wanted a fake Rolex or some dodgy Viagra.

Sort it out, she told herself sternly. This trip was proving to be far more unsettling than she'd ever imagined. So far she'd nearly made the hideous mistake of forgiving Richard, had wound up her biological clock at a very inconvenient time, and was now in danger of making an idiot of herself with a man whose ex-wife was clearly hoping for a reconciliation. It had the makings of a comedy fit for the stage.

Perhaps it was something in the water here in Picton, making her feel all warm and happy like Yorkshire's equivalent to Puck's love juice? She hoped it would wear off soon. The quicker she got back to London and normality the better.

Paul's smile was still floating Cheshire Cat-style before Charlotte's eyes when she eventually returned to the hotel. Scolding herself for being ridiculous – she hardly knew Paul after all – she ordered a sandwich and soup from Archie and prepared herself for a long afternoon battling budgets and writing reports.

She booted up her laptop and spread her papers across the four-poster, but no matter what she did, she couldn't focus. Her thoughts were just drifting away like hot-air balloons cut adrift from their moorings. So she decided that checking in with the London office was a priority – it was easier to concentrate on a phone call.

The files on YORC and Hope were open just in case her boss wanted some data. *See*, she told herself firmly, *you are professional! You are in control. You do not need Richard Sinclair!*

'Hi, Charlotte!' trilled Dave's PA, Annabelle. 'Dave's not in the office right now, can I take a message?'

'No, it's fine. I was just checking in,' Charlotte said quickly. Annabelle was a lovely girl but she had a brain like honeycomb. She could be relied on for the contents of the latest edition of *Heat* every week, but she was notorious for not passing on messages. Still, underneath the fake hair and Cheddar Gorge cleavage, was a heart of gold and an encyclopaedic knowledge of the goings-on in the office. If anyone knew why Richard had really gone zooming back to the capital, it would be Annabelle. 'Actually there is something you can help me with,' Charlotte said carefully, not wanting to betray her interest. 'What did Dave need so urgently that Richard had to be recalled? It's really going to slow up my work here,' she added self-righteously, just in case Annabelle should think she was pining for her ex.

'Dave didn't make Richard come back. Suzie did,' Annabelle said, before dropping her voice to a stage whisper and adding, 'Suzie was going nuts at the thought of you guys being away together. She was snapping at everyone and when I made a comment that maybe you'd get back together, she totally flipped!'

A nasty, mean, evil streak of Charlotte's was delighted to hear this. Trouble in paradise, eh? Glancing around the beautiful room, still romantic even though it was now strewn with discarded tights, laptop cables and phone chargers, she totally understood why Suzie was so unhappy about the idea of her and Richard sharing it. After all, who knew better than Suzie how easy he found it to forget his partner?

'They've been rowing loads,' Annabelle continued breathlessly. 'This afternoon they were shouting so loudly we could hear them from through Suzie's door. In the end Dave had to tell them to keep their private lives out of the office!'

Charlotte was staggered. Lunchtime snogging aside, Richard and Suzie were usually extremely business minded. Rowing in public was unheard of. Things really must be bad.

Charlotte's mean streak did a victory dance.

'I probably shouldn't repeat this,' Annabelle continued, clearly bursting to share even more juicy details, 'but Cally in accounts said she overheard Suzie accusing Richard of still being in love with his ex-wife!'

Charlotte didn't breathe for a moment.

'His ex-wife is you!' Annabelle pointed out.

Charlotte couldn't respond because her mind was spinning so fast she felt queasy. Had Richard been telling the truth? Did he still love her?

'Isn't it romantic? You guys are meant for each other. I just know it! It's like something out of a fairy tale!'

'One written by the Brothers Grimm,' muttered Charlotte darkly but Annabelle – an avid reader of Mills and Boon – was well and truly carried away now.

'You guys are just destined to be together! You're like . . . like . . .'

'Sickness and diarrhoea?' offered Charlotte, unable

to bear the sound of cogs grinding as Annabelle struggled to find a comparison.

'No, silly! Like . . . Posh and Becks!'

Charlotte's soup and sandwich started to trampoline in her stomach. 'Annabelle! For Heaven's sake! Richard and I are not meant to be together. We're divorced. And just for the record, he's sleeping with someone else.'

'Duh! David Beckham slept with someone else, and this week's *Heat* says they are more in love now than they ever were,' Annabelle said airily.

Unable to bear a minute more of this saccharine conversation – she could feel her teeth rotting by the second – Charlotte ended the call on the pretext of having to answer someone on the other line, before chucking the phone down on to the bed and thumping her head against the pillows.

Why was everything so complicated? Did Richard really still love her? Was that what he and Suzie were rowing about? And was there still hope? Is that what the psychic had been alluding to when she'd said that love would only come to her through hope?

Stop it! she told herself firmly. Richard was weak and faithless. She needed to put him out of her heart and mind once and for all and move on. There were plenty of nice genuine guys out there – like Paul, for example – she didn't need Richard.

But what if I can't move on? Charlotte thought in despair. *What if I do still love him? What if I was too hasty ending the marriage? Maybe I do want to try again after all? What if he's the one?*

What if? What if? What if? It was enough to drive a girl crazy and Charlotte felt like screaming. Why couldn't things be straightforward?

Luckily she was saved from going totally round the bend, which actually wasn't quite as far to travel as she would have liked, by Archie ringing up to her room.

'I'm sorry, lass, I forgot to tell you that Heath called for you.' As a secretary he was even worse than Annabelle. 'Won't that make the ladies of Yorkshire jealous?' And he was just as much of a gossip.

'Thank you, Archie. I'm sure it'll be regarding Arts Council business,' she said, setting him straight and hoping it didn't sound like she was protesting too much.

She glanced at her watch. Nearly half five. Heath was bound to be home by now. Dialling his number and listening to the ringing, she wandered back to the window. Pushing it open, she breathed in deep lungfuls of afternoon air, pinched with the nip of autumn's frosty fingers and scented with a faint sweetness of heather. Somewhere beyond those blue and purple hills was Heath's house.

'Charlotte, hi!' Heath sounded delighted to hear from her, or at least Charlotte thought he did. It was hard to tell, because it sounded as though he was at a thrash metal concert. 'Thanks so much for calling back. Look, do you mind holding on a second while I take this upstairs? Joel's watching Scuzz and I can hardly hear myself think!'

There was a brief pause and a thud of footsteps followed by a door shutting.

'That's better!' Heath said with feeling. 'You know you're getting old when you start telling the kids to turn the music down!'

She laughed. 'All part of the joys of raising teenagers, I guess!'

He sighed. 'I love them dearly but my poor ears haven't been the same since Joel discovered Five Fingered Death Punch.'

'I've never heard of them,' admitted Charlotte. 'I'm afraid my musical knowledge stops with Take That – the first time around.'

'You're lucky; I hear it nonstop. Still, it gives me a bit of street cred at YORC. Anyway, enough of my domestic woes.'

'We've all been handling woes recently,' she sighed.

'You're not still worried about Richard getting drunk, are you?' asked Heath, picking up on exactly what she was thinking. 'Please, don't give it another thought if you are. We've all been there. I thought he was pretty well behaved, all things considered.'

Hmm. That was easy for him to say. Heath hadn't had to help Richard into bed or listen to him trying to resurrect their marriage, had he? But, of course, she didn't say this. Heath was just a business associate and though he was easy to talk to, he didn't need to know that her relationship with Richard was so complicated that it made the theory of relativity look like basic maths.

'Seriously, I had a great time last night,' Heath was saying. 'Richard was hilarious, especially his jokes!'

Personally, Charlotte found her ex-husband's jokes

about as funny as a dose of swine flu, but it was sweet of Heath to be so kind.

'I was wondering if you'd like to come out for dinner again sometime,' Heath said finally, once he'd finished being polite about what had been a hideous event. 'In fact, how about this evening? To be honest, my ear drums could do with a rest!'

'That's really kind of you, Heath, but I'm afraid Richard's had to shoot back to London,' Charlotte said.

'Actually, I wasn't asking Richard, I was asking you,' Heath said slowly. 'There's a great pub up on the moors, not too far from here, actually, and I think you'd really like it. The views are amazing and their Yorkshire puddings are even better!'

'Oh dear, I really must look like a girl who likes her grub,' sighed Charlotte.

'You look like a girl I'd like to get to know better,' Heath said warmly. 'But if you've already eaten, then how about a drink? I'll be sober because I'm driving. You won't have to carry me into a cab!'

Shocked, Charlotte inhaled sharply. What the hell was Heath playing at? As far as he knew, she and Richard were a happily married couple! What kind of man deliberately targeted a married woman the moment that he thought her husband was out of the way? And if that wasn't bad enough, what about poor Cassandra, the woman he'd taken out for lunch today and who was clearly crazy about him?

Men! They were all the same. Cheating, opportunistic and disloyal!

'So, what do you say?' Heath wanted to know. 'I'll just need to make sure my hordes are fed and watered, but I can pick you up in about an hour.'

'That won't be necessary,' Charlotte said, hoping that the ice in her voice would give his ear frostbite. 'I'm far too busy to go out tonight – or any other night, in fact. Besides, I really don't think it's advisable to blur the professional boundaries. After all, your funding application rests on my decision. It might look as though you were trying to bribe me or sway my opinion.'

'You don't think that, do you?' Heath sounded horrified. 'I just thought it might be nice to get to know you a bit better, somewhere away from prying eyes. Well, here's another idea. How about you come over here tomorrow and I'll cook for us? I do a really good cheesy chicken dish. I've disguised the vegetables so well that even the kids eat it!'

She said nothing. If she didn't know that he was seriously involved with Cassandra and that he knew she was married, she'd almost have thought he was genuinely interested in her.

'And I promise that the kids are pretty tame. They haven't bitten anyone for ages!'

In spite of her anger she laughed. She felt a connection with him that was more than just physical attraction, even though he was undeniably attractive with those dancing sea-spray eyes and that slow sexy grin. She'd felt that somehow he'd understood her, that he'd *got* her, but then she guessed that was how guys like him operated. They made you feel really interesting and special and then they pounced.

At the thought of his strong tanned body pouncing on hers Charlotte's stomach flipped and her pulse skittered.

'The answer's no,' she said firmly.

'Fine.' Heath even had the nerve to sound hurt. 'I won't keep you, then. I'll catch you tomorrow.'

'Tomorrow,' Charlotte said brusquely and, ending the call, flung the phone on to the dressing table.

Pacing round her room she felt more annoyed with the entire male gender with every passing second. She decided to take it out on a nice bottle of wine and an indulgent over-order on the room service.

She didn't need a man. She didn't need Richard. Of course she didn't!

But why, then, did her life feel so desperately empty without him?

10

The next morning back at YORC, Charlotte was rubbing her temples like they were a genie's lamp. *Either Zak is talking at about fifty decibels*, Charlotte thought as she massaged her throbbing temples, *or that Sancerre was stronger than I realised . . .* More likely the stress of dealing with her ex was getting to her! A bucket of strong coffee and two Nurofen for breakfast had made her feel slightly better, but it would take more than pills to get rid of this headache. Right now decapitation felt like a good option!

Dragging her concentration back to the interview, and trying not to wince as sneaky slices of sunlight slipped through the blinds to slice into her eyeballs, she asked Zak if he felt YORC had given him the chance to try new things and express himself.

'That's the whole point of YORC,' Zak pointed out pityingly. 'Although I could express myself anyway. You've seen my file.'

Charlotte gulped. It had looked like a great question when she and her team had devised it back in a London think-tank session but now it sounded really patronising. From the case file she'd seen on Zak – passed from foster home to foster home since he was five – joy riding wasn't so much expressing himself as a big fat cry for help. The same had gone for Kylie, whom she'd interviewed earlier. Her poor arms looked like the tube map, all purple and crimson scratches underlined with ghostly traces of previous scars. Self-harming was a new concept to her but, after chatting to Kylie – 'It hurts so much, so I don't think about other stuff' – she got it clearly. After all, wasn't a wine binge just a thirty-something's equivalent?

'Miss, you look like shit,' Zak said sympathetically. 'I'll get you a Red Bull. That helps when I'm hung over,' he added, possibly using it as an excuse to put the questions on pause. It was a tactic Charlotte knew well.

'I'm not—' She started to protest, but right now, anything that might help was worth a shot.

As Zak fetched her drink she noticed Heath heading over. Great, just what she needed. For a second she toyed with the idea of scuttling away on the pretext of needing the loo, but knew that then she'd be behaving like a teenager. She'd just have to stick it out and hope he was going to be professional.

'So why won't you have dinner with me?' Heath asked straight away, blowing all hopes of small talk out of the water. Perching on the edge of the pool table he fixed her with puzzled green eyes and ran a tanned hand through his thick golden mop, making tufts stand up in confusion. 'Have I offended you or something?'

Charlotte's headache went up a gear. 'I told you, it

just isn't professional to socialise with clients. It would raise all sorts of awkward questions, too, with funding issues.'

Heath laughed. 'That's an excuse, if ever I heard one.'

'Think what you like, but it's the truth.'

'I don't buy it. When I worked in business most of my deals and networking were done over meals and nobody ever accused me of trying to bribe them with a Yorkshire pudding. Come on, Charlotte, have dinner with me tonight. Who knows, you might even have fun.'

The irony was that she didn't doubt this for a second. Heath was great fun, warm and generous too, and Charlotte was sorely tempted to throw caution to the wind. There was a twinkle in his eyes which made her stomach cartwheel and in spite of herself she felt the strong pull of attraction. That broad-shouldered, long-limbed body and those strong arms, corded with muscle from working his smallholding rather than pumping weights in a city gym, certainly ticked all her boxes. When he smiled at her she couldn't help her own lips twitching upwards in reply.

Could it really hurt? It was only dinner. She didn't have to sleep with him or anything.

What! Where the hell did that come from? She had no intention of sleeping with Heath! Not at all. The thought had never crossed her mind – well, not until a second ago! The trouble was that now that it had, it was all she could think about. Reading Charlotte's mind would be enough to make even Jackie Collins blush!

'Come on!' cajoled Heath, sensing she was weakening. 'You know you want to. I can tell.'

Her face flamed. 'I do not!'

'Fibber.' Heath grinned.

'How many times do I have to tell you? I'm not having dinner with you,' she said, dragging her gaze away from his strong arms, downed with hair, spun gold in the sunshine. 'It isn't right.'

Heath crossed his arms and regarded her through narrowed eyes. 'I think there's more to it than *professional distance*. I think you're scared.'

'Scared? Of you? Hardly!' she scoffed.

'Not of me exactly,' he said thoughtfully. 'More of what having dinner with me would represent. It would be a step off the normal path, wouldn't it? A bit of a risk? And I don't really see you as a risk taker.'

Of all the cheek! Of course she took risks! She took them all the time, like when she . . . when she . . . Er . . . Well, so what if she couldn't instantly find an example? There were just too many to remember, that was all!

Charlotte decided to change the subject. 'If you don't mind, I'd really like to get on with these interviews.' And then go and lie down, she added silently, wincing as the sun glared in through the blind. How ever did Archie drink all that whiskey and coke night after night and still function the next day? Practice, she supposed.

'Hangover kicking in?' Heath teased. 'That'll teach you to sit in your empty hotel room knocking back wine like Bridget Jones when you could have been listening to Black Sabbath at mine.'

'It's a migraine, not a hangover!'

'Course it is,' Heath said, swiftly exchanging the role of therapist for doctor. He walked to the window and twiddled with the blind until the room was plunged into shade. Charlotte could have wept with relief, especially when Zak returned with a can of Red Bull and two Anadin.

'That's what I always used to get my mum,' he explained as he handed them over. 'Always used to perk her up after a bender.'

'It's a migraine,' Charlotte insisted again, but nobody was listening so she took the tablets and washed them down with the sugary drink anyway. Who did Heath think he was, calling her Bridget Jones? Bridget was a sad singleton whereas as far as he knew, she was a happily married woman.

God, he was annoying!

'How many more interviews have you got left?' Heath wanted to know.

She glanced down at her list and, miracle of miracles, this time her brain didn't feel like someone was bashing it with a mallet. Hooray for Red Bull!

'Only two, then I've finished. I'm going to take some time to look at the city before getting back to the hotel to work on my files. All night. Alone. With my phone switched off.'

'You don't want to have dinner with me. I get it.' Heath looked hurt but he didn't press the point. 'I've got to nip to Picton now and shift some scenery for Cass. If you see Justin, could you remind him about the hike tomorrow?'

'Hike?'

'We're walking six miles from Haworth to get us into the mindset for *Wuthering Heights*. Maybe you'd – no, of course not,' Heath said swiftly when she glowered at him. 'Those spiky heels would never make it. See you later – here, I mean! Although my offer still stands, if you want to change your mind.'

Heath was lucky one of those spiky heels didn't end up in his head. Charlotte gnashed her teeth in annoyance. The man was made of Teflon! Rejection and brush-offs just seemed to slide off him. With a sigh she turned to a new page in her notebook and pasted a welcoming smile on to her face when Justin sauntered in.

By the time the interview was over, Charlotte's smile was genuine. Her headache had lifted and the light was no longer using her irises as punch bags. Justin was funny, too, and although he was still intent on becoming the next Banksy, she'd managed to convince him that art school could be the way forward rather than graffitiing the streets. See, it wasn't only Heath who could help teenagers change their lives, she thought.

'Art courses are great these days,' she concluded. 'There's more to them than bowls of fruit and nude models. A girl I know, Fern Moss, did an Art and Drama course and now she designs sets for theatres and TV shows. I think she's involved with the latest Luke Scottman movie.'

'Cool.' He grinned. 'I like the sound of that more than painting fruit, although I wouldn't mind the nude models too much!'

'Dream on, they're usually old ladies,' laughed Charlotte.

Justin grinned at her. 'That's fine by me! I like older women! In fact, you're not too bad for a wrinkly.'

She rolled her eyes. 'Well, if I ever need to do a spot of babysitting to boost the old-age pension, I'll bear you in mind. Now, I think we've just about covered everything and, bang on cue, here's Ruby!'

Sure enough, Ruby was shuffling in, lumpy body swathed in shapeless black combats and baggy Korn hoodie, her eyes downcast and lank curtains of hair shielding her pale face. Charlotte's heart went out to her. Being a teenager was so painful. It only felt like five minutes since she, too, had been shuffling along trying to hide her boobs under baggy jumpers and dyeing her hair any colour that would disguise its distinctive carroty hue. Underneath Ruby's heavy fringe was a stunning pair of blue eyes and her skin was clear and creamy, the extra pounds concealing cheekbones you could ski off. *If only she could have a bit more faith in herself*, Charlotte thought sadly. Maybe being involved with the play would give her the confidence she needed?

'All right, Rubes?' Justin gave her a cheeky wink as she shuffled past. 'I haven't seen you for ages. Give us a bell, yeah? If you're not too busy being Emo, of course.'

Ruby's face glowed crimson through her hair and

she fixed her eyes firmly on the floor as though the scuffed tips of her Doc Martens were the most fascinating things in the world. Charlotte wanted to give her a hug. Although she'd spent her teenage years looking after Steve and worrying about her father rather than hanging out with her friends, she could still remember that excruciating sensation of fancying someone and desperately pretending not to be interested.

Actually, that kind of behaviour wasn't reserved solely for teenagers . . .

'Laters!' Justin chirruped with a thousand-watt smile which Ruby pointedly ignored. Justin didn't seem offended, though, blowing her a kiss and saying, 'Enjoy the interrogation, Rubes.'

'Idiot,' muttered Ruby, but her eyes were shining and Charlotte could see that even in her clompy boots she was floating above the floor. Young love, eh?

Moving towards the bean bags and indicating for Ruby to sit next to her she took a deep breath. After what Heath had said the other day regarding being honest with the kids she was going to come straight to the point. She just hoped Ruby wouldn't be offended.

'I hope you don't mind me asking, but how did you end up at YORC?' she asked.

Ruby sighed. 'It's not very exciting. I got caught shoplifting. It was so lame. I didn't even need the stuff I nicked. Half of it was the wrong size anyway.'

'So what made you do it?'

'My mum died,' whispered Ruby. 'I know that's no

excuse for being a thief, but it was a really horrible time. Everyone was too busy looking after my little brothers to notice what I was doing. So I thought I'd give it a try.'

'I understand,' Charlotte told her. 'My mum died when I was young too, and it's really hard. How did your dad cope?'

Ruby shrugged. 'I dunno. I don't know him. We live with my stepdad.'

Charlotte's pen hovered over the notebook. 'And how do you get on with him?'

Ruby pulled at her fringe. 'All right, I suppose. He lost it a bit when Mum died, but he's getting better. Since I was charged he's spent a bit more time with me and my brothers, but sometimes I hear him cry when he thinks we're all asleep.' She paused. 'Actually, he hasn't done that for a while. Do you think that means he's forgotten her?'

Charlotte's eyes filled. She'd felt exactly the same way when she'd realised that she hadn't cried for her own mum for a few weeks. The guilt had burned like acid. 'I'm sure he still misses her, Ruby. It just means he's coming to terms with it.'

'Yeah.' Ruby's monotone belied what she was feeling. Charlotte knew it.

'You've had a really tough time,' Charlotte continued, her heart twisting in sympathy for the unhappy girl. 'Has being involved with YORC helped you?'

'A bit,' Ruby admitted.

Goodness, talking to teenagers was hard work! How could she evaluate the effectiveness of this project and its suitability for more funding if nobody told her it had made a big difference? She could *see* the difference in the kids when they were on the stage, but how on earth did you quantify that?

'You stopped stealing things, though, didn't you?' she said encouragingly.

There was an awkward silence before Ruby's shoulders began to shake. To her horror, Charlotte realised that beneath the curtain of hair tears were running down Ruby's cheeks. Thick black eye make-up made tracks down her face and dripped off her chin. How on earth had this happened? All she'd done was chat about YORC and, as advised by Heath, been up front about Ruby's criminal record and now the poor kid was in floods.

'I didn't mean to upset you, Ruby,' Charlotte said, mortified. Yet again she'd messed up. Unintentionally, of course, but poor Ruby was distraught. Fishing in her bag she plucked out a packet of tissues and offered one to Ruby. 'It was a stupid thing to ask. Of course you don't steal things any more.'

'You're wrong!' Ruby blew her nose loudly. 'I stole something a few months ago but I didn't have any choice. I didn't want to, but I didn't know what else to do.' She buried her face in her hands. 'I really, really want my mum!'

She was howling in earnest now, her whole body shaking with grief. Abandoning her clipboard Charlotte put her arms around Ruby and held her tightly, smoothing her hair back from her hot, wet face and murmuring to her that it would be all right, she'd see, things would get better. Eventually Ruby quietened and, wiping her face with a baggy sleeve, gave Charlotte a watery smile.

'Sorry, Miss.'

'Don't apologise. Whatever it is, I'm sure we can sort it out,' Charlotte promised, with a confidence she didn't quite feel. After all, if Ruby had stolen something major, then it was going to be very tricky indeed to talk her way out of it. Still, how bad could it be? She didn't look the type to rob banks or joyride Ferraris. 'We can return whatever you took to the shop and say it was a mistake,' she added firmly.

'That's a nice idea,' Ruby sniffed. 'But I don't think they'd want it back now.' She paused. 'I stole a pregnancy test.'

Charlotte felt the hard floor beneath her turn to sinking sand. Oh. Shit.

This wasn't on the job description!

'I felt sick and I'd missed periods. I had to know for sure, didn't I?'

Charlotte nodded.

'I did two tests and they were both positive.' Ruby looked up at her, her eyes two big, blue circles of despair. 'I'm only seventeen! What am I going to do?'

Charlotte gulped. Where was Heath when you needed him? She was just an assessor from the Arts Council! She was useless at all this emotional stuff. Ruby needed someone motherly like Zoe, or worldly like Libby, not someone like her who'd made a mess of her own life. All she knew was that she'd been looking after Steve when she was Ruby's age and much as she loved her brother she'd never wish that kind of responsibility on somebody so young.

'What about the baby's father? Can you tell him?'

Ruby shook her head. 'He isn't really interested in me; it's not like we're together or anything.'

There went that option. 'What about your stepfather? Could you talk to him?'

Ruby looked horrified. 'No way! He'd be so disappointed; first the shoplifting and now this. Please, promise you won't tell him!'

'No, no of course not.' Charlotte knew this chat had to remain confidential but her mind was whirling. What should she say? What should she do? They hadn't prepared her for this back in the office, that was for sure.

'How will I cope with a baby?' Ruby said in despair. 'I can hardly cope with my A-levels.'

'You do have options,' Charlotte pointed out gently. 'You don't have to have the baby, if you don't want to.'

'You mean an abortion. I couldn't do that.' Ruby looked horrified.

'That's just one option,' Charlotte said quickly. 'What about adoption? That's something you might want to consider. There are lots of lovely couples who'd love children but can't have them. That way you would be able to know your baby had gone to people who really wanted it.'

Ruby blotted her eyes with the corner of her hoodie. 'They'd have to be really nice. Would I get to meet them?'

'There are people who'd sort all that out for you,' Charlotte assured her and Ruby nodded thoughtfully. Surely this was the ideal solution for a girl Ruby's age? She should be out having fun at seventeen, not be burdened by responsibility.

'Maybe you could adopt my baby?' Ruby said hopefully. 'You're old enough and you're really kind.'

Charlotte was really touched. The truth, of course, was that she'd be a hopeless parent but it was sweet that Ruby had faith in her. 'I don't think I'm the right person, Ruby,' she said gently. 'For one thing, I'm not married any more, and I work full-time, for another. But I promise that adoption agencies have lots of really nice suitable couples who'd love to bring up your baby, if that's what you choose to do. But it's a big decision to make and you shouldn't do this alone. You really need to see a doctor, too. Maybe you could make an appointment and talk things over with your GP?'

Ruby swallowed. 'I know I should. Maybe she could help sort the adoption thing out?'

'I'm sure she could,' Charlotte agreed. 'But it's a huge decision. You also need to talk to your stepfather.'

The girl nodded. 'I know. I can't hide it for ever, can I? But at least I can start to put some plans in place. I feel better now I know there's something I can do.' She gave Charlotte a watery smile. 'Thanks, Miss. You've really helped.'

Those words stayed with Charlotte for the rest of the morning. Maybe she wasn't quite as useless as Richard thought? Finishing off her notes she powered down her laptop and wandered outside for some fresh air. No matter what she did her head was filled with thoughts of Ruby and she wondered how Heath managed to cut off from the troubled teenagers when he went home. She'd have to ask him.

Outside, a spiky wind had got up, skittering leaves across the car park and whisking crisp packets and sweet wrappers into eddies. The sunshine had leached away and left the sky the colour of dishwater. She shivered and pulled her cardigan closer, as she sat down on a low wall. A storm was on the way, she thought as she perched on the wall and raised her face to the breeze, just as a storm was coming for poor Ruby and her family. It was so sad and she really felt for the girl. She just hoped she'd been some help to her. Nobody that young should feel so alone and frightened. If only she'd had someone to talk to when she was Ruby's age, it might have made life easier to bear.

'Budge up, you, don't hog all the wall,' Heath said, joining her and perching that sexy, tight denim-clad backside next to her. She gulped and shifted away slightly so that his thigh wasn't resting against hers.

'Busy morning?' he asked.

She smiled at him. Those sparkling eyes, bright and merry as the summer sea, just made her lips curl upwards. There was no point trying to control them. 'Busy doesn't even come close. I feel drained! How on earth do you do this, day in and day out?'

'I guess because I can see a difference in the kids. It isn't always easy, though, but it's the most worthwhile thing in the world,' Heath said thoughtfully. The wind blew his thick golden hair across his face and to Charlotte's horror she discovered that her hand was itching to reach up and push it back. Burying both hands deep within her cardigan pockets she gave herself a mental slap on the wrist. He'd only just returned from seeing his girlfriend!

'Take Justin,' Heath continued, turning to look at Charlotte with a gaze so intense that she decided to study a skittering crisp packet instead. 'He's got a track record for vandalism and graffiti but when I just bumped into him in the pool room, he was buzzing about going to Art College. Good work!'

She laughed. 'I think it was the idea of nude models that sold it to him, not me!'

'That would have worked for me, too.' Heath grinned. 'But seriously, Charlotte, well done for that. Kids like Justin are hard to inspire. They fail at school and feel that there's nothing they can succeed at, but you've managed to get through to him. That's a real achievement.'

Charlotte felt so warm from his praise that it was as though the sun had come back out. She could see why the kids loved Heath so much. He made you feel as though you could do anything. 'Thanks! If only they were all as easy to help as him.'

'Problems?'

She sighed. 'One girl asked me for advice about a problem she had. It really got to me, actually. I hope I've been able to help her.'

Heath smiled. 'Counselling young adults is a major part of what we do here but it can be quite a strain. The trick is to give them options but allow them to make their own minds up.'

She nodded. That was what she'd done, wasn't it? She'd given Ruby the adoption option and then suggested she follow it up with the doctor. Still, there was something so open about Heath that she couldn't help wanting to share her morning's dilemma with him and moments later she was spilling more beans than Heinz. Leaving out Ruby's name she filled him in on all the major details, finishing by telling him how she'd come up with adoption as the best solution.

'It really will be the best thing all round,' she concluded, totally assured she'd done the right thing. 'That way the baby gets a good home and the girl gets to enjoy her life and finish her education.'

Heath was staring at her. 'Run that by me again? You told this girl that having her baby adopted was the best course of action?'

'I didn't quite put it like that but, yes, I did. How can a girl her age cope with a child?'

'Plenty of them do,' Heath pointed out. 'Adoption's certainly one option but it's her decision. You can't make up her mind for her.'

'Heath, this girl's bright and has her whole life ahead of her! Giving her baby up for adoption is the best thing!'

'Best for whom?' Heath demanded, his eyes now dark green of an angry ocean. 'The baby? The poor confused girl? The father – who, I bet, hasn't got a clue this conversation's taken place?'

She stared at him. Just how ungrateful could you get? He should be thanking her for helping Ruby, not having a go. The girl had been a mess whereas now she had a plan of action.

'Her, obviously! And the baby too, in the long run. Honestly, Heath, she was a mess to start with but she felt much better after we'd talked.'

But Heath was looking shocked, not impressed. 'Charlotte! Didn't you stop to think about just how vulnerable and impressionable she is? You can't go telling young people what to do. That's totally irresponsible!'

'It bloody well wasn't!' she shot back. 'No one else was bothered to help her, the father isn't on the scene and she's terrified of telling her family. At least this way she's still got options. Having a child would mean kissing goodbye to her own childhood and a whole heap of opportunities. Believe me, I should know.'

His eyes narrowed. 'Who exactly are we talking about here?'

'Stop twisting my words! She asked for my opinion and I gave it to her. If that's OK with you?'

'No it isn't OK with me! Far from it, actually!' Heath leapt up from the wall and glowered down at her. 'It doesn't matter what's happened to you in the past. When you're working with young people you have to be neutral. Your own feelings and experiences can't come into it.'

They glared at each other. Charlotte had never felt so misunderstood in her entire life.

'But I was counselling her!'

'That wasn't counselling! You let your own personal feelings cloud your judgement and told her what to do.' Heath was looking seriously angry. 'She could spend the rest of her life regretting any decision made on a whim and longing for her baby. That's what I'd call a ruined life, not being a teen mum!'

Suddenly Charlotte felt cold to her bones. Like poisoned darts, Heath's words flew straight to her heart and, with a sickening lurch to her stomach, she realised he was right. She'd been so certain she was doing the right thing advising Ruby to pursue adoption, had been totally assured in her belief that no seventeen-year-old girl should be raising a child when she could be out having fun. She'd been giving Ruby the escape route that had been denied to herself, superimposing her own feelings and experience on to the younger girl's situation. But every person is different. Every situation is different. Of course having a baby of your own was totally different to having to care for your little brother and alcoholic father, wasn't it?

What had she done?

'You don't have children of your own,' Heath continued, every line of his lean, sculpted body rigid with anger, 'so what on earth gives you the right to judge what's right for someone else? But then, I shouldn't really be surprised at any of this, should I? After all, you make snap judgements about everyone and I don't suppose you're ever wrong, are you, Charlotte?'

'And just what is that supposed to mean?' Charlotte demanded, anger at his self-righteous tone replacing her self-reproach. 'You can't say things like that; you don't even know me!'

'No, but I think I'm starting to. You judge by appearances and you make all your decisions based upon them without stopping to ask any questions,' he told her.

'That's not true!'

'Isn't it?' He shrugged his broad shoulders. 'Well, let's all hope, for her sake, that you've got it right this time.'

And, jumping up off the wall, he turned sharply on his heel and strode away, leaving Charlotte staring after him with hot tears stabbing her eyes. Was Heath right? Did she judge people too swiftly, leaping to conclusions without pausing to sift through the facts? If she was honest, she did tend to make up her mind quickly – as Richard had discovered to his cost – but that was a strength, wasn't it? She was a strong woman who could make decisions, however hard, and stick to them even when her heart was crying out for her to do the opposite. Only weak people prevaricated and gave second chances out like sweets. People like that got trampled on.

And no one was ever going to trample on Charlotte Sinclair again.

A wise man once said: when the going gets tough, the tough go shopping.

Frustrated with herself, Charlotte headed into York for some serious retail therapy. Comfort shopping was better for her waistline than comfort eating. Besides, after the terrible morning she'd had, Charlotte figured that she deserved to treat herself.

Two hours and a serious dent in her overdraft later she drifted into Topshop, seduced by the upbeat music and the knowledge that Kate Moss had designed a range for them.

Never mind that the only thing Kate and I have in common is that we are of a similar age, thought Charlotte as she flicked through the rails and selected a neat pencil skirt and frilly white blouse. If this was good enough for supermodels, then it was good enough for her.

Five minutes later, her arms filled with clothes, Charlotte headed for the changing rooms, determined to spend away the misery that was gnawing in the pit of her stomach.

The changing room was crowded, crammed with slender teenaged girls pouring themselves into skinny jeans and belly tops or pirouetting in front of the mirrors squinting critically at non-existent cellulite or fat bits. Feeling every one of her thirty-four years, Charlotte shot into a cubicle and yanked the curtain closed behind her. The room was buzzing with excitement as the teenage customers chatted about their plans for the weekend or what a minger so and so was or how well fit Gavin in Year Twelve was, and as she listened Charlotte felt about a hundred and thirty-four. Had she ever been that young? When she'd been a teenager she'd been wandering around Asda trying to find the two-for-one offers, not parading through Topshop or trying on bling in Claire's Accessories.

Putting the events of the morning behind her, Charlotte studied herself in front of the mirror. The skirt fitted just fine. The shirt was smart and shapely. But there wasn't anything more she could say than that. Compared to the other shoppers, she looked like a dull brown moth hanging about with a flutter of rainbow-hued butterflies. Her skin was pale, her eyes shadowed, and there was a dull droop to her mouth.

Oh my God, she thought in horror. *I look worse than old. I look . . . boring!*

Quickly changing back into her own clothes and dumping the skirt and blouse with the changing-room assistant, she whirled around the store again, this time selecting bright jewel colours and soft, flowing fabrics, skinny jeans and glittery T-shirts. She tried on some purple velvet boots with four inch heels; instead of buckles, they had gold cat heads with glittering diamond eyes. Normally Charlotte would have written them off as totally impractical, clashing with everything she owned and more difficult to walk in than stilts, but this afternoon she was throwing caution to the wind and leaving her usual boring self behind for a bit. Diving back into the changing rooms she tried on everything, smiling when she saw how the colours brought out the deep violet of her eyes and made her hair glow like the sunset. If Zoe could see her now!

Twenty minutes later she was still smiling in spite of nearly maxing out her credit card. She headed back out on to the street, this time wearing a soft, flowing moss-green sweater dress which clung to her curves in all the right places, the killer purple boots and, best of all, a new mock-crocodile skin bag in matching purple. A trip to Browns led to a free makeover at the Benefit counter and catching a glimpse of herself as she left the shop, Charlotte hardly recognised the slim woman in bright eye-catching clothes, her hair pinned up into a tousled up do and her eyes enhanced with clever, smoky make-up.

She looked years younger, Charlotte decided happily as she headed back out on to the street.

She was so busy stealing glances at her new look that she failed to notice Paul cross the road, waving cheerily as he strode towards her.

'Charlotte? Hey, it *is* you!' Paul called as she looked round. He smiled at her appreciatively, his merry eyes sweeping over her body. 'I thought Angelina Jolie had dyed her hair and come to visit Yorkshire.'

That was fifty quid well spent, then, Charlotte thought with relief.

'Thanks, Paul.' She smiled back, delighted to see a familiar face. 'I've been flashing the plastic a bit. I think there's still smoke coming off my Barclaycard!'

He laughed and glanced down at his shopping bags. 'Mine's melted. It's Isla's birthday next week and I may have gone a bit over the top. I never knew there was so much pink glittery stuff in the world. Actually, I was just about to have a coffee and rest my feet. Would you like to join me?'

For a second she hesitated. Then she thought, *why not?* After the horrible morning, the least she deserved was a cup of coffee with someone who didn't think she was the female equivalent of the child-catcher.

'That'd be great,' she said. 'I haven't walked far in these boots yet but my feet could do with a rest!'

He whistled. 'I'm not surprised! Isla would go mad for those. She loves kitsch stuff like that.'

I've got cool kitsch shoes, thought Charlotte proudly as she settled on to a sofa in Starbucks. She could tell from the admiration in Paul's eyes that she looked good and her ego, so recently given a good kicking by both Richard and Heath, started to feel a little less bruised. Paul was attractive and good company and although she had no intention of doing anything but chat and flirt a little, it was nice to be appreciated.

As they sipped their coffee and shared a blueberry

muffin they chatted easily. Paul was fascinated by her job at the Arts Council and, in turn, she found his stories about making a Viking longboat mesmerising.

'Come back to my workshop and see it, if you like?' Paul offered. Then he flushed bright red. 'Oh dear, that sounds terrible. And if I say, "come and look at my longboat", it will sound even worse.'

Poor Paul looked so flustered that Charlotte took pity on him. 'It's certainly the most original offer I've ever had,' she joked, draining her skinny latte and pushing away the last crumbs of muffin. She was really interested in the idea of the replica ship and spending time with Paul was also helpful, seeing as he was so involved with the Hope Foundation. At least, that's what she told herself.

As they strolled across the city centre they chatted about the Hope Foundation. 'I think I enjoy it even more than Isla does,' he admitted with a wry smile. 'It's supposed to be for the kids but actually us lonesome single parents need the company, too.'

Charlotte cast her mind back to when she'd spent the afternoon with Paul making the boats. He'd had such a natural way with the kids and he'd been so kind to her, too, after the paint-drinking trauma. *He is a genuinely nice man*, she thought warmly. Good-looking, too, although not in a flashy, groomed manner like Richard or an instant stomach-flipping way like Heath. Paul was grounded and straightforward but nonetheless attractive. Elise must have been crazy to throw away such a genuinely good man and she was intrigued to know more about him. Like her, Paul hadn't been able to forgive and forget and she wondered whether he ever would. But unlike her, he hadn't hurtled straight into the divorce courts. He was biding his time and making sure that separation was the right option. So maybe Heath had a point. Maybe she was too quick to judge and make decisions?

Arrah! Bloody Heath! He was right there inside her head, swishing around like water trapped in one's ears after swimming, and she couldn't forget what he'd said. It was very, very annoying. The sooner she got back to London and left Mr Heath Holier-than-Thou Fulford the better.

Paul's workshop was a good mile from the city centre and with every step he seemed to relax more.

'Here we are!' Paul said proudly, flicking on the light. 'And there she is, the love of my life! *Nordic Princess.*'

As the workshop was flooded with light Charlotte gasped in awe. Towering above her, like something out of Norse mythology, was the great hull of a longship, complete with snarling dragon's head and covered with intricate carvings of fearsome sea serpents. Her fingers stretched out, of their own volition, touching the wood and tracing the carvings, recoiling in distaste as they reached the pointed fangs of a snake so realistic that she could practically hear it hiss.

'My God,' she breathed, looking at Paul with new admiration. 'It's awesome. You made this yourself?'

He nodded. 'It's been a labour of love, that's for sure.

But I've enjoyed every minute. It's taken my mind off other things, I suppose.'

Charlotte understood. When life was rubbish, work was an excellent panacea.

'This is fantastic,' she said, walking around slowly and drinking in every detail, the pain in her feet totally forgotten. 'How long has it taken? Did you design it yourself?'

Paul laughed before answering all her questions patiently and with understandable pride, but eventually he placed a gentle hand on her shoulder and said, 'That's quite enough about me for one afternoon! You know just about everything there is to know about me now, but I know hardly anything about you.'

She shrugged. 'There's nothing to tell. I certainly don't have your talents.'

'Maybe not for woodwork, but I bet there're lots of things you're good at?'

'Making lists? Being organised? Upsetting people?' Charlotte said drily. 'Take your pick!'

'You're too hard on yourself,' said Paul. 'You're warm and funny and generous but you constantly doubt yourself.' Stepping closer he gently tucked a lock of hair behind her ear. 'Who knocked the confidence out of you? Or perhaps I shouldn't ask?'

She gulped. Paul was so close she could smell the warm scent of his skin and the spicy tang of his aftershave. 'Nobody did anything to me. I'm fine.'

He shook his head. 'I don't believe you. Please tell me.'

Charlotte felt as though she was poised on the edge

of the high diving board, teetering over the water. Paul's hand was still on her shoulder and she wondered whether now was the right time to jump in? Who would understand the hurt and humiliation better than this man?

'You remember the colleague I was with the other day?' she said slowly, daring to bear her soul. 'He and I were married for seven years and then he slept with someone else. To cut a long story short, we ended up getting divorced. Even though I know it was the right thing to do, it's been hard, you know?'

Paul sighed. 'Oh yes, I know all about that, believe me. For what it's worth, he's an idiot to have let you go.'

'He didn't let me go; I divorced him!' Charlotte said firmly. 'No one was going to treat me like that. I couldn't be with someone I didn't trust.'

'So you don't love him any more?'

She deliberately put Richard's drunken ramblings out of her mind.

'I . . . er . . . I tolerate him as a colleague, but that's as far as it goes.'

'Are you sure about that?'

She wasn't, but she couldn't let Paul know. She couldn't let anyone know the turmoil she'd been through. 'Honestly,' she said, 'we're ancient history.'

He squeezed her shoulder sympathetically. 'I bet he kicks himself every day for losing you.'

Charlotte wished she could believe that, but it was pretty hard to when every day she saw Suzie wrapped round Richard like a chest bandage.

Paul's hand rose up to touch her cheek. 'You look so sad. I wish there was something I could do to make things better.'

The closeness of his body only inches from hers was actually doing a great job of making her feel better, Charlotte realised with surprise. Maybe if she spent some time with a lovely guy like Paul who was the antithesis of her ex-husband she could erase the bad memories and move on. All she needed to do was take one step closer, stand on her tiptoes and brush her lips against his and she'd be well on her way to forgetting the misery of the past eighteen months.

And why not?

'There is something,' she whispered, moving a fraction closer so that she could feel his breath fluting against her skin, and all of a sudden, as though by magic, desire was fizzing through her bloodstream and her heartbeat accelerating.

Paul gazed down at her. 'Charlotte Sinclair,' he said huskily, 'I love the way your mind works!'

His lips were only a heartbeat away and she closed her eyes in delicious anticipation as he wrapped his arms round her and pulled her close. Tilting her chin upwards she waited for the butterfly-soft touch of his mouth.

'Daddy! Daddy! Guess what? I'm getting a Barbie Castle for my birthday! And it's pink!'

Paul let go of Charlotte so abruptly that she stumbled backwards on her purple heels. Steadying herself against the smooth hull of *Nordic Princess* she quickly slapped a delighted smile on to her face as Isla bounded into the workshop and hurled herself into her father's arms.

'Hello, sweetheart! What a lovely surprise!' Paul said, scooping her up and hugging his daughter tightly. 'Where's Mummy?'

'Mummy can't run as fast as me!' Isla said proudly. 'I beat her. She's coming.'

'Oh goody,' Paul said, smiling ruefully at Charlotte.

She pulled a wry face. Much as she adored Isla, the child had lousy timing!

'Hello, Charlotte!' Isla beamed. 'Why are you here? And why is your face all red again?'

'Charlotte's come to see the boat,' Paul said quickly.

'It's lovely, just like the pictures you painted the other day,' Charlotte added, smoothing her hair back from her hot cheeks and hoping desperately that she wasn't looking too flushed and glittery eyed. Thank heavens Isla hadn't arrived a minute later! Who knew how it would have affected her to see her daddy kissing someone who definitely wasn't Mummy?

Paul must have had the same thought because suddenly he was the other side of the workshop showing Isla the latest dragon that had been carved on to the hull. He couldn't have felt further away from Charlotte if he'd suddenly been beamed *Star Trek*-style to another galaxy. Feeling awkward, she pretended to be totally absorbed in the design sketches pinned to the wall, hoping that her heartbeat would calm and her Edam face would cool down before Elise caught up with her daughter.

'Sorry, Paul, I know you're busy but Isla was adamant we popped in,' Elise was saying, breezing into the workshop and plopping herself on to a tatty sofa with the easy familiarity of one who'd been there many times before. 'Oh! I didn't realise you had company,' she added, catching sight of Charlotte skulking in the corner. She didn't exactly look delighted to see her.

'I just came to have a look at the longboat,' Charlotte said quickly. 'It's amazing, isn't it? Paul's so talented.'

Elise gave her a cool, measured stare.

'Yes, he is,' she said finally after a silence so long that Charlotte practically expected tumbleweed to start blowing across the workshop. 'Paul has many talents, but most of all he's a wonderful, wonderful father. And that's the biggest talent of all, wouldn't you say?'

Following her gaze across the room Charlotte watched Paul as he lifted Isla up on to the deck of the boat. The expression on his face was so full of love that her throat tightened. Elise was right; Paul was an amazing father and he deserved to be with his daughter. More than that, he deserved to be with his family and the wife who clearly still adored him. Where there was love there was always hope, as Steve liked to say. Normally that kind of guff made Charlotte snort with derision but seeing this couple and their beautiful daughter together made her stop and think. There had to be a reason why Paul hadn't hurtled into divorce. Maybe he still had feelings for Elise after all? Either way, getting involved with him would only make the poor guy's situation even more complicated.

At this thought she scooped up her shopping bags. It was time to beat a hasty retreat.

'Paul, thanks so much for showing me the ship. It really is fantastic. I'll head off now and leave you guys to it. I've got a tonne of work to do before tomorrow.'

Turning away from the small family she shouldered her new purple bag and set off out on to the street. But no matter how fast she walked or how many people turned to admire her new boots, she couldn't escape from the knot of sadness tightening in her stomach. Today really had been a bad day and she couldn't wait for it to be over.

And to be on her own once again.

12

'And everything's going well? Even having to work with Richard?'

It was eight o'clock in the evening and Charlotte was on the phone to Zoe while sitting on a squashy sofa tucked away in a lamp-lit corner of Archie's bar, her legs curled beneath her and a large glass of white wine in her hand.

'It's all been absolutely fine,' Charlotte assured her sister-in-law. Well, that wasn't a lie, was it? Work had been fine, it was everything else that had gone hideously wrong. 'Actually, Richard isn't here. Suzie got nervous about him spending too much time with his stunning ex-wife and summoned him back to London.'

'And how do you feel about that?' wondered Zoe.

'I couldn't care less. OK, I must admit there's a part of me that's pleased to see Suzie getting a taste of her own medicine but that's where it ends. I don't want to be with him any more. I promise.'

'Right.' Zoe sounded doubtful. 'So if Richard came back right now and said he's made a terrible mistake and that he's loved you all along, you wouldn't be tempted to try again?'

'No way!' Charlotte insisted, pushing away the memories of the other evening when she'd come dangerously close to doing just that.

'Working with him must be hard, though,' Zoe was saying. 'It isn't natural to have to be in such close proximity to your ex-husband and his new partner. Why don't you look for another job, Charlie? I know it's daunting making a new start, but it might be exactly what you need.'

'Exes can be friends, you know,' Charlotte told Zoe airily. Then, to change the subject, she added, 'There's this guy here, Paul, who's one of the dads at the Hope Foundation and he's on really good terms with his ex. He's got the cutest little girl who absolutely adores him. He's a fantastic father.'

'It sounds to me as though you think he's pretty fantastic, too,' teased Zoe.

'Hardly. He's just someone I've had to chat to for work,' Charlotte said lightly, crossing her fingers as their almost-kiss replayed in her mind. 'Besides, what is it they say about mixing business with pleasure?'

Zoe sighed. 'There's nothing wrong with having a bit of fun, Charlie. There must be some gorgeous guys up north? I've been picturing all these rugged types with rippling muscles and brooding stares.'

'The men up here are just as bad as the ones in London. This one guy, Heath, he's handsome and brooding, all right, but guess what he did: Richard and

I couldn't be bothered to explain our mutual surnames so we allowed everyone to think we are still married. Yet Heath keeps asking me out! The nerve of the man.'

Zoe's reaction was not the outrage Charlotte had expected. 'He sounds interesting,' Zoe said thoughtfully, 'are you going to take him up on it?'

'Hardly,' scoffed Charlotte. 'What kind of guy hits on another man's wife? There's no way I'd get involved with someone like that.'

'Let me get this straight,' Zoe sounded like she was talking to an imbecile. 'You're *not* married but you don't like Heath because he thinks you are? Isn't that just a bit silly?'

'I admit it's a little arse about face, but you can see my point.'

Zoe sighed. 'Look, here's a novel idea; why don't you tell him the truth about you and Richard? Or are you making excuses?'

Charlotte rolled her eyes at the ceiling. Zoe *so* wasn't right this time. 'No, hon, I just think anyone who'd knowingly date a married person isn't to be trusted.'

'OK, forget Heath for a moment. This Paul person's single,' her sister-in-law pointed out, starting to laugh. 'Maybe you should bear him in mind? After all, he's involved with the Hope Foundation and according to your prophecy that makes him your one true love! "Love will come to you through hope alone", wasn't it?' Zoe laughed.

'Who am I to defy fate?' said Charlotte drily, but beneath the cool façade, her mind was spinning. If Charlotte believed in all that psychic stuff – which of course she didn't – she might have been really unnerved because the coincidence was certainly uncanny. But Paul wasn't her one true love, was he?

Ending the call with Zoe's words ringing in her ears, Charlotte gulped down her drink and turned her attention to the fat pile of magazines she'd bought. She was trying to concentrate on the latest celebrity gossip when Heath strolled into the bar. *Oh great*, she thought, her heart plummeting, just what she needed, another lecture. She sank into the cushions and pretended to be engrossed in her magazine but it was too late; Heath was already heading in her direction, waving cheerily across the room as though the last time they'd met they hadn't been rowing furiously.

'You look nice and cosy,' Heath commented. 'Can I buy you a drink and join you?'

Was he insane? As if she wanted to drink with him after all the harsh things he'd said. It would take more than a drink to make up for the verbal lashing he'd given her.

'No thanks. I'm fine.'

'No, you're not; you're still annoyed with me about earlier on, and I don't blame you,' Heath said with a sigh. Perching on the arm of the sofa he fixed her with his clear green eyes. 'Look, Charlotte, I'm really sorry about that. I was far too hard on you, and it wasn't fair. You're not a youth worker and you were only trying to do your best. It's just that sometimes I get a bit carried away when it comes to the kids. I can't help feeling protective of them.'

'So I gather,' Charlotte said coolly. 'Well, I'm sorry we can't all meet your high standards, Heath. Some of us are only human, I'm afraid.'

'I'm as human as anyone, believe me. If we had a few weeks, I'd tell you about some of the mistakes I've made. In fact, forget weeks, we'd need years.' Those green eyes twinkled at her winningly.

Charlotte dragged her gaze away. Heath's criticism had really stung and she wasn't inclined to let him off the hook, no matter how appealing she found him or how apologetic he was. But with that fit, lean body only inches from hers she felt her resolve wavering, which was very annoying indeed. She wasn't attracted to Heath Fulford in the slightest, not really, she tried to tell herself.

'Come on, Ms Sinclair. One drink and I promise you can call me all the names you like. In fact, how about I save you the trouble and do it for you? I was judgemental, hasty and ungrateful. Inconsiderate, too, because you could have just sent that young woman on her way and said it wasn't your business, but you didn't. You took the time to talk and even if I don't agree with what you said, I don't doubt for a moment that your intentions were good. It wasn't your fault you got it wrong.'

'That makes me feel so much better,' said Charlotte sarcastically. 'Is that how you make people feel good? I think I'd rather be insulted.'

Heath ran a hand through his thick golden hair. 'I'm not great with words, Charlotte, and I'm making a hash of trying to apologise, aren't I?'

Her raised eyebrow told him all he needed to know.

He laughed. 'OK, I'm useless. Look, I'm really sorry I had a go at you. I didn't think for a minute how hard you must have found it, having to deal with all that emotional stuff. I can see it wasn't easy for you.'

'And what exactly is that supposed to mean?'

'Nothing nasty, it's just that you don't strike me as a person who likes to open up and discuss her feelings.'

She folded her arms across her chest. 'I like to keep my private life private, if that's what you mean.'

To her surprise he nodded. 'I totally understand. And the last thing you needed after having to handle all that was some self-righteous idiot going off on one. You must have felt like punching me!'

'Why have you put that in the past tense?'

Heath smiled. 'I'm always telling the kids that they need to listen to both sides of the story but I'm not very good at taking my own advice, it seems!'

Charlotte remained silent. She was still annoyed, but she couldn't help admiring his passion and dedication.

'Look, please let me get you a drink,' Heath said. 'I know it doesn't compensate for everything, but it's a start.'

Charlotte swallowed. She wanted to tell him to get lost but, on the other hand, part of her wanted to have a drink with him. Annoyingly, this part won.

We have to work together, she told herself as Heath went to the bar, *so I have to be professional*. But if she was honest, wanting Heath to stay had less to do with talking about second-stage funding and more to do with the weird way that being close to him made her fizz with sheer excitement. She needed a drink to cope with that.

Returning with a glass of white wine for her and a Guinness for himself, Heath plopped himself down on the sofa.

'To a successful working relationship,' he said, chinking his glass against hers. 'And to me keeping things in perspective in the future. Friends?'

'Don't let's get carried away,' Charlotte said coolly. 'I might forgive you for earlier, but don't push your luck.'

'So I am forgiven, then? Phew!' Heath mopped his brow in mock relief. 'I'm not sure how clean Archie's carpets are but I was prepared to kneel down and beg if necessary.'

They both glanced down at the lurid swirly seventies carpet. It was hard to tell what was grime and what was part of the original design.

Charlotte's resolve started to weaken. 'I think we can safely say that grovelling won't be necessary,' she told him. 'Besides, you'd stick to that carpet and never get up again!'

Heath laughed. 'I'm nearly forty; I'd probably never get up again, anyway!'

She cast her eye over his body and looked away hastily in case he thought she was checking him out.

Trying desperately to keep her mind on track she said, 'To be honest, Heath, you don't really need to apologise. I was the one in the wrong. I should have asked the girl in question to talk to someone else, someone trained to deal with teenagers. I'm useless with children, it's about time I just admitted defeat and stopped trying.'

'Charlotte, that wasn't what I meant at all!' Heath said, looking horrified. 'She chose you out of all the so-called experts because she felt she could trust you. That's really important. She needed you and you were there for her. You could have turned her away or sent her to find another youth worker, but you didn't! You gave her your time and did your best to help.'

There was a lump in her throat the size of a rugby ball. 'But I gave her the wrong advice.'

'You gave her the advice you thought was best,' Heath said firmly. 'Your motives were good. And, who knows, you may see her again and talk some more or she may choose a totally different course of action. Maybe adoption *is* right for her. I wasn't there, and I don't know the situation. Things will work out for the best, you'll see.'

'Will they?' Charlotte was doubtful. In her experience things tended to work out for the worst, not the best. Take her decision to think carefully about having children, for instance, that had effectively ended her marriage, hadn't it? But, of course, she couldn't say any of this to Heath; he didn't need to hear the sordid details of her messy life. He was her client, not her therapist.

He took her hand and squeezed it. 'I promise.'

Her hand lay in his. For a second Charlotte let it rest there, her fingers curled in the warmth of his palm, before sliding it away. The last guy's hand that had held hers had been Richard's and it felt strange to glance up and see Heath instead. Not strange nasty, just strange different.

'We're out hiking tomorrow. I'm hoping to give the kids a taste of the moors to prepare them for the play,' Heath was saying, smiling gently at her and not looking at all offended that she'd pulled away from physical contact. Then again, why should he be offended? Heath was with Cassandra, it wasn't as though he was interested in her. He was only being kind. Kind and probably thinking about the future funding for YORC, added a cynical little voice. After all, it wouldn't do to fall out with the person who had the power to decide the future of your project, would it?

'Would you like to come too?' Heath asked. 'We're only doing six miles and the forecast's good. You can't come all the way to Yorkshire and not see the moors.' He glanced down at her feet, still encased in the purple boots, and looked up again with twinkling emerald eyes. 'Don't wear those, though! I'd have to carry you all the way!'

Charlotte had a sudden mental image of herself clasped tightly against Heath's chest as he strode across the moors, her red hair sweeping the heather like something from the cover of a bodice ripper novel and her cheeks flamed. What was the matter with her tonight? A brisk walk in the cold Yorkshire air was probably exactly what she needed.

That or a cold shower!

'I'll come on the hike,' she said impulsively. 'And

don't worry about my footwear; I've got walking boots. You won't have to carry me.'

'Pity!' Heath gave her a cheeky wink and Charlotte couldn't help laughing.

'I've eaten so much here that you'd need a crane,' she sighed.

'Rubbish, you've got a fantastic figure,' Heath said firmly, his eyes sweeping her body appraisingly and making her blush again. Something crackled in the air between them and Charlotte found she could hardly breathe. Then Heath leaned closer and murmured, 'In fact, I think—'

Hard wired to protect herself, she pulled back quickly and ignored the part of herself that was longing to lean in and see what happened next. 'Do you know what, Heath—'

Heath sighed, as though recognising that Charlotte was so hard to get she was mission impossible. 'No, and don't tell me. I don't think I'll like it.' He was giving up. Heath stood and shrugged on his tattered Barbour. 'I'd better get home before the kids trash the house!'

'You don't have to go.' Charlotte was surprised to find herself protesting. She was disappointed and relieved in equal measure. She didn't want him to go and yet she didn't want him to stay, either. Not if the night was heading in the direction she thought it was. She couldn't bear to be with another man who was going to let her down and hurt her. But she found herself saying, 'Stay and have another drink.'

'I'd love to, but I really do need to get back!' Heath

brushed her cheek with his lips. Golden stubble rasped against her skin and she shivered.

She'd blown it!

Gritting her teeth so hard that it was a miracle they didn't shatter, Charlotte waved goodbye to Heath and wanted to kick herself. Whatever it was she'd felt between them had vanished like mist in the sunshine and now he was giving her a cheery wave and promising to collect her bright and early the next morning.

Just then, her mobile rang and Richard's number flashed up. 'What is it?' she barked into the receiver.

'And hello to you too,' said Richard cheerfully. 'Bad day?'

'It is now,' she snapped. 'Anyway, it's not as if you're interested, is it? Not when you've bailed out on me.'

'That's why I'm ringing, Lottie. I feel really bad about that and I need to explain why I left.'

Charlotte counted to ten. Anger was rising up inside her like red-hot lava. 'You don't need to explain. Suzie clicked her fingers and you came running. I understand.'

'You don't, though,' he protested. 'Suzie called me back because she sensed something was going on between you and me. And she was right, wasn't she?'

Her breath caught in her throat. She couldn't deny it. It might not make life easy but, in spite of everything, she did still have feelings for Richard, of course she did. She'd once loved him enough to marry him, for heaven's sake. He was the only man she'd dared to trust. Even though he had damaged that trust, there was always a chance they could build it up again.

'There's still something there, something that neither of us can deny,' pressed Richard. 'Admit it, Charlotte! I know you feel it too.'

Charlotte didn't know what to say. She was far too confused. The other evening when Richard had made his drunken declaration of love she'd thought that maybe there was still hope for them but then he'd wrecked it by running back to Suzie with his tail between his legs. Then there was her almost kiss with Paul earlier and the white-hot attraction she'd just felt for Heath only moments ago . . .

Her head was starting to hurt again.

'I meant every word I said the other night,' Richard told her softly. 'I know I was drunk but I was speaking from my heart. I still love you, Charlotte. I've never stopped loving you. I know things have got a bit complicated but surely what we had is worth fighting for? I've never stopped hoping for a reconciliation.'

'Richard, you live with another woman,' she said slowly, as though talking to an idiot. 'We're divorced, in case you'd forgotten. That's not exactly a minor detail.'

'Yes, yes,' Richard said impatiently, as though minor details were exactly what these were. 'I know all that, Lottie. But surely what really matters is that we're together again?'

Richard never failed to amaze Charlotte. He was like an emotional weapon of mass destruction. Never mind that he'd be breaking Suzie's heart and totally disrupting all of their lives.

'Richard, it's been a really long day. I've had to do

two people's jobs,' she told him wearily, 'and I really don't want to have this conversation. Not tonight. Only call me if it's work, OK?'

'But this is far more important than work!' Richard protested. 'This is the rest of our lives I'm talking about.'

'Goodnight, Richard. Give my love to Suzie,' she said coolly. Then she hung up on him, cutting off Richard's protestations with a very satisfying bleep.

'All the young men are after you tonight,' teased Archie from his usual position at the bar, nursing his whiskey and coke. 'They've certainly put the colour in your cheeks, too!'

'If I'm flushed, it's because I'm angry,' she snapped. 'And I'll thank you not to eavesdrop on my private conversations!'

And turning on her heel she stomped out of the bar and up to her room, her head pounding with every step she climbed. A painkiller and an early night would soon sort her out, Charlotte decided as she sank on to the bed and buried her pounding head in her hands. Dealing with her headache was the easy bit, sorting out her feelings for her ex-husband was proving to be far more complicated.

'Glad you came?' Heath asked the next morning as they paused for a breather. It had been a great hike up into the peaks and valleys of some of the most desolate but wildly beautiful landscape that Charlotte had ever seen. The kids, looking like tortoises beneath their bright rucksacks, had moaned and whinged to start with but, a couple of hours into the hike, they had plugged in their iPods, munched through their sweets and resigned themselves to the ordeal. They'd even given up asking if they were nearly there yet.

She knew *exactly* how they were feeling. Charlotte was longing to flop down into the bracken except that would make it look as though she was struggling and there was no way she was going to let Heath see how hard she was finding it. He hadn't said anything but the way he'd looked at her walking gear and raised his eyebrows told her that he thought she was a hopeless city girl.

Well, so what if she was? She'd show him! She'd like to see Mr Heath Macho Fulford negotiate the Hanger Lane gyratory system during the rush-hour!

Charlotte gave him a sideways glance. Even dressed in a bulky red anorak, sage combats and seriously chunky walking boots he still looked like an advert for Calvin Klein, all unshaven and rugged and with his thick hair wind-blown and tussled. His eyes were sparkling and there was a glow about him from the fresh air and exercise. He was clearly in his element, striding along and pointing out views and landmarks to the teenagers. Charlotte wished that the biting wind had the same effect on her, but rather suspected that her hair had been whipped into a knotty rat's nest and that her nose could put Rudolf out of business. Knowing her luck she probably looked more like an advert for Lemsip than high fashion!

'It's stunning up here,' she said diplomatically, 'although you might have warned me that you were running a boot camp! That last hill was nothing short of torture. What sort of sadist are you?'

Heath laughed. 'I never mentioned a relaxing stroll, Charlotte. I said we were hiking! Healthy exercise is just what these guys need.' He gestured towards the teens who were shrugging off their rucksacks and sprawling out on the coarse grass for a quick rest. Or, in Justin's case, a sneaky fag. 'They might moan a bit but, trust me, they're having a great time. I also have a theory that if they're worn out from fresh air and exercise they'll stay out of trouble.'

'Too exhausted to move, you mean?' Charlotte knew exactly how they felt.

'They're tougher than they look, believe me. I'm

more worried about you. Will you make it?'

Charlotte hated looking weak so there was no way she was admitting to Heath that her legs were screaming for leniency or that her feet were pleading for a quick death.

'Of course I will,' she said airily. 'I'm loving every minute.'

Heath gave her a sceptical look.

'Glad to hear it. We've done the easy bit, there's a tough section ahead now.' He grinned and bounded ahead to round up the teenagers.

That was the easy bit? Resigning herself to a few more miles of misery, Charlotte fell into step behind him and tried to ignore her throbbing feet.

'Are you enjoying the walk, Miss?' Ruby asked, joining her.

'I don't think *enjoying* it is quite the right word,' admitted Charlotte. 'But the scenery's amazing and the weather is beautiful, so I can't really moan.' Glancing down at Ruby she noticed that the younger girl was red in the face and struggling with the incline they were climbing. Even her breath was coming in painful rasps. Alarmed, she asked, 'Do you think you ought to be doing this hike in your condition?'

Ruby shrugged. 'Don't have a lot of choice, do I? My stepdad made me come. He said some fresh air and exercise would do me good.'

'I take it you haven't told him yet?'

'How can I?' said Ruby, her voice trembling. 'He's been through enough crap without me adding to it.'

'He sounds like he'd be there for you whatever,' Charlotte said carefully, aware now that she mustn't steer Ruby towards any course of action. 'Maybe he'd want to help.'

But the young girl wasn't having this and shook her head vehemently. 'No way! I'm not dragging him into my mess. Not until I have to, anyway. Like you said the other day, there're lots of nice people who'd love my baby and once I've sorted that I'll tell him. Then it won't be any hassle for him.'

Charlotte groaned, and not because the ground had suddenly become steeper. 'Ruby, I was wrong to encourage you to give up your baby. There are loads of other options available too. You don't have to handle this alone.'

Underneath her sweaty red cheeks Ruby paled. 'You're not going to tell anyone, are you? Please, Miss! You promised you wouldn't!'

'Of course I won't,' Charlotte assured her. 'If that's what you want, then I'll keep it a secret. But Ruby, I really think you need to talk to someone soon. The more time that goes by the more limited your options are.'

'I already told you I'm not having an abortion,' Ruby said. 'No way. I'm going to find this baby the best mum and dad I can find and then everything will go back to normal, won't it?'

Charlotte's heart went out to her. It was such a childlike sentiment. Make everything all right, was what Ruby was really saying, make it all go away. Charlotte might not have been a mum herself but she'd seen enough of her friends becoming parents to know that life was never the same again once you'd given birth.

'You'll always know you've got a child, Ruby,' she said gently. 'Adoption won't make that disappear.'

But Ruby wasn't listening. As far as she was concerned the decision was already made and nothing Charlotte could say now could sway her to explore other options. Watching her stomp miserably over to join Justin and Zak, head bowed and shoulders hunched defensively, Charlotte could only hope that it was the right decision because, no matter what she said now, it seemed that the damage was done. Ruby's mind was well and truly made up.

At about half twelve they arrived at a pub where Heath planned to stop for lunch. Situated at one of the highest peaks on the moors it had hovered on the horizon like a mirage. For the last mile, only the thought of collapsing in front of a roaring fire had motivated Charlotte to keep going. At long last she could sit down and unlace her boots and have a drink and a sandwich. At the idea of food her stomach rumbled so loudly that Heath heard it and laughed.

'I should have taken Archie up on his cooked breakfast after all,' Charlotte sighed, sinking on to a battered leather sofa. 'I am absolutely starving.'

'That's what real exercise does for you,' Heath teased, plopping down next to her and reaching across to grab a menu. His arm brushed against her breast as he did so and he pulled away abruptly as though scalded.

'Sorry!'

'It's fine,' she replied and then could have ripped her tongue out. It's *fine*? That sounded like an invitation to come and touch her up! 'What do you recommend?' she added quickly, fixing her eyes on the menu as though reading about toasted sandwiches required the concentration of translating Beowulf from the original.

'I'm well hungry,' Justin announced. 'What's good here, man? They don't have burgers, do they?'

'No, but the steak and kidney pie is amazing,' Heath was saying.

'The shepherd's pie is mint,' added Ruby, which confused Charlotte until she remembered that *mint* was teen speak for good. A discussion then followed with ten teenagers all yelling about what was better to eat. Panninis were *gay*, apparently, but sausage in a basket was *class*.

'It's a whole new language, isn't it?' Heath said as he scribbled their orders on to a beer mat. 'Don't worry, though; hang out with me for a bit longer and we'll soon have you fluent in teen.'

Does that mean he wants me to stick around? wondered Charlotte as he went off to order the food. And maybe, even more importantly, did she want to? Glancing across the pub her gaze was drawn to his broad-shouldered frame leaning against the bar as he chatted easily to the pretty barmaid. She was certainly impressed with him, Charlotte couldn't help noticing with amusement. Red Rum couldn't have tossed his mane any more energetically and if she batted those false eyelashes any more she'd do herself an injury. Heath threw back his head and laughed at something the girl had said and Charlotte wondered whether he was flirting with her.

It was just hunger that had made her stomach twist, that was all. Lack of food was playing tricks on her brain.

The sooner she ate the better . . .

Lunch was indeed *mint* and Charlotte didn't think she'd ever eaten anything as delicious as the steak and kidney pie. The pastry was light and golden, the meat so tender it dissolved on her tongue and the gravy rich with wine. She wolfed down every mouthful and mopped up the last of the dregs with a hunk of delicious rye bread. She'd needed that!

'So, who's walking the last two miles back and who's going to wimp out and take the bus?' Heath wanted to know once the plates had been cleared away and the teenagers were starting to get restless. 'It's mostly downhill, remember, and it shouldn't take too long.'

'No way!' Justin said, in horror. 'I'm knackered.'

The others nodded and murmured in agreement. Ruby was slumped in her seat and didn't look as though she could put one foot in front of the other to walk out of the pub, let alone hike back to the minibus. Charlotte was relieved that she'd be getting a ride back to town. She didn't know much about being pregnant but she was pretty sure six-mile hikes weren't recommended.

'Wimps,' said Heath good-naturedly.

'Teenagers need more sleep than old fogeys, man; it's official. I read it somewhere,' Zak told him.

'Well, even though I'm an old fogey, *I'm* walking back,' said Heath. Grinning at Charlotte, he added, 'Would you like to join me? Unless you're too tired, of course. It must be a total shock to encounter real exercise and not machines in a gym.'

Charlotte hadn't seen the inside of a gym since about 1995 but she wasn't about to tell Heath this. Let him think she spent her spare time pumping iron if he wanted. It was better than the reality, which was eating Häagen-Dazs and crying over her wedding video. Besides, Zoe thought she was holding back on living because she was scared of being hurt. What better than to prove her wrong by walking home alone with a man as undeniably attractive as Heath Fulford?

'A couple of miles are exactly what I need to work off lunch,' she declared, leaning back in her seat. How she managed not to wince as her muscles screamed was nothing short of a miracle. 'Don't worry, guys, I'll make sure this old fogey gets back in one piece!'

Heath groaned. 'You're as bad as they are! There's life in me yet! Right, Sinclair. Last one back's a loser!'

'Come on, then,' said Charlotte mischievously, jumping to her feet and grabbing her small rucksack. 'Or does the old man need help getting out of his chair?'

'Now you've done it!' In the blink of an eye Heath was up and pulling on his jacket.

After making sure the kids were safely back on the bus home, they strode along the deserted road that led from the pub and back down to York. The rugged moors swept above them, each peak standing like a sentinel against the bright blue sky. Map in hand, Heath turned left and away from the road, leading her along a track where the bracken was flattened by countless walking boots and the earth was freckled with rabbit droppings.

'You didn't think we were going on the road?' he asked, when Charlotte expressed surprise at the route. 'That would be far too dull. Besides, don't you see enough tarmac in the big smoke? This track takes us past a ruin right out of *Wuthering Heights*.'

'Do you come here often?' she teased.

'This is one of my favourite parts of the moors,' Heath replied. 'I was out here the other weekend, actually, with Cassandra.'

Charlotte had forgotten about the founding member of the Heath Fulford fan club. Hearing her name now, as they walked companionably together through the yellow gorse and the purple heather, came as something of a shock. She'd been on the verge of flirting with Heath, Charlotte realised, which was a pretty stupid thing to do seeing as he was attached. The half of cider she'd had at lunch must have gone to her head.

'It's beautiful out here,' she said quickly. 'What an amazing place to share with your partner.'

Heath stopped dead in his tracks and Charlotte cannoned off him. Turning round to face her he said firmly, 'Cassandra's not my partner, she's my friend.'

Charlotte's inner cynic was snorting. Yeah right! The sort of *friend* he met for lunch and took for romantic walks on the moors.

'Cassandra's a great person but there's nothing

between us,' Heath insisted, seeing the doubt on her face. 'She's certainly not my girlfriend.'

'Really?' Charlotte couldn't have been more incredulous if he'd told her the moon was made of cream cheese. Cassandra had been very keen to give the impression that she and Heath were an item; she had even hinted they had a past. Why on earth would she bother to lie? Heath, however, was a man and therefore genetically programmed to tell fibs.

'Really,' said Heath. He stepped closer and his eyes narrowed thoughtfully. 'Cassandra is not my girlfriend. Why does it bother you so much that she might have been?'

Charlotte's mouth dried. Something had shifted and she could feel a definite current of attraction between them. There was a fluttery feeling deep inside her that she struggled to identify for a split second before realising with surprise that it was hope. But what exactly was she hoping for? She turned her face up to his which was framed by those golden curls, his green eyes darker now with emotion. Then Heath smiled, reached out to brush a strand of red hair back from her cheek, and she realised with terror exactly what she was hoping for.

She was hoping that he would kiss her.

Horrified at this realisation she stepped away from him, digging her hands deep into her pockets rather than letting them reach up to touch his face as they were longing to.

'What you do in your personal life is none of my ·

business,' she said crisply. 'You don't owe me any explanations.'

'I know I don't,' Heath said gently. 'But I want you to know the truth about me and Cass.'

For a second they held each other's gaze. Charlotte looked away first.

'Cassandra was my wife's best friend,' Heath began. 'She's my friend too. We grew up together, actually, but it was Rachel she was closer to at the beginning. Anyway, when Rachel got sick Cass was always there for her and for me and the kids too.' He closed his eyes as though tortured by memories too painful to voice. 'Cancer's an evil disease. It doesn't just rob you of your life; it robs you of everything you hold dear. Rachel lost her dignity, her looks and, when the cancer reached her brain, she even lost that very part of her that made her who she was. She didn't recognise any of us towards the end. Not me, not Cass and not even the children. That was the cruellest thing of all.'

'I'm sorry.' Charlotte slipped her hand out of her pocket and almost without knowing she was doing it, made a small move to take his. For a split second their fingers brushed before catching hold and entwining.

Heath sighed. 'I wasn't a great deal of fun to be around. I was angry; I felt cheated and so totally and pathetically sorry for myself. How selfish was that? My wife was dying and I was sitting around concerned only about me. Cassandra, though, she was brilliant. She spent time with Rachel and made sure the kids were fed while I fell to pieces.'

Charlotte said nothing; she just squeezed his hand. Cassandra was blatantly in love with Heath but she wasn't surprised to hear that she was a good person. The work she did for Hope proved that.

'She has feelings for you, though,' she said softly.

Heath sighed. 'Her parents and mine were always the best of friends and I guess they'd hoped we might end up together, but I'd never seen her in that light. As Rachel got worse, Cass and I were pretty much thrown together and, what can I say? She was there for me. She understood what I was going through and maybe that led her to believe that one day there could be more between us. Perhaps we shouldn't have got so close. But I swear to God, Charlotte, I never meant to betray Rachel by letting Cassandra think there could ever be anything more than friendship between us. I never intended to give her the wrong idea.'

Charlotte could hardly believe what she was hearing. Unless her ears were playing tricks on her, Heath Fulford had just confessed to cheating on his dying wife with her best friend, citing his loneliness as an excuse! As though loneliness was a valid excuse for infidelity! For a second she froze before snatching her hand away from his.

'How could you?' she hissed, hating herself for still being so horribly attracted to him. 'How could you sleep with another woman while your wife was dying? That's the most despicable thing I've ever heard in my entire life!'

And hurtling away from him through the bracken as

fast as her sore feet could carry her, she ran and ran until her breath was ragged and painful.

'You've got it wrong!' Heath was calling after her. 'Charlotte, come back and let me explain!'

But Charlotte was beyond listening. Men! She was sick of all of them. They were useless and faithless, every single one!

'Charlotte, don't be stupid!' Heath was shouting now, his voice filled with fear. 'No matter what you think of me, please don't run off on the moors. It's dangerous out here. You'll get lost!'

Ignoring Heath's warnings Charlotte continued running. How hard could it be to get back? Surely if she kept heading downhill she'd end up in York? The city was only two miles away. Ducking to the right and crouching down behind some lichen-crusted rocks, she watched Heath run past, still calling her, before she turned and followed what looked like the path homewards. See! It was easy to find her way. Like that old saying about women needing men like fish needing bicycles – never a truer word spoken.

But, twenty minutes later, Charlotte was starting to regret her outburst of temper. A brisk wind had got up, whipping the hair from her face and stinging her cheeks, and the sky was no longer periwinkle blue but as dark and as heavy as lead. Mist was starting to billow upwards from the wetlands below and before long the peaks and rocky outcrops were no more than faint pencil sketches against the greyness. The mist crept up on her and muffled the world eerily so that all she could hear was the harsh scraping of her own breathing against the stillness and the slapping of her feet against the wet peat. Damp was beading her fringe and dripping from her hood and suddenly she felt a lurch of unease. Hadn't she just passed that rocky outcrop there? She paused for a moment, her heart hammering against the bone cage of her ribs. Was she going around in circles? Or headed in the wrong direction?

Slipping her rucksack from her shoulders she delved inside for her mobile, moaning in despair when she saw that there was no signal. All colour had totally faded now and ethereal wraiths of whiteness wrapped themselves soundlessly around any remaining landmarks until the entire landscape was flooded with a terrifying blankness. Trying to fight a growing sense of panic, Charlotte peered around her but, try as she might, she couldn't distinguish a single thing. Nothing existed any more except this terrifying emptiness and the chill that was slowly seeping into her bones.

She was well and truly lost.

Pulling her jacket closer she began to shiver. Why had she been so silly? Why did she run off in a huff just because she was unnerved by her sudden feelings for a handsome, complicated man? A normal person would have allowed Heath to explain how hard things had been when his wife was dying rather than jump to ugly conclusions. Who knew better than she did what it was like to live with someone who was in the grip of a cruel and unrelenting disease and just how lonely and desperate that could make you feel? She'd jumped on her high horse and now look where it had got her: lost and alone in the middle of the Yorkshire moors where she'd probably die of hypothermia if she didn't stumble into a marsh first, of course.

Tears stung her eyes and, for once, Charlotte didn't struggle to hold them back. What would be the point? There was no one here to see her cry, no one who'd be bothered that tough old Charlotte Sinclair was actually cracking. Burying her face in her hands she sobbed and sobbed until her eyes were swollen and her cheeks raw.

When she finally looked up she saw a light moving slowly through the gloom and for a split second she was terrified. What was it?

The light drew closer and a shadow drifted beside it, growing longer and darker as it drew nearer. Then to her utter joy she saw that there was nothing ghostly about this form, unless ghosts had red puffa jackets, torches and a mane of thick blond hair beaded with moisture. Striding towards her out of the fog was Heath. He was wet, worry had darkened his face and water dripped from the peak of his hood, but he'd never looked more beautiful to Charlotte. Forgetting their earlier row she hurled herself at him, shuddering with relief when his arms closed around her and held her tightly. She was still lost on the moors in the thickest fog she'd ever seen but everything would be fine now that Heath was here.

'I'm so sorry,' she sobbed into his chest.

Heath rested a hand on the top of her head, an amazingly gentle and tender gesture for such a big strong man. 'It's OK, sweetheart. Don't cry. It doesn't matter; I'm here now.'

She looked up at him, taken aback by the unexpected endearment. Was he teasing her? But those green eyes fringed with lashes spiked from the damp were filled with relief not mockery.

'I'm not just sorry about getting lost. I'm sorry about what I said earlier. I should have let you explain about Cassandra. I understand that things are complicated.'

Heath smiled. 'More than you know! You're a true fiery redhead, that's for sure! But don't blame yourself too much. Didn't I tell you yesterday that I'm not much good with words?'

'Well, I'm even worse at listening to them,' she sighed.

'I want you to know that I never cheated on Rachel. Not with Cassandra or anyone else.'

Charlotte was relieved, and when his arms tightened around her, she wanted nothing more than for him to dip his head and kiss her. In spite of the damp and chill she felt as though some deep secret part of her was thawing after a long hard winter. But then Heath released her and the moment passed.

'There's no mobile signal here,' Heath was saying, checking his phone just in case. 'So I think what we ought to do is try and retrace our steps back to the path, very slowly. Once we find it we'll be safe but until then we'll need to be really careful. The ground here can be treacherous.'

Charlotte nodded. Whatever Heath thought best

was fine by her. She was through with trying to fight him. Lacing his fingers tightly with hers he began to pick his way downhill, but the ground was wet and bumpy and several times they lost their footing. Heath's furrowed brow spoke volumes about how worried he was. Then she tripped again, ricking her ankle and crying out with the sharp pain.

Heath shook his head in despair. 'That looks quite bad,' he said, crouching down to where she was sprawled on the damp bracken and casting an experienced eye over her ankle. 'This isn't going to work. We'd better unlace that boot in case your foot swells and sit it out.'

'You mean we've got to stay here? All night?' Charlotte was horrified at the thought of spending a night outside on the moors.

'I'm afraid so. Even if you could walk, which I doubt, it's too dangerous in the fog and fading light. We'd better find somewhere to shelter.'

Cautiously and slowly they made their way over the treacherous ground to a rocky outcrop. It was shelter of sorts, Charlotte supposed bleakly as she leaned back against the rough stone and drew her legs up against her chest. It was bloody cold, though, and unless somebody was playing the castanets nearby those were her teeth she could hear chattering. The damp felt like it was seeping through her sodden clothes and into her bones. Even her goosebumps had goosebumps.

'This spot looks safe enough,' Heath said, dropping down next to her. 'The ground seems firm and we're out of the wind. All we need to do now is sit tight, keep warm and wait for the morning.'

'I'll have hypothermia by tea time,' Charlotte said, dismayed.

'We're going to have to get close and share body heat,' Heath told her. 'It's an old survival trick but skin-to-skin contact really does work.'

Skin-to-skin contact? She gulped. Was Heath saying that they needed to get naked if they were to survive? She wasn't sure she could trust herself not to become a molten puddle of desire if he undressed.

'The things men do to get women naked,' she tried to joke but the quaver in her voice gave away her fear.

Heath gave her a serious look. 'Don't look so worried. I don't think we need to go quite that far, but if we huddle together we will feel a lot warmer. Is that OK with you?'

She nodded and he slid an arm round her shoulders, pulling her close against his chest and tucking her against him under his padded jacket. Immediately she felt the warmth of his body and moments later the violent shivering subsided only to be replaced by a trembling of a very different kind.

'Warmer?' asked Heath and she nodded. Warmer didn't come close. Being so near to him was raising her body temperature to ridiculous proportions, especially since she could feel the hard muscles of his chest pressed against her back and his hot breath tickling her neck.

'Much warmer, thanks,' she agreed, the merest brush

of his hand against her thigh causing the rising tide of desire to tsunami through her nervous system. If only he wasn't the kind of guy who would hit on a married woman, she'd be tempted to get even warmer by slipping her hands inside his sweater . . . then maybe even a little lower . . .

Dear Lord, maybe she ought to step back into the cold? How could she bear a whole night of lying this near to Heath Fulford? She'd be a nervous wreck by the morning.

'I'm sorry if you feel awkward,' Heath said, mistaking her expression of anguish for a sigh of horror at having to be in such close physical proximity. 'But look on the bright side, at least this way we won't freeze to death.'

Hardly, thought Charlotte; she was about to spontaneously combust! Trying her best to ignore the hand placed on her thigh, she pretended to doze off, but it was practically impossible when every nerve ending in her body was on red alert. It was torture! Heath seemed totally at ease and slept peacefully, clearly having no idea how much of an effect he was having on her. Charlotte wasn't sure if that made her feel relieved or annoyed.

As the light began to leech from the sky Heath woke up and broke away to fish a slab of Dairy Milk out of his rucksack.

'My secret supply,' he explained as he offered her some. 'If I let on I had this with me the kids would have mugged me for it.'

She laughed. 'If I'd have known, I'd have mugged you for it too!'

They ate the chocolate and talked about the teenagers, trying to keep their minds off their situation. The conversation turned back to the young pregnant girl and whether or not she would follow Charlotte's advice.

'I saw so much of myself in her,' she sighed. 'Not that I was a teen mum, but when my own mum walked out I was basically left looking after my little brother. It was really hard. Even though I loved him I resented missing out on doing all the things that my friends were up to. I'd hate to see anyone else go through the same thing if there was another option.'

'What about your dad? Didn't he help out?'

'He was an alcoholic,' she said quietly. 'He still is, actually. So when it came to looking after Steve it was all down to me.'

Goodness. She'd never told anyone that before. Even Richard had only found out months into their relationship. There was something about Heath, though, that inspired confidence.

His arms tightened around her. 'That must have been hard. I understand now why you wanted that young girl to have the chance of a normal teenage life.'

Charlotte sighed. 'But like you said, how much of what I said to her was really about me? What's normal anyway? How do you get it right?'

He shook his head, showering her with moisture. 'If it makes you feel any better, I don't think anyone ever does. There are thousands of adults in therapy who prove that! All you can do as a parent is trust your instincts and act out of love and concern. Mostly they ignore you and sometimes they say they hate you, but at least you've done your best. My stepdaughter certainly hates me today. She spends far too much time moping in her bedroom so I made her come out hiking and get some fresh air.'

Charlotte suddenly felt cold to the marrow, and this time it was nothing to do with the icy mist. Oh dear Lord. Surely not?

'Is your stepdaughter Ruby?' she whispered.

'Yes. Didn't you know that? I thought I'd told you?'

No, she could safely say that he hadn't. Great. Now she was in even more of a predicament. Suddenly all the pieces fell into place. The mother who'd died, the stepfather who'd been heartbroken but tried to hold it together, the involvement with YORC. Of course Ruby was Heath's stepdaughter. Why hadn't she realised earlier? Now Heath would think she'd deliberately been keeping secrets from him. She'd have to keep Ruby's secret, too, because she'd promised that she would.

Luckily Heath couldn't see her horrified expression. Instead he carried on chatting about Ruby.

'I'm so pleased that she's got the part of Cathy,' he was saying. 'I know it's a big responsibility having the lead role but it could be really good for her. She doesn't have much confidence and she's been so withdrawn lately.'

'She does seem a bit troubled,' Charlotte offered. Hint, hint.

Heath sighed. 'Ruby was never the most outgoing kid but she's so introverted now. She hardly ever sees her friends and she spends hours in her room listening to music. Cass says it's just typical teenage behaviour but I'm not so sure. Something doesn't feel right.'

'Try talking to her,' Charlotte suggested. Even though it would be a shock Charlotte knew it was the best course of action.

'She needs her mum,' Heath said sadly. 'Rachel would have known exactly how to handle it. She was brilliant with the children, such a natural. I try my best but stepdads just aren't the same.'

He sounded so bleak that she reached for his hand and squeezed it. 'From what I've heard it sounds like you do a great job. To be honest, I really admire anyone who's brave enough to be a parent. Just the thought of it terrifies me.'

'You've got nothing to be terrified about!' Heath said firmly. 'I've seen you with the kids at YORC and you're great with them. Besides, you wouldn't be doing it on your own. You'd have your husband around to help out.'

Charlotte swallowed. 'Actually, Heath, there's something you need to know.' She had to tell him she had misled him about Richard and her still being married. 'Maybe I should have made it a bit clearer. The truth is . . . I would be on my own because I'm not with Richard any more. We're divorced.'

Although it was dark she could feel the heat of his gaze searing into the back of her head.

'Why didn't you tell me before?' Heath asked softly.

For a moment she paused. There were reasons lurking just below the surface that were too complicated to try and explain. She wasn't even certain that she understood them herself or even wanted to.

'Didn't you trust me to understand?' he added.

Charlotte shook her head. 'That wasn't it. I didn't say anything because you'd just assumed that we were together and it seemed easier to let you carry on thinking that. I don't like talking about the divorce much, and by the time I did consider telling you the truth, it just felt too complicated.' She paused because Heath didn't seem at all taken aback to hear any of this. In fact, he didn't seem surprised at all.

'You already knew,' she whispered. 'You were just waiting to hear it from me, weren't you?'

'Guilty as charged,' Heath admitted. 'The day after his drunken antics Richard called to apologise. He was really embarrassed and said that if you hadn't already divorced him you would have done now for his performance at dinner. I was a bit taken aback, to be honest, because he seemed to adore you. Then I thought what an idiot he must be to have let someone like you slip through his fingers.'

Charlotte was glad it was dark so that Heath couldn't see her face. She was struggling to adjust to this new world view because it made things look very, very different. When Heath had called and asked her out for dinner he wasn't a sleaze hitting on a married woman. He'd known she was single! Which meant . . . which meant . . .

Heath Fulford was a genuinely nice man.

Yet again it seemed she'd managed to get him totally and utterly wrong.

Charlotte wasn't sure how it happened, but somehow she managed to slip into a doze and the next thing she knew, Heath was shaking her awake. The mist had gone and pearly daylight was stealing over the moors. It was beautiful. Charlotte and Heath made their way back to the track, his strong arms supporting her with her wobbly ankle. After only about twenty minutes of walking they reached the road where a kind farmer picked them up and drove them back to the hotel.

Heath was desperate to get home and see the kids. He'd already phoned a frantic Cassandra and spoken to Ruby and the boys. She felt a pang of regret that there was nobody who was frantic with worry for her; Archie was probably the only person who'd noticed her absence. This was quickly replaced by annoyance when she dragged herself into the lobby to discover Richard waiting like an angry Victorian father.

'Where the hell have you been?' her ex-husband demanded, his furious eyes dark as coffee beans.

'Calm down,' cut in Archie, who'd been hovering in the background. 'The lass looks right poorly. Let her sit and have a brandy, lad.'

Richard glowered at him but bit his lip. Charlotte

felt exhausted and now the elation of being back and safe was ruined. The last thing she needed was another round of blame slinging with her ex.

'What are you doing here?' she asked wearily, still leaning against Heath who helped her on to a chair and eased off her walking boot. 'I thought you'd gone home to Suzie. Surely she hasn't let you out again, not with your wicked ex-wife on the prowl?'

'This isn't about Suzie,' thundered Richard. 'It's about you! What were you thinking, going for a hike on the moors? Anything could have happened. I was worried sick when I heard you'd gone missing. I came up here to find you.'

Charlotte glanced down at Heath, who raised a curious eyebrow as he tugged off the boot. The fact that Richard must have driven all through the night to get to the hotel wasn't lost on him. It was hardly standard behaviour for an ex-husband.

'This looks nasty,' Heath said, gently touching the swollen purple flesh. 'It might be worth getting it X-rayed.'

'I'll look after her,' Richard said quickly. 'I'm sure you've got other things to do.'

'I'm happy to stay,' Heath said softly to Charlotte, his hand still on her skin.

She smiled down at him. 'Go on and get back to the kids. One night of cold and discomfort is more than enough for anyone.'

'You were out together all night?' Richard looked slowly from her to Heath, hardly able to conceal his dislike of this thought. 'Alone?'

'Get a grip, Richard!' said Charlotte, finally finding her voice after being taken aback by his jealousy. Was this proof that Richard really did still love her after all? 'Yes, I spent the night with Heath – on the moors and in the freezing fog! I fell and hurt my ankle and when the mist came down we couldn't get any further. If Heath hadn't stayed with me I'd have died of hypothermia!'

Richard held his hand out to Heath. 'I can't thank you enough for looking after her. I owe you.'

'No problem,' said the ever-generous Heath, shaking his hand. 'It was the least I could do after all the help Charlotte's given me.'

Richard still didn't look overjoyed that she'd spent the night with Heath, even if it was in wet and miserable circumstances, but he managed to curb his jealousy and offered to drive him home. Declining, Heath said he needed to pop into YORC and that Cassandra would pick him up from there and run him home.

Good old Cassandra again. *She does a lot of partner-like things for someone who isn't his partner*, Charlotte found herself thinking and then gave herself a mental shake.

Who sounded jealous now?

That was ridiculous. She wasn't jealous of Cassandra!

'I'll be off, then,' Heath said. His hand slipped from her foot and Charlotte felt a jolt of longing. 'Take care, Charlotte. I hope the ankle gets better. Have a safe journey back to London.'

London. Of course. Charlotte's time in Yorkshire was over and today she was due to return home and back to her normal life. No more chatting to Archie in the evenings, playing with Isla or talking to Heath. She'd be back in the office and back to her usual routine of double espressos, funereal suits and feeling bitter over her failed marriage. Her heart sank with the inevitability of it all. Only days ago she couldn't wait to go home and go back to normal.

So what had changed since then?

14

The sky was blazing pinks and crimsons when they finally arrived back in London later that evening. As before, it was a quiet journey with just the two of them in the car, but this time the lack of conversation was more to do with Charlotte sleeping most of the way, rather than a falling out. A trip to the hospital in York had revealed that her ankle was badly sprained, but nothing more. The strong painkillers that they'd given her, mingled with the brandy from Archie, had made her woozy. It came as something of a surprise when she opened her eyes and realised that they were cruising round the M25, only half an hour from home.

Or, only half an hour away from the empty flat she *called* home.

'Hello, there,' Richard said, as she yawned and stretched. 'I was starting to wonder whether you'd ever wake up.'

'It was a bit of a long night. I hardly slept. And before you start, not because of anything worth staying awake for.'

Unfortunately, she thought to herself. Heath had had

every opportunity to take advantage of her if he'd wanted to but he'd been the perfect gentleman. She supposed that meant he didn't find her attractive and that his dinner invitation really had been work related. It was just as well she was back in London; she'd been in danger of making a fool of herself if she'd stayed in Yorkshire for much longer. She'd most likely never see Heath Fulford again, which was probably a good thing.

But if it was a good thing, why did the thought make her want to crawl into bed and never emerge from the depths of her duvet?

'I'm so sorry about earlier,' Richard said, mistaking her sigh of regret for one of irritation. 'It was just that seeing you with *him* . . . for a moment I really thought there was something between you and I couldn't bear it. Honestly, Charlotte, I thought I'd lost you.'

'You lost me months ago,' she pointed out. 'Although *lost* isn't quite the right word, is it? *Discarded* would be more accurate.'

Richard's eyes slid from the road to hers. 'Despite what you think of me, I love you, Charlotte. I've always loved you and I always will. We're meant to be together; I know we are.'

She looked away, preferring the blur of ugly industrial estates to his pleading expression. Once it had really moved her and she'd have done anything to make Richard happy, but after his betrayal with Suzie she'd had to learn to cut out any tender feelings she had. It was the only way to survive.

'You're with Suzie now,' she said dully. 'We shouldn't even be having this conversation.'

'Getting involved with Suzie was stupid, a moment of weakness, and I should never have allowed it to get this far. But I was angry, Lottie! You were so quick to file for divorce and you wouldn't even hear me out.' He hung his head. 'I suppose I was hurt that you could give up on us so easily; that was why I let things move so fast with Suzie.'

'Yes,' she said, simply. The black and white was blurring to grey and she was beginning to see that Richard had a point.

'I wrecked what we had and I have to live with that,' said Richard hoarsely. 'But you never ever gave me a chance to make it up. *You* bailed out on the marriage, not me. I would have given anything to try again.'

Was she quick to judge? After all, it hadn't taken her very long to make assumptions about Heath and Paul, had it? She did tend to fly off the handle and leap to conclusions. Had her marriage deserved a second chance?

'I don't mean to be judgemental,' she said slowly, 'and perhaps you're right, perhaps I was too quick to give up on us. But you really hurt me, Richard.'

Richard didn't say anything but his hand slipped from the wheel to find hers. It felt familiar, the fingers long and slim, the nails manicured and the skin soft. City hands, she found herself thinking, not like the large, calloused but infinitely gentle hands that had held hers earlier. But she shouldn't be thinking about Heath any more. Heath was gone and Richard was here. And Richard was telling her he still loved her.

'I was so scared of having a baby,' she said quietly. 'I'd already had to basically raise Steve alone and I was terrified of being in that position again. So when you slept with Suzie it was like having all my worst fears confirmed. That's why I filed for divorce. Not because I didn't love you. Of course I bloody well loved you.'

'I'm so sorry,' Richard told her and this time Charlotte actually believed him. The way he slumped in the seat spoke volumes, as though all the fight had been knocked out of him. Richard wasn't the pantomime villain she'd built him into. He was just a person, as flawed and confused and as human as anyone else. Richard loved her. He'd just driven hundreds of miles to be with her and the worry written on his face when he'd thought she was missing said more than any words and protestations.

'I know you are,' she said softly, reaching out and covering the hand now looped over the gear stick. 'And for what it's worth, I'm sorry too. I think maybe part of me used what you did with Suzie as an excuse to not have to face my fears about having children. The adult thing to do is talk things through, not lock your feelings in a box and throw away the key. Richard, I'm sorry about how I treated you. If I could turn the clock back, I'd behave so differently. I feel so differently about everything now.'

Richard took the next exit off the motorway, pulled into a side road and killed the engine. Turning to face her properly he asked, 'Are you trying to tell me there's still hope for us?'

She started at his choice of words. Still hope. Love would come to her through hope alone, Angela had said. Was this the completion of her prophecy? Suddenly fear of the unknown took hold of her and Charlotte felt her hands tremble. She clamped them together and looked up at him. That sensation of being back on the highest diving board was back. But then she'd just risked life and limb out on the moors, hadn't she? Maybe it was time to stop being cautious and to live her life?'

'I think I'm ready to try again,' she told him softly. 'If you still want to, that is?'

'Do you mean that?'

Her heart was thudding. It was time to jump. 'Yes, Richard. I really do.'

His face, as familiar to her as her own, split into an enormous grin. He pulled her into his arms, as best he could since they were squashed in his tiny car, and brushed her lips tentatively with his. Charlotte closed her eyes and held on to the sense that she was doing the right thing. She'd loved Richard once; she could get that back and everything would be fine.

Sometimes taking risks paid off.

A week later Charlotte wasn't quite so certain whether things could ever return to normal, whatever normal meant. Although she'd spent lots of time with Richard since then, the majority of it had been in the office as they worked to finish their reports on YORC and the

Hope Foundation. He was very sweet and attentive, buying her lunch and sending flowers to the flat, but outside of the office he was more elusive than the Scarlet Pimpernel. There was the tricky issue of Suzie: although he made all the right noises, Richard had yet to tell her it was over.

'I'm just waiting for the right time to break it to her,' Richard insisted whenever Charlotte pressed him on the issue. 'Suzie's vulnerable, you know?'

Charlotte didn't know, but she'd caught Suzie watching her and Richard together with such an unhappy expression on her face that she felt horribly guilty. No matter what she thought of her boss, Suzie was still Richard's partner. She also found that unless she was very strict with herself, her thoughts kept slipping back to Heath and the night she'd spent with him on the moors. During a lull at work or last thing at night before she drifted off to sleep, she found she was reliving the way it had felt when he'd held her close to keep her warm. The sense of safety and acceptance still puzzled her. What was it about Heath that, although he constantly challenged and often infuriated her, made her feel she could tell him anything? She'd shared some of her deepest, darkest fears with him; he'd seen her mess up; yet she'd felt as though he'd really understood her in a way that nobody else ever had, not even Richard.

Charlotte abandoned her paperwork and sighed. This was ridiculous. Heath was just a client. He'd probably been kind because he was desperate for his project to get the funding, nothing more. She should put him right out of her mind and concentrate instead on mending her marriage. Mooning around like a lovesick schoolgirl when she was thirty-four was just pathetic.

'That's a big sigh,' Richard said, sitting down beside her. 'Are you missing me?'

'Like a blister,' she said, but the curve of her mouth belied the sarcasm, as did the fact that only an hour earlier they'd sneaked a kiss in the stationery cupboard. Teenage behaviour, but oddly enjoyable!

'So cruel,' Richard said to nobody in particular. 'Come on, leave all this paperwork behind and come out for lunch. My shout.'

Charlotte was hungry. But she'd booked the afternoon off work to go shopping with Zoe to find a dress to wear to the prestigious charity awards ceremony she was attending that evening. It was being held at the V&A and a host of celebrities were rumoured to be presenting the awards. The female contingent of the office was almost hysterical with excitement because Luke Scottman, one of the hottest actors on the planet, was presenting an award and those lucky enough to have an invite had been planning their outfits for months. All except for Charlotte. Luke Scottman was certainly hot enough to melt the polar ice caps but those blue eyes didn't really do it for her. No, a mosaic of emeralds and jades was all she needed—

Stop it!

She'd been planning to wear her trusty black Next dress until Zoe's horrified reaction made her think again. Now she was doomed to trawl Selfridges until her sister-in-law was satisfied. Once upon a time Charlotte would have protested but she was surprised to find that actually she was looking forward to going shopping. She'd even worn her purple boots to surprise Zoe.

After those few days in Yorkshire she felt different, as though she wasn't quite herself.

Weird.

'I'm meeting Zoe for lunch,' she told Richard. 'And I've already told you that we're not going on any kind of date until you've spoken to Suzie properly.'

'Meet me for drinks before the awards ceremony, then?'

She was just about to point out that he was taking Suzie to the ceremony because he hadn't broken up with her yet, when Suzie came charging towards them like a paratrooper, her face clouded with anger and suspicion.

Uh oh, thought Charlotte. Was this the point where Suzie abandoned her policy of never bringing the personal into the office and walloped her?

But instead of asking them what they were whispering about, Suzie just took a deep breath and demanded Charlotte's reports by the end of the day.

'You can have them now if you like,' Charlotte said calmly. 'I've just finished. I think both organisations should continue to receive funding; they both do amazing work.'

Suzie nodded. 'Email them now and I'll have a read through. But I doubt that the board will approve both when they come up for appraisal.' Then she turned on her heel and returned to her office without so much as a thank-you.

'Oh dear,' said Richard. 'Not a happy bunny.'

Charlotte watched her leave with a sinking heart. Suzie's unhappiness really upset her. Gathering her bag and jacket she frowned at Richard.

'I can't keep doing this,' she told him. 'You need to have that conversation with Suzie. I know it won't be pleasant and you feel bad about hurting her, but you're not being fair to anyone otherwise.' He began to protest so she told him again. 'Don't call me until you do. It's not right.' And, shouldering her bag, she stalked from the office leaving Richard open mouthed behind her.

Charlotte pulled her pashmina around her shoulders as she stepped out of the cab. Although it was only late September, the nights were drawing in and tonight a cloudless black velvet sky was sprinkled with frosty stars. The strapless frock Zoe had helped her choose might have made her chilly, but at least she knew she looked good. It was worth it, even if she did die of starvation tonight. The boned bodice was so tight that she could barely breathe, never mind eat.

The V&A was ablaze with lights and the road crawling with taxis and limos. There was Dame Judi Dench, looking as collected and stylish as always, ahead of her was Peter Andre, looking darkly handsome in a white tux. And in a blaze of flashbulbs was none other than Victoria Beckham, looking stunning in skin-tight black Cavalli.

Charlotte gulped. No wonder the girls at work had been planning their outfits like a military operation! This was a serious stylish event. She just hoped her dress wasn't too loud. Maybe she should have stuck to black, like Posh?

'No more black, Charlie!' Zoe had insisted as they combed every department in Selfridges in the attempt to find the perfect dress. 'It's a Charity Awards Gala, not a funeral!' Frog-marching Charlotte away from a black Coast sheath and up to the designer floor, they'd rummaged through Valentino and Ralph Lauren, goggling over the prices. Finally ending up in Jaeger, Zoe had plucked a bright emerald silk dress with a crystal-studded bodice and a fishtail skirt. Trying it on, Charlotte had thought all she needed to complete the look was a goldfish bowl. But Zoe had been in raptures.

'You look amazing!' she'd squealed, grabbing Charlotte by the shoulders and forcing her to look in the mirror. 'Just look!'

So Charlotte had looked. And she'd been amazed! The dress clung to her curves in all the right places, cinching her waist to a hand span and giving her the most spectacular cleavage. Against the bright silk her skin glowed like polished glass and the jewel-bright hue made her eyes aquamarine and her hair like flame.

'It's amazing what good tailoring can do,' she'd said, studying herself from several different angles.

'Good tailoring, my bum!' snorted Zoe. 'This is all

you. Haven't I been telling you for years that you'd look stunning in colours? You are *so* buying this dress!'

And with that Charlotte had been escorted to the till, via the shoes, bags and pashminas, of course, and ended up blowing a good chunk of her savings.

Next stop: the salon, where her hair was tonged into corkscrews and piled up on to her head with glittery clips. At the time Charlotte had thought all of this a ridiculous extravagance but now that she'd seen the fashionistas she was rubbing shoulders with, she could have kissed Zoe.

That ancient cocktail dress from Next would *so* not have done!

Once inside, Charlotte accepted a glass of champagne from one of the waiters, trying not to look as though she was staring at the host of celebrities. She spotted Luke Scottman looking ridiculously handsome in his tuxedo, flanked by beautiful women as groomed and glossy as thoroughbreds. Charlotte recalled Zoe saying she'd been friends with Luke Scottman at Uni. Charlotte decided to introduce herself if she got a chance; it might be nice for Luke to remember that he had real friends rather than fans. On the other hand, she saw his on/off girlfriend Trinity place a possessive hand on his arm. Her sullen pouting seemed genuine, not just for the cameras. *Trouble in Tinseltown*, thought Charlotte. Maybe she would stay put. She had no desire to have a Manolo buried between her eyes.

Leaving the celebrities to pose, she decided to work the room. After greeting colleagues and clients, all of whom were really sweet about her dress, Charlotte decided to venture into the atrium for some fresh air. She was just leaning across the ornamental pond to see if her cheeks were as flushed as they felt when a second reflection floated next to her like a wraith. Dear Lord! She was going stark raving mad! For a moment she'd really thought she'd seen Heath. Teetering on the edge of the lake she would have fallen in if two strong hands hadn't grasped her waist and steadied her.

'I'm so sorry! I didn't mean to make you jump.' Although it was dark, Charlotte could sense a smile in the velvety blackness and instantly her heart went into freefall.

'What are you doing here?' she gasped.

'Sometimes, Ms Sinclair, I'm allowed to venture down to the big smoke. I don't even need a passport!' Heath's cheeky grin turned into a look of pride as he said, 'YORC's been nominated for an award.'

'Congratulations!'

'Thank you.'

Heath's gaze lingered on her figure before returning to her face. Admiration was written all over him.

'I couldn't believe it when I saw you,' he murmured, his eyes locking with hers. In spite of the chilly night air, Charlotte suddenly felt very warm indeed. 'You're looking amazing. Better than amazing. You look absolutely beautiful.'

Charlotte opened her mouth to make the usual sarcastic self-deprecating remark, but closed it again. Heath wasn't being sleazy; he was being genuine.

'Thanks,' she said. 'You look pretty good yourself.'

That was an understatement. Dressed in a black tux with his bow tie loosened, golden stubble already shadowing his firm jaw line and his blond curls cork-screwing over his collar, Heath looked like he, rather than Luke Scottman, had just strolled off a film set.

'So how's the ankle?' Heath was asking.

'It's fine. It was only a sprain,' Charlotte assured him.

'Does that mean I may be able to have a dance later?' he asked softly, reaching out to push a stray curl behind her ear. 'If you want to, of course. And if Richard lets me. I know you're divorced but I've seen the way he's looking at you tonight.'

Richard? Charlotte had almost forgotten about him. Trying to work out how she felt about her ex was harder than running through treacle, while her feelings for Heath were easy to fathom: she wanted to dance with Heath, very, very much.

'I think Richard can let me out of his sight for one dance!' she said.

Heath stepped closer, so close that his eyelashes were almost brushing hers. 'Then he's a fool,' he said softly. 'Because I wouldn't.'

With that, the last of the frost in Charlotte's heart melted and suddenly she realised that she wanted nothing more than for Heath Fulford to kiss her. *This will never do*, she told herself sharply. She was back with Richard. She just was on the brink of trying to explain this to Heath, easier said than done when her heart was racing like she was running the marathon, when they were interrupted by Cassandra, channelling Barbie in a pink frilly frock, armed with champagne and canapés.

'Heath! There you are. I've managed to find some food. And Charlotte! Hello! Tuck in; I've got enough for us all!'

Charlotte was so taken aback to see Cass that before she even knew it she was chomping on a mini Yorkshire pudding. Heath and Cassandra had come to the gala together. Did that mean that they were now an item? From the easy way Cassandra tucked her hand into the crook of Heath's arm, she supposed it must.

'You look lovely, Charlotte!' Cassandra said, as sunshiny as always. 'Doesn't she, Heath?'

'Yes,' Heath agreed, but couldn't quite look Charlotte in the eye.

Charlotte wondered how it was possible to lurch from hope to despair so quickly. Moments ago she'd felt fantastic in her dress but in comparison to the petite Cassandra she suddenly felt clumsy and awkward.

'It's great to see you guys again,' she said brightly, slapping a smile on to her face, relieved that it was too dark for either of them to see that it was more of a grimace. 'I'd love to chat but I think Richard will need me. I'll catch you later, maybe?'

And, leaving them in the romantic glow of the fairy lights, she fled back into the hall where, vowing to avoid Heath Fulford for the rest of the night, she busied herself networking and entertaining various dignitaries. At one point she even got chatting to Luke Scottman. He was friendly and down-to-earth. She brought him up to date with Zoe's news, laughed with him at Libby's exploits and even managed to persuade him to contact YORC and discuss doing a workshop with the kids.

'Anything for Zoe's sister-in-law,' Luke said gallantly, whipping out his BlackBerry and punching in her number. 'Besides, I know what a difference drama can make. It wasn't so long ago that I was a bored teenager myself.'

'It feels like for ever to me,' sighed Charlotte.

'You don't look a day over nineteen,' he fibbed kindly. 'I'll give you a call when I'm next in town and we'll sort something. Maybe fly up to York in the helicopter? And perhaps have a drink afterwards?'

'That would be fantastic. Thanks so much!' said Charlotte. Wow! Had she just been propositioned by a movie star? As she took his number she felt someone's gaze burning into her back with the force of a blowtorch. Turning slowly, she expected to see Trinity charging over for a *keep your hands off my man* showdown. What she didn't expect was to find it was Heath staring at her. Catching her eye, he raised his glass in congratulations before following Cassandra into the dining room.

'We're on different tables,' Richard complained when Charlotte joined him by the seating plan. 'How annoying! I don't know anyone I'm sitting with.'

'Where's Suzie sitting?' she asked.

Richard shrugged. 'She hasn't come. We had a row and she refused to come. Bloody unprofessional, in my opinion.'

'Was it about us?'

Richard shook his head. 'But I will tell her!' he insisted when Charlotte raised her eyes to heaven. 'Tonight. When I get home, I promise.'

The word 'home' was like a slap in the face. Richard and Suzie had a home together. This wasn't a game he was playing. Real people and real emotions were involved and the more Richard prevaricated the more painful and messy the situation would become.

'Do whatever you think best, Richard,' she told him wearily. 'Either you love me or you don't. Just make up your mind and let me know.'

Leaving him by the seating plan she made her way to her table, trying to swallow down her annoyance so that she could at least manage a starter. Unlike her ex she did know someone at her table, and waving delightedly she took her seat next to Paul. She hadn't seen him since the *almost* kiss but, as he pecked her cheek and said hello, she was delighted that there was no awkwardness between them. She realised now that it had never been more than a flight of fancy. But Paul was a nice guy and she liked him a lot.

'You look wonderful,' Paul said as she took her seat. Charlotte murmured her thanks but couldn't quite return the compliment. Paul was still his smiley self but his big bear-like body seemed uncomfortable in the constraints of a tux. He'd also had the most severe haircut since Britney Spears and looked as though he'd wandered on to a sheep farm and been shorn by mistake.

'I know, I know, it's horrendous.' Paul laughed at the surprised look on her face. 'I foolishly let Isla paint *Nordic Princess* and ended up with half a pot of red paint on my head. Unlike you, being a redhead doesn't suit me so I had to get Elise to shave the lot.'

'Paint plus kids equals disaster.' She winked at him, knowing he'd remember her experience. 'But how is Isla? And Elise?'

'Isla's great, still talks about you non-stop,' Paul told her, whacking butter on to a bread roll. 'You were a big hit.'

She smiled sadly. At least somebody loved her!

'Elise is good, too. Actually, we've become quite close again.' Paul dropped his voice and leaned closer. 'We've talked a lot since she saw you and me together in the workshop.'

'I hope you told her nothing happened!'

'Of course I did. And to be honest, I'm glad nothing happened,' said Paul. 'Not that I don't think you're amazing,' he added hastily.

Charlotte smiled to let him off the hook. He was right. One silly moment was all it had been, and thank goodness they had stopped before it was too late. Being involved with Paul would have made it impossible for him to sort things out with his wife.

Hang on a minute. That sounded familiar . . .

Had it been the same for Richard and Suzie? If she'd been less judgemental, less afraid, less set on divorce, might his fling with Suzie have remained just that? A fling?

'I think I might be ready to forgive Elise,' Paul was saying, his expression thoughtful.

Charlotte recalled how Elise's eyes had filled with tears when she'd admitted why she and Paul had broken up. She would have staked her last penny that Elise was still in love with him. 'I'm sure Elise is sorry. From what you've told me you guys were going through a tough time. Making mistakes is only human.'

If only she'd been this wise eighteen months ago! Paul's situation mirrored her own; yet he was willing to forgive and move on, whereas she'd been so unforgiving of Richard's imperfections.

'And to forgive, divine,' said Paul.

Charlotte was clearly no angel.

She'd had enough of schmoozing, especially as a million thoughts were making her head whirl. Or was that the champagne? She crept out of the grand doors on to the steps outside and shivered at the blast of cold night air against her skin. Scanning the street for a cab, the touch of a warm hand on her bare shoulder practically sent her into orbit.

'Sorry,' Richard grinned, looking anything but, 'didn't mean to make you jump. What are you up to?'

'Dancing the tango, obviously,' quipped Charlotte, her heart hammering.

'Oh, well, I'm waiting for a cab.' Richard smiled weakly. 'Although I'm not quite sure where it's going to take me. I've just called Suzie and she's told me not to bother coming home.'

Charlotte sighed.

'I was supposed to do an errand for her today and I totally forgot.' Richard looked so woebegone that only someone with a heart of stone could have resisted feeling sorry for him. 'I suppose I'll end up in a hotel room somewhere,' he continued, those melting Malteser eyes wide and hurting. 'But it's probably for the best. It's not where I want to be any more. I want to be with you.'

Charlotte's heart of stone crumbled. She looked deep into his eyes. 'Why don't you ask if you can come home with me?'

'I love the way you always cut to the chase,' Richard said softly. 'Of course I want to be with you.'

She opened her mouth to point out that he hadn't felt quite this way last year, but stopped herself. Maybe it was time to stop snapping at him and cut Richard some slack?

'In that case, come and stay at mine. Or should I say, *ours*?' she replied and was rewarded by a smile of such sweetness that she was reminded exactly why she'd fallen for him in the first place. When he wasn't driving her round more bends than a Formula One star, Richard could be very loveable. Even his terrible jokes were endearing to her.

When Richard's cab arrived he gave the driver Charlotte's address, and in spite of herself she felt a tingle of excitement. There was something illicit and undeniably thrilling about hurtling through the deserted midnight streets in the back of a taxi. When the car braked suddenly, throwing her against him, she liked feeling Richard's arms close around her. Moments later they were kissing – hot, hard, urgent kisses which were familiar, yet half forgotten. It felt like coming home. Charlotte closed her eyes and gave herself up to the warmth of his mouth, kissing him back and pulling him closer and closer. For a fleeting second the thought of Suzie gave her a twinge of guilt but then his kisses grew deeper and more demanding, driving away all thoughts save the pressure of his lips against hers.

While Richard settled the fare Charlotte decided that the sooner she got into a cold shower the better. She may have decided to try again with Richard but she'd intended to take things slowly. Ripping his clothes off in the entrance hall probably wasn't the best idea!

'Can I come up for a coffee, then?' asked Richard with a wicked grin as she unlocked the front door.

'You don't drink coffee any more,' Charlotte reminded him. 'Suzie says it has far too many toxins.'

He grimaced. 'Suzie talks a load of bollocks sometimes. If I never see another glass of wheatgrass juice again it'll be too soon. Besides,' he added, moving closer and pulling her into his arms, 'it's over with Suzie, so I can drink what I like, go where I like, sleep with whom I like . . .'

Charlotte pulled away and sprinted up the stairs with a speed that Libby would have admired. 'You can't while you're still with Suzie,' she called over her shoulder.

'It's only a technicality,' Richard protested, catching

his foot in the tear in the carpet – which had tripped him up practically every day since they'd first moved in. He almost fell down the stairs. 'Shit! I haven't missed that. Don't laugh, you! I could have broken my neck!'

But Charlotte was giggling so much she could hardly get the key in the front door. Some things never changed. But one thing *had* and it couldn't be ignored: she wasn't going to do to Suzie what Suzie had done to her.

'Spare room,' she said firmly, pointing down the hall. 'Alone.'

'Oh come on, Lottie. I'll call her first thing tomorrow and tell her. You know it's you I really want to be with. Why wait?' protested Richard.

'Nice try,' Charlotte said, giving him a shove in the small of his back, 'but I'm not falling for it. You can stay with me once you've sorted things out properly and not before. If you don't like it, you know where to go.'

Richard knew his ex-wife well enough to quit while he was ahead. Looking most hard done by, he pushed open the door, sighing as though he'd been sent to the Gulag, not to the spare room. Hands on hips Charlotte watched him beadily, shaking her head and mouthing 'no' when he turned round for yet another plea.

'OK, you win,' Richard said, finally defeated. 'I'll sleep in the box room if it's what you really want.'

Of course it wasn't what she wanted! But one of them had to be strong and Charlotte knew, much as she might love him, that this was never going to be Richard. Cute, fun, sexy, yes. Responsible grown-up? Err, no. But she realised she loved him just the same.

Charlotte wasn't a morning person, which Richard should have been very well aware of after seven years of living with her, so she wasn't best impressed when the curtains were flung open at an ungodly hour and bright sunshine blasted her awake.

'For pity's sake,' she hissed, diving under the duvet. 'Some of us are trying to sleep!'

'It's nearly ten-thirty! High time you were awake, sleepy head!' Richard, who was always annoyingly chirpy in the morning, pulled back the covers and got in beside her, settling into 'his' side of the bed as though it was the most natural thing in the world. 'Cheer up, grumpy. I've brought you breakfast in bed and a bunch of your favourite flowers!'

Charlotte didn't care if he'd brought her Johnny Depp naked and covered in chocolate sauce; all she wanted to do was sleep. It was Saturday morning and she fully intended not to stir until at least lunchtime.

'I'm not hungry,' she muttered. 'Go away.'

'You always were a grouch in the morning!' Richard laughed and reached under the duvet to ruffle her hair. 'Come on, I've been out and bought croissants, double espressos and the papers.'

Double espresso! Now he's talking. She sat up and before long they were scattering crumbs everywhere and kissing buttery croissant flakes from lips and fingers. It was a lovely romantic gesture, so sweet of him to go to all this trouble. Nestling against Richard she thought how easy it was to slip back into their old routine, and how very comforting.

She dropped a kiss on to his cheek. 'You look deep in thought, Rich. What are you thinking about?'

'I was thinking how scruffy the bathroom looks,' Richard said idly. 'I'm not very keen on that funny yellow colour, either. I think I'll redo it in black and chrome, or maybe—'

'You bloody well won't!' Immediately Charlotte straightened up, irritated by his assuming tone.

'OK, babe. Don't have a cow,' said Richard cheerily. 'It was just an idea. How about some under-floor heating, though? I'd forgotten how chilly the lounge is first thing.'

Charlotte felt alarmed. He'd only stayed the night in the spare room but as far as Richard was concerned, he was back for good.

'Slow down,' she said firmly. 'I haven't even asked you to move in yet and already you're changing the blueprints.'

'Sorry, babe,' he said through a mouthful of croissant. 'I was only trying to—'

'Well don't,' Charlotte snapped. 'Honestly, Richard, why do you have to be so full on?' She frowned as a horrible thought occurred. 'Did you deliberately set last night up so that you could come back here? Did you really row with Suzie?'

Richard looked hurt beyond belief at her distrust.

'Is that really what you think of me? I can't change

the past. But if it's always going to be such a huge issue, what chance do we stand?'

'But it isn't the past, is it?' Charlotte felt like throttling him. How could he so not get it? Like *duh*, as Libby would say. 'You're still with Suzie! You haven't told her about us and I don't think you've got any intention of telling her. You just thought you could get your feet under the table here and then she could find out the hard way.'

He stared at her. 'You're wrong.'

'Am I?'

Richard leapt out of bed and strode from the room. 'Yes, you bloody well are,' he yelled over his shoulder. 'You're so quick to think the worst of me. As usual. But you're wrong and I can prove it.'

Charlotte placed her head in her hands. She was doing it again. Would she ever learn?

'Look at me,' she heard Richard say as he returned to the bedroom. 'Lottie, look at me. Please?'

Reluctantly, she did as she was asked. It was just as well that she was sitting down in bed or she would have fallen over. Richard was kneeling before her with a perfect diamond solitaire in his hand!

'Charlotte Sinclair,' he was saying, a catch in his voice, 'I love you with all my heart and I'm more sorry than I can ever say that I screwed things up. Please would you do me the honour of marrying me, again, and being my wife? I swear I'll be the best husband in the world if you give me a second chance.'

For a moment, time seemed to stand still and he was

frozen there on the laminate floor, looking so vulnerable in his boxers, and so full of hope. Suddenly tears were pouring down her cheeks and before she knew it, Richard was kissing them away and slipping the ring on to her finger. It was beautiful, an antique square-cut diamond set into white gold – exactly the kind of thing she had always wanted.

'I know,' Richard said proudly when she choked this out. 'I chose it especially and I've been waiting for the right moment.'

Charlotte felt a pang of guilt so sharp she was amazed it didn't draw blood. There she was, accusing Richard of being a cynical opportunist, when he'd obviously been planning this for weeks. She really was a horrible, untrusting person and she didn't deserve him. Well, no more! She was going to change.

She stretched out her hand, turning the ring round on her finger and watching it play with rainbows of light. It was a bit loose, but it was stunning. Surely this was evidence just how much Richard loved her?

'So?' he whispered, taking her hand.

Charlotte glanced up from the ring and met his gaze. Richard's eyes were so full of love and hope that a lump filled her throat. How could she possibly resist?

'Yes, I'll marry you,' she said.

He sat on the bed, but before he could take her in his arms she held up a warning finger. 'I want to take it slowly, Richard. We've still got a lot of things to talk through first.'

'Sure. Yes. You're right. Absolutely,' Richard agreed

willingly. 'Whatever you think best is fine by me. I'm the happiest person in the world right now.'

'Me too,' Charlotte replied. Well, she *was* happy. It was just that she couldn't really feel it properly yet. Not until he'd told Suzie and made everything right, anyway. Then she'd feel happy.

'I'm not wearing this ring or telling anyone until you've spoken to Suzie,' she warned him, slipping the ring off and back into its back velvet nest. 'And I'm not doing *that* either!' she added, pushing him away playfully as his hand slipped down to caress her breast.

Richard glanced down ruefully at the promising bulge in his boxers. 'Then I think I'd better phone her asap.'

'Yes, you'd better,' she agreed, laughing. But as he kissed her she found herself hoping that he wouldn't tell Suzie just yet; she'd like a little bit more time to get used to the idea herself.

That was only natural. Wasn't it?

15

'So Priya's all loved up,' Zoe had said, sloshing more wine into their glasses. It was the Sunday night following the awards ceremony and Charlotte had met up with Zoe for a meal. She'd not minded in the least when Priya had joined them; although she'd only met her on the hen night, Charlotte had liked her directness and sharp sense of humour. But Priya had just returned from filming in India and, newly loved up, couldn't stop singing the praises of her new man.

'But what about you, Charlie? Anything to report about that nice man you met in Yorkshire?'

Charlotte had smiled. 'No, nothing happened there . . .'

'But?'

Charlotte had bitten her lip. She supposed she'd have to break the news sooner or later. She wasn't worried as such about her decision to take Richard back, but she knew it would probably come as a big shock to her friends and family.

'But I am seeing someone. Richard. We're getting married again.'

'Say that again?' Zoe was staring at Charlotte, her mouth hanging open in shock. 'I think I must be going mad. For a minute there I thought you said you were thinking about getting back with Richard.'

'She didn't say she was getting *back* with him,' chipped in Priya, her unusual hazel eyes wide with disbelief. 'She said she was getting *married* to him again! I don't think it's you who's going mad, Zoe!'

'Richard, the one you said should have his gonads made into maracas? *That* Richard?'

Had she said that? Well, she may have done. After all, she had been incredibly angry.

Well, anyway. Yes. That Richard.

'Everyone's entitled to make a mistake,' Charlotte said calmly. 'Richard's really sorry for what he did and he's adamant he's going to make it up to me.'

'But he cheated on you!' Priya exclaimed. 'How could you ever trust him again?'

It was a good question, and not one that Charlotte felt quite able to answer. Taking a sip of her drink she dodged the issue by trotting out her standard line about everyone deserving a second chance. She'd been thinking about this a great deal since Richard had proposed the day before and she was almost ready to believe it. Besides, if Paul could forgive Elise, why couldn't she forgive Richard?

'Babes, it's totally your decision,' Zoe said carefully, leaning forward and squeezing her hand. 'And if you truly think Richard's the one for you and that he really is genuinely sorry, then of course Steve and I will support you. But please be careful. He hurt you so badly and we'd all hate to see that happen again.'

So would I, thought Charlotte. 'Well, if it does, then I guarantee Richard will be wearing his testicles as earrings!' she joked but the other two weren't laughing. In fact, Priya was frowning and even her choppy bob seemed confused.

'So is he The One?' she asked. 'Is Richard the love of your life?'

Charlotte laughed. You could tell Priya was still in her twenties! Bless, she still believed in soulmates and true love. Maybe even in Santa?

'I'm not sure if I believe there's "a one",' she said with an indulgent smile. 'Maybe there are lots of "ones" and we just have to pick the best of the bunch we come across. I'm thirty-four, Priya, and I want to settle down and have a family before it's too late.'

The younger girl looked at her as though she was insane. 'That's total bollocks! You shouldn't settle for second best just because you're afraid your ovaries are shrivelling up.'

'Thanks for that.' Charlotte winced.

'Sorry,' Priya said, looking anything but. 'What I meant was that you shouldn't limit your hopes. Somewhere out there your perfect match is waiting for you.'

For a split second Charlotte saw eyes as green as sea grass and a crinkly smile that made her feel as though she was immersed in a warm bath. Then she pushed the images away. There was no use in longing for things you could never have.

'Well, I'll stick with Richard because, knowing my luck, my soulmate's on the other side of the world,' she said with a smile.

'So what if he is?' cried Priya. 'Wait for him.'

Changing the subject quickly, Charlotte started to tell them about her visit to Yorkshire. By the time they'd scraped the tiramisu bowl clean and polished off another bottle of wine, Charlotte and Priya had forgotten about their earlier squabble and Priya had even voiced an interest in filming YORC for a documentary. *That could be fun*, Charlotte thought. If Priya filmed, she could go back to Yorkshire and catch up with the friends she'd made there. She might even see Heath again. Just thinking about bumping into him made her heart lurch, which was rather alarming now that she was engaged to someone else.

Maybe she should remarry Richard sooner rather than later?

Monday was such a hectic day at work that Charlotte barely had time to grab a coffee or nip to the loo, let alone fret about Richard. She was just shutting down her computer when a summons to see Suzie took her by surprise.

This is it, she thought, as she grabbed a notebook and pen on her way through to Suzie's private office. Richard will have broken the news about leaving Suzie and wanting to pick up the fragments of his marriage. An icy hand squeezed her heart. Would Suzie be in tears? Would there be shouting? Was she ready to deal with this yet?

'Ah, Charlotte, come in,' said Suzie briskly when she rapped at the door. 'Take a seat.'

Sliding into a black leather chair Charlotte sneaked a glimpse at her boss and was relieved to see no evidence of red eyes and tear stains. In fact, as Suzie perched on the edge of the desk and leafed through a thick wad of papers she looked every inch the consummate professional, from her immaculate French pleat to the tips of her neat Jimmy Choos. Exhaling slowly Charlotte felt an overwhelming sense of relief that she hadn't been summoned for a confrontation.

'Your report has recommended that both YORC and the Hope Foundation continue to receive Arts Council Funding,' Suzie said slowly.

Charlotte had been so certain that they were about to have a fight over Richard that she'd failed to notice exactly what the papers clutched tightly in her boss's fingers were. Now, looking closely, she realised that they were the reports she'd slaved over.

She nodded. 'In my opinion these projects offer invaluable services to the young people they work with and the results of both are quantifiable, as Richard's figures show.'

Suzie waved her hand dismissively. 'Yes, yes, I've read the reports, Charlotte. I don't require a précis. But surely one must have outweighed the other in terms of overall efficiency of funds and value for money?'

Even though Charlotte was used to the realities of sparse funding it was strange to hear YORC and Hope suddenly discussed in such a cold and mercenary manner. 'Both projects were fantastically successful in their own way.'

'That makes things very difficult.' Suzie's mouth set in a tight line as she glanced back down at the report. 'The board's looked at your suggestions but I'm afraid it's bad news. They've only got enough money to fund one project. I was rather hoping you could make this a little easier by giving me some idea of which we should plump for.'

Charlotte stared at her, totally horrified. 'Isn't there some way they can both get funding? There's no way I can choose. Honestly, Suzie, if you'd have been there, you'd feel exactly the same way.'

Suzie shrugged. 'Perhaps. I just can't help feeling you've got far too close to these organisations and it's clouded your objectivity.'

What? Charlotte leapt from her chair infuriated. How dare Suzie question her professional opinion? 'I can assure you that's totally untrue! If I was impressed it's because both of them are exactly the kind of charities that the Arts Council should be supporting. Richard will back up everything I've written.'

Her boss gave her a long, cool stare. 'Oh, I don't doubt that for a minute. We all know just how closely you and Richard have worked on this.'

Charlotte felt hot all over. Even the ends of her hair were blushing.

'I guess I have no choice but to travel up to York and see these projects for myself,' Suzie said. 'And seeing as you feel so passionately about them I'm going to take you with me. You can give me all the inside information.'

'I can't!' Charlotte was distraught at the idea of going back to Yorkshire for the sole purpose of signing the death warrant for one of the charities. It felt like a total betrayal. And if she was honest, she wasn't sure she could spend that amount of time with Suzie either. The guilt would crucify her. 'Can't you take Richard?'

'Richard and I are barely talking,' said Suzie and the words *thanks to you* hung in the air. 'Besides, you're the expert because you were there longer than him.'

Charlotte's heart plopped into her purple boots. How could she face all her new friends up north knowing that she was going to condemn one of their charities? She opened her mouth again to protest but this time Suzie pulled rank, leaving her with no choice. If she wanted to keep her job, then she'd better do it, her boss told her, unless she wanted to face a disciplinary.

'Fine,' Charlotte said miserably. 'I'll go. I don't seem to have much choice.'

'No, you don't,' Suzie said coldly. 'Your job doesn't always involve jollies with other people's boyfriends.'

Riled, Charlotte looked her in the eye. 'It was really kind of you to book us into the honeymoon suite. It had been a long time since *our* honeymoon.'

Suzie paled and for a few seconds they stared at each other like cats squaring up for a fight. Then she looked away.

'Sorry, Charlotte, I guess I deserved that. Look, no

matter what's going on in our personal lives you and I still have to work together. Do you think we could maybe just concentrate on the job in hand and leave the rest of it for another time?'

Charlotte shrugged. 'Sure.'

'Good,' Suzie said crisply. Glancing down at her watch she added, 'I'll book us on to a flight up to York so we'll need to be at City Airport for half six. Go home, pack a bag and I'll meet you there.'

'Fine,' said Charlotte. But inside she felt far from fine. Her head was buzzing and there was a knot of anger in her chest at being backed into this corner. She was off to York to play Judas and, even worse, she was going to be stuck for days with the one person she desperately wanted to avoid. The only saving grace was that Richard hadn't yet plucked up the courage to break the news to Suzie. Charlotte may have been really angry about this before, but now she felt relieved.

Richard could break the news when they returned. At least this way she wouldn't have to deal with Suzie's wrath while they were away together.

'It's right good to see you again lass.' Archie beamed as, much later, Charlotte and Suzie checked into the hotel. 'Welcome back to York. And hello to your pretty friend too. The men in London must be mad letting two crackers like you out of their sights!'

Suzie curled her lip at this, but Charlotte took it in the manner it was intended and hugged him.

'It's good to see you too,' she told him and was

surprised to discover she meant it. There was something really fatherly about Archie, although that was probably less to do with his welcoming hug and strong cups of Yorkshire tea and, sadly, more to do with him and Geoff both being alcoholics.

'You've certainly made some charming friends,' Suzie observed, her nose wrinkling in distaste as she glanced across the bar at Archie, who was searching for their keys as though it was a challenge from the *Krypton Factor*. 'I can't believe you'd let a revolting old drunk like that anywhere near you, let alone give you a hug.'

Unfortunately, just as Suzie said this, the music on the ancient jukebox came to a halt and the last part of her sentence was practically shouted into the bar. Archie didn't say anything but Charlotte saw his face redden beneath the drinker's rosy hue and felt mortified on his behalf.

'Don't be such a stuck-up cow,' she hissed at Suzie. 'He's one of the kindest people you could meet. When I was lost on the moors it was Archie who alerted the rescue people.'

'Sorry, sorry.' Raising her hands Suzie backed away. 'I was only saying.'

'Well, don't,' snapped Charlotte, shoving Suzie's room key at her and almost taking her boss's eye out. Suzie, embarrassed, escaped to her room.

'I'm really sorry about her,' she said to Archie who joined her with his habitual whiskey and coke.

He shrugged. 'Aye, she's caught the northern

bluntness, that's for sure, lass. Still, there's nowt wrong wi' that. She was only saying what you'd already thought.'

Charlotte stared sadly into her wine glass. 'Maybe, Archie, and I'm sorry for it, but I can't help being a bit uneasy around heavy drinkers.'

And slowly she told him about Geoff and just how hard she'd always found it having to deal with his drinking. Archie listened sympathetically, never interrupting but just nodding and agreeing from time to time.

'Aye,' he said thoughtfully once she'd come to a stop. 'Living wi' an alcoholic isn't much fun; that's for sure. My wife, God rest her soul, was an angel to put up with me the way she did. If it hadn't have been for her I'd never have found the strength to give it up.'

Charlotte stared at him. 'You don't drink?'

'I haven't touched a drop for nigh on ten years!' he said, proudly.

'So you're not an alcoholic?'

Archie shook his head. 'Oh, I'm an alcoholic all right. I always will be, lass, but I'm a recovering one. One day at a time is how I take it.'

She glanced down at his drink.

'That's just coke,' laughed Archie, following her gaze.

'I'm so sorry, Archie. I just assumed . . .'

She had done it again. It was time she believed a bit more in the good bits of human nature rather than focussing on the negatives.

Her fingers closed on the ring, pushed deep into her

jeans pocket, and she smiled. Forgiving Richard was definitely the right decision. The sooner she got home and sorted everything out the better. Suddenly she couldn't wait for them to begin their marriage anew.

Suzie pulled the hire car up outside Picton Village Hall. 'Is this it? The Hope Foundation meets here, miles from the city? That's not economical for a start.'

While she stared critically out of the window Charlotte pulled a face at her back. Childish, yes, but Suzie was driving her crazy. She'd moaned all the way to Picton and had refused to let Charlotte phone to tell Cassandra that they were on their way, insisting that she wanted to catch the charity off guard. *What did she think was going on?* Charlotte had thought angrily, *child labour?*

'It's a great venue,' Charlotte said, keeping calm by digging her nails into the palms of her hand. Only one hour into her mission with Suzie and she'd almost made it through to the bone. Not a good sign.

'It's a village hall, not the O2 Arena,' Suzie said briskly. 'I'm sure there are others a lot closer to the city.'

Briefcase in hand she slammed the car door and stalked up the path. Sighing wearily, Charlotte followed her, her stomach heavy with dread.

'Hey, Charlotte! This is a nice surprise,' Paul called, looking delighted to see her. He was helping some children decorate a giant Viking mural and, wiping his hands on a rag, left them to it to come and give her a hug. 'Couldn't keep away, eh?'

'I'm back on Arts Council business,' she told him, her heart sinking at having to keep the truth of her visit a secret. 'I've got another colleague with me this time. Suzie, this is Paul, one of Hope's project workers.'

'Nice to meet you.' Paul shook Suzie's hand and treated her to a twinkly smile. 'Thanks so much for lending us Charlotte for a bit. We've loved having her here.'

'Really?' Suzie couldn't have looked more amazed if Paul had told her Charlotte had been helping the kids to split atoms.

'Really,' nodded Paul, draping an arm round Charlotte's shoulder and giving her a friendly squeeze. 'She's been fantastic with the kids. My daughter's nuts about her.'

Suzie raised her eyebrows. 'It seems she isn't the only one,' she murmured. Luckily Paul didn't hear because Isla bounded over to deliver a painting to Charlotte, shrieking loudly about the green paint not being quite dry. As her boss and Paul chatted about Hope, and paint dripped all over the floor, Charlotte found herself really hoping Suzie didn't get an inkling that anything had gone on between them. That would make it seem as if she was biased in favour of Hope.

Fortunately, Cassandra appeared at this point and soon took Suzie away, leaving Paul and Charlotte alone.

'My God,' he breathed, miming mopping his brow. 'She's a force of nature, isn't she? I felt like I was being interrogated.'

Charlotte sighed. 'She's on a mission to dot all the i's

and cross all the t's, I'm afraid. Hopefully she'll not take long and then we'll be off to YORC and will leave you guys in peace.'

'Ah, off to see the award-winning Heath? That'll put us well and truly in the shade,' teased Paul.

She swatted him on the arm. 'Don't be silly. You're doing great things here.' And will continue to do so if Suzie doesn't decide to pull the plug, she added silently.

'Thanks, Charlotte.' Paul gave her a sweet smile. He ran a hand over his short hair. 'I made a decision after the awards ceremony; I've decided that I want to try again with Elise.'

'That's great news,' Charlotte said. 'Isla must be made up, as you lot say up here!'

He laughed. 'Aye, that she is! Seriously, though, I don't just want to try again because of Isla. I actually want Elise back; she's my wife and I still love her in spite of everything. She's the love of my life. I just hope she still wants to be with me.'

'I totally understand,' Charlotte said softly. 'And I really hope things work out for you both.'

Charlotte smiled, remembering her conversation with Steve when they'd joked about love coming to her through *hope*. Some psychic Angela had turned out to be. She'd got that totally wrong!

Later on that day they arrived at the York Play House where YORC were rehearsing for their production of *Wuthering Heights*.

Catching sight of Heath lugging props about

backstage, Charlotte's heart started to break-dance. Almost before she knew it she was walking over to say hello.

'Hey, this is a nice surprise!' said Heath, catching sight of her and instantly abandoning his work. 'What are you doing here?'

Charlotte gulped. She could hardly tell him the truth, could she?

'Just tying up some loose ends.'

'Well, I'm glad,' said Heath softly and they smiled at each other. The atmosphere seemed to tingle and it was only broken when Kylie raced over to tell Heath that Ruby had gone missing.

'What do you mean, missing? When did you last see her?' Heath asked, his face ashen.

Kylie shrugged. 'About an hour ago? We went for a burger but she said she didn't feel too good. She said her tummy hurt. No one's seen her since.'

Charlotte felt cold to her bones. Please God, no!

Instantly they were surrounded by a crowd of teenagers, all of whom were panicking that the play would have to be cancelled.

'Sorry, Charlotte,' Heath apologised. 'We'll catch up later. I have to sort this out.'

'It's fine,' she assured him. 'Can I help?'

But Heath wasn't listening. He was already on his mobile, his brow furrowing when Ruby didn't answer.

'Bloody Ruby,' snarled Nick. 'Just before her big scene, too. I knew she'd bottle it.'

'She's playing Cathy,' Zak told Suzie who was

looking confused. 'She's our lead and if she does a runner now, she'll screw up the entire play.'

'She's too lardy to go far,' Kylie said nastily. 'She's probably stuck in a doorway somewhere, fat cow.'

The whole group of teens sniggered and Charlotte felt like banging their heads together. Reminding herself that they were just kids, she asked who had seen Ruby last, only to be met with shrugs and blank looks.

'Heath seems very concerned,' remarked Suzie. 'If she's over the age of sixteen, what's the fuss about?'

'She's his stepdaughter and she's had a really hard time since losing her mum,' Charlotte told her, biting back panic. A missing pregnant teenager was a serious issue, especially when no one else knew about her condition. Her heart started to play squash against her ribs. What if the stress of taking the lead role had prompted a miscarriage? They had to find her!

'In that case, I'm hardly filled with confidence,' Suzie was saying. 'If Heath can't even keep tabs on his own stepdaughter, what's he going to do with a large budget? Hide it in the biscuit tin and forget about it?'

But Charlotte wasn't listening. Instead she was busy organising a search. Suzie's tick boxes could wait.

'Nobody is to stop until they find her, OK?' she told the gathered teens, who unplugged their iPod earphones and nodded. 'I'll search the stage and dressing area, Kylie and the girls can do front of house and Zak is going to go up into the gods and lighting.'

'Thanks for helping, Charlotte,' Heath said,

reappearing at her side. His eyes were like open wounds and his face was white with worry. 'I'm so sorry,' he added to Suzie. 'This has never happened before. Rubes is normally so reliable.'

Charlotte felt terrible. If only she could tell him.

'We have to find her,' he continued, his voice throbbing with emotion. 'She's been so low. I'm worried she might have done something silly.'

There wasn't much Suzie could say to this. 'It's all part of working with vulnerable teenagers, I guess,' she said.

'Not really,' said Heath. 'There's more to this than meets the eye, I know it. Ruby's been acting strangely for weeks.' He shook his head and then gathered himself visibly. 'Right, I'm going to search outside.'

Everyone scattered in their different directions. Charlotte searched through the dressing rooms, opening cupboards and calling Ruby's name until her voice was hoarse, but to no avail. She trawled through the creepy bowels of the theatre, down a narrow corridor that led beneath the stage to the props store. Wishing she hadn't watched so many episodes of *Most Haunted*, of which a disproportionate number seemed to be set in theatres, she pushed open the door to the props cupboard, nearly leaping out of her skin when she heard a noise coming from the inky blackness.

Her heart hammering, Charlotte froze, her ears straining against the silence. Then the noise came again, louder this time, more distinct; it was very definitely a sob.

'Ruby?' she called, stepping forward into the darkness. 'Is that you?'

There was a sniff and another muffled sob. Someone was definitely there and, unless the Phantom of the Opera was on holiday in York, Charlotte was pretty sure it was Ruby. She slid her hand along the wall, crying out in triumph when her fingers brushed against a switch. She pressed it down and the cupboard was flooded with light. Blinking furiously as her eyes adjusted, Charlotte saw Ruby huddled in a corner, her arms wrapped around her shuddering body and her cheeks raw from weeping.

'Ruby, thank God!' She dropped to her knees and crouched down beside the trembling girl. 'We've been so worried about you! Are you OK? You're not in pain are you? Is the baby all right?'

In answer Ruby just nodded, before flinging her arms round Charlotte and howling into her shoulder. There she cried for a good five minutes while Charlotte patted her back and smoothed damp fronds of hair back from her face. Eventually the storm of weeping subsided to a few hiccupping sobs.

'I can't do this any more,' she said, so quietly that Charlotte had to strain to hear.

Tears sprang to Charlotte's eyes and she hugged the trembling girl tightly. 'Oh sweetheart, there're so many people who'll be there for you, if you'll only let them in.' She paused as a thought occurred. 'Are you thinking that you might be ready to tell the baby's father?'

Ruby raised doleful eyes. 'He needs to know. I can't hide this for much longer, can I?'

Charlotte squeezed her shoulder. 'I know you can't, sweetheart. Will it be easy to get in touch with him?'

'He's already here. I think he's guessed that something's up. He kept asking me what was wrong; that's why I ran away. I was going to ruin the play because I knew I couldn't go on stage with Justin watching my every move.'

'Justin? He's the father?'

'Don't sound so surprised,' Ruby said with a watery smile. 'We've been out a few times. He's all right.'

'I know he's all right.' Charlotte felt certain that although, understandably, Justin would be shocked, he'd be there for Ruby. He might like to play Jack the Lad but underneath the jokey exterior was a thoughtful and sensitive young man. She jumped to her feet and held out her hand to Ruby. 'Come on, I think it's time you guys sat down and had a heart-to-heart, don't you?'

Slowly, with her arm still around Ruby's shoulders, Charlotte guided the young girl back upstairs and towards the green room where some of the cast members were waiting to hear what was happening. While Zak went in search of Justin she shooed them out and then texted Heath to let him know Ruby was safe.

The panic in his eyes was frightening; being a parent must be the most terrifying thing in the world, she thought, but also, judging by the overjoyed message he sent back, the most marvellous.

Maybe now she was getting back together with Richard she'd get to find out.

'Rubes! Zak says you wanted me? Wassup?' Justin asked as he tore into the green room. 'Shit, man! You look terrible. What's happened?'

Ruby's eyes, wide and terrified, held Charlotte's. 'Will you stay with me while I tell him?'

Charlotte squeezed her hand. 'Of course.'

'What's going on?' Justin looked from Ruby to Charlotte. 'Rubes? If there's a problem, please tell me. Has someone hurt you?'

Ruby swallowed. 'I'm pregnant.'

Justin stared at her. 'Pregnant? With a baby?'

In spite of her tears and terror, Ruby laughed. 'Yes, a baby. And before you ask, I know it's yours.'

'I wasn't going to ask that,' Justin said, sounding offended. His face was a perfect study in shock and even his gelled-up quiff looked surprised. 'Blimey, Rubes, I knew something was up but I never imagined you were pregnant. No wonder you've been acting so weird. I thought you hated me or had found another guy or something. I was well pissed off.' He shook his head. 'Actually, I'm still pissed off and I still don't understand why you dumped me. I really like you. Shit!' He slumped on to a chair and buried his head in his hands. 'I'm going to be a dad! Why didn't you tell me?'

'I thought you wouldn't want to know.' Ruby was crying again. 'I was so scared. I didn't have anyone to talk to until Charlotte came.' She gave Charlotte a weak smile.

'You should have talked to me.' Justin was crying now too. 'I'd have been there for you.'

'Charlotte said I had to tell the baby's dad but I was too scared.'

Justin wiped his eyes with the back of his hand. 'She was right, Rubes. You shouldn't have had to go through all that on your own. We can sort this.'

Ruby looked hopeful for the first time since Charlotte had met her. 'Do you mean that?'

'Course! We're in this together, aren't we?' Justin insisted.

Then he crossed the room and threw his arms around Ruby murmuring, 'It's going to be OK' into the top of her head and wiping away her tears with his thumb. He was still visibly shocked, but the way he'd stepped up to the mark was very impressive.

Charlotte snuck out of the room, shutting the door gently behind her and leaving the two young people alone for some much-needed privacy. Then something inside her frayed and she found herself crying her heart out. It didn't seem to matter any more that other people would see her red eyes and know that cool and controlled Charlotte Sinclair wasn't quite so cool and controlled after all. She wept for relief that Ruby was safe, for pity that her young life had been so hard, and she then cried for herself, too, for the shattered dreams and all the disappointments and her own lost childhood.

'Hey, there you are!' She recognised Heath's voice instantly by the shivers it caused to run down her spine. 'I've been looking all over for you. I want to say thanks—' he stopped when he saw her face, which must have made her look like Alice Cooper. 'Hey, what's up?' Leaning against the door frame Heath peered down at her. 'You've been crying.'

She shrugged. Being so close to him stole her words away.

Heath reached out and touched her cheek, smoothing away a strand of hair.

'Don't worry. She's safe now.'

She nodded, unable to look into those searching eyes of his, knowing that if she did, Heath would see right down to the depths of her most secret self.

'You're crying about more than just Ruby,' Heath said softly. 'I don't know why you're so upset, Ms Sinclair, but there is one thing I do know for sure and that's if ever a time does come when you feel ready to open up, then I promise I'll be there for you.'

His hand slipped down to touch her cheek before his fingers wound their way into her hair. Then he tipped her head up and, almost before Charlotte realised what was happening, his lips had grazed hers so softly that it was as though a butterfly's wings had brushed against her mouth.

'I promise,' he whispered again and then he was gone as quickly as he'd arrived, leaving Charlotte staring after him, her heart in freefall.

Deep inside her jeans pocket Richard's ring dug into her leg and the ground beneath her feet seemed to dip and spin. Charlotte touched the chilly diamond but the familiar loving feelings refused to flood through her hand and up into her heart. Suddenly she was viewing her life through a kaleidoscope as Richard's brown eyes and chestnut curls fragmented, replaced by Heath's green eyes and heart-stopping smile.

Charlotte's hand rose to her mouth in shock. This wasn't supposed to happen!

The next day, as Charlotte wandered around the stalls at the Picton Autumn Fair, her mind was less on the tombola and jars of pumpkin chutney and more on Heath's delicious kiss the day before.

The Hope Foundation had played a big part in planning the fair. The children had made the bright banners and flags, designed the posters, and had baked cinnamon biscuits. Elise had made bramble jelly; Paul was selling wooden toadstools, and the children were helping out too, busy showing parents their handiwork. Even Suzie looked impressed, Charlotte was relieved to see. Surely she could see just how much of a positive influence the charity was having on the children and their families?

The pièce de résistance was a vast pink and green hot-air balloon which floated above the green while tethered to the earth, giving paying customers a bird's-eye view of their village. It was here that Charlotte had arranged to meet Paul and Elise. She'd been thinking long and hard about the estranged couple and the more she dwelled on them the more silly it seemed that they were apart. They were made for one another and seeing them waste time was infuriating. As soon as she'd clapped eyes on the balloon Charlotte thought she'd found the perfect plan.

'Hey there,' Paul said, kissing her on the cheek. 'What's all this about?'

'Yeah, why did you want to meet us here?' Elise asked. She was holding Isla's hand tightly and, stepping close to Paul, she added, 'Is something wrong?'

Charlotte took a deep breath. 'No, of course not! You guys have been so welcoming and helpful since I came to Picton and I've been thinking of a way that I can say thanks. When I saw the balloon I thought it would be perfect if I paid for you all to go up in it and look at your village from the air.'

Paul frowned. 'That's a lovely thought, Charlotte, but it really isn't necessary.'

'Rubbish!' Charlotte said brightly. 'Besides, I'd love to contribute to the fund-raising without eating any more fudge!'

Paul opened his mouth to protest further but Isla was pogoing up and down and begging to be allowed to go in the balloon.

'I'm not sure,' he said, looking at Elise. 'What do you think?'

Goodness, Charlotte thought impatiently, *what a fuss!* It was a trip up in a balloon, not the first manned mission to Mars.

Elise shrugged. 'It's only a few minutes. It'll be fine.'

'Yippee!' shrieked Isla. 'We're going in a balloon! Thanks, Charlotte! You're the best!'

'You guys get in whilst Isla and I go and get us all some ice creams,' Charlotte instructed, taking Isla's hand. 'We can eat ninety-nines and admire the view.'

Pulling a face and telling her that he didn't want an ice cream, Paul lifted Elise into the basket and then clambered in after her.

'Let the rope go!' Charlotte hissed to the balloon operator. 'Now!'

The balloon operator was only too happy to oblige, paid off by Charlotte's fifty-pound donation. As the balloon rose into the air she could hear Paul yelling but his words were snatched away by the wind and muffled by the roar of the gas.

'Daddy! Mummy!' screamed Isla. 'Wait for me! I want to go in the balloon too!'

'It's OK, sweetheart,' Charlotte reassured her, bending down and ruffling the child's blond hair. 'Mummy and Daddy will stay up there for a bit so they can be on their own. We can go later.'

'Why can't I go with them?' said Isla, looking worried.

'Because I'm hoping that if Mummy and Daddy are alone, they'll remember how much they love each other. It's my plan to get them back together again.'

Hearing this, Isla beamed from ear to ear and Charlotte felt a twinge of unease. She hoped her plan worked; she'd hate to get Isla's hopes up for nothing. Still, nothing ventured nothing gained, right?

'Can you leave them for about half an hour?' she

asked the balloon operator who was only too glad to abandon his post for a bit and investigate the rest of the fair. Crossing her fingers that Elise and Paul would end up in each other's arms rather than in pieces, Charlotte bought Isla her promised ice cream and followed the excited child from stall to stall. They went into the hall and played hoopla, hooked ducks and even managed to win a purple teddy on the tombola. Isla's funny comments made Charlotte laugh so much that her cheeks hurt.

'You look like you're having fun.' The deep voice, lightly laced with a Yorkshire burr, caught her attention. Turning away from the lucky dip, Charlotte saw Heath smiling down at her and her heart skipped a beat, just as though the kiss was happening all over again.

What was the matter with her? She was engaged to Richard, she shouldn't be obsessing over another guy, let alone kissing him! Maybe it was because Richard still hadn't told Suzie about them? But try as she might to rationalise it, Charlotte couldn't recall any kiss ever affecting her so deeply. Luckily Isla saved her from her growing sense of panic by chattering away nineteen to the dozen.

'Thanks for yesterday,' Heath said, once Isla paused for air and he could get a word in.

Charlotte flicked her hair back from her face and smiled up at him. 'I was happy to help. I'm really fond of Ruby.'

Heath shook his head. 'I wasn't talking about *Ruby*. Charlotte, I—'

'There you are Charlotte! For goodness' sake! I've been looking everywhere for you!' Suzie's shrill voice could have grated granite. She elbowed her way through the children clustered around the stall to give Charlotte a disapproving look. 'What on earth are you doing playing hoopla? We're supposed to be evaluating this event, not joining in!'

Heath looked taken aback at this abrupt interruption but Isla glared at Suzie and said, 'Charlotte's looking after *me*. My mummy and daddy are in a balloon.'

Suzie raised a perfect eyebrow. 'Good Lord, Charlotte. This child's parents are foolish enough to leave her in *your* care? Do they want to see her again?'

Charlotte was used to Suzie's snide comments. After all, she was renowned for being useless with children, but Heath's eyes widened in surprise and Isla was really offended.

'That's not a very nice thing to say,' Isla said in her shrill, clear voice. 'You must be a really horrible person to say nasty things about Charlotte!'

Suzie's cheeks flushed strawberry pink. 'I'm sorry if that sounded harsh, Charlotte, but we've got so much to do. Dave has just called and he wants our decision by Monday afternoon at the latest.'

'Decision?' Heath looked from Suzie to Charlotte, confusion clouding his face. 'What decision? I thought you said you'd come back to finish the paperwork?'

'That's one way of putting it,' said Suzie, with a grimace. 'The board will only approve one project, I'm afraid, so—'

'You've come to decide which charity gets the funding,' Heath finished for her. 'Or maybe I should say, you've come to decide which one of us you want to bin?'

Charlotte suddenly felt as though she was in an elevator descending at about a million miles an hour.

'Heath, it really isn't like that!'

'Explain it to me.'

'I promise, I didn't—' But Charlotte's attention was suddenly drawn to a crowd of people gathered around the hot-air balloon. The hot-air balloon that was most definitely earthbound rather than floating romantically above the village green.

'My daddy!' shrieked Isla, pointing to a slumped figure on the grass. Tugging Charlotte in her wake she ran towards the wicker basket and hurled herself at Paul who, sure enough, was flat out on the ground.

'What's wrong with Daddy?' Isla wailed. 'Why's he such a funny colour?'

'Daddy doesn't feel very well, darling,' Elise told her, shooting Charlotte a furious look. 'He suffers from extreme vertigo and being stuck high up in a balloon has made him very poorly.'

Isla's face crumpled. 'But Charlotte said if you and Daddy went up in the balloon you'd get back together again.'

'Oh she did, did she?' Elise looked incredulous. Over the top of her daughter's blond head she hissed, 'Are you out of your mind? How dare you say that to her?'

'I'm so sorry,' Charlotte whispered. 'I was only trying to help. I didn't think.'

'No, you didn't,' agreed Elise. 'And I tell you what, why don't you go and *not think* somewhere else?'

Charlotte saw such disdain in Elise's face that it took her breath away. Suddenly she wanted nothing more than to run off and hide from all these people that she'd unwittingly upset and betrayed. They'd trusted her and this was how she'd repaid them.

Her head drooping and tears pooling in her eyes, she didn't blame Elise or Heath one bit for despising her.

How could she? She felt exactly the same way.

'Charlotte, open the door. Please?' There was a sharp rap of knuckles and a pause before Suzie added, 'I'm worried about you. If you don't answer, I'm going to get Archie to open up.'

It was late afternoon and although it was still light outside, Charlotte had drawn the curtains and was lying on her bed staring at the ceiling. The pillow was damp and crumpled-up balls of tissue dotted the duvet. Her eyes were sore and heavy and she felt as though someone had superglued her nostrils together.

'Come on,' Suzie was saying. 'You've been in there for ages.'

Suzie was right. As soon as they'd reached the hotel Charlotte had raced up to her room, locked the door, and cried and cried and cried. Even as she unlocked the door to let her boss in, she started to weep again. Once upon a time she would rather have died than let Suzie see her in such a state but, oddly, this no longer mattered.

'My God!' Suzie looked shocked at the sight of her. 'You look terrible. Have you been crying all after-noon?'

Charlotte nodded and a tear rolled down her cheek and splashed on to the carpet. 'Sorry,' Charlotte sniffed. 'I don't know what's up with me.'

'I do,' said Suzie. 'I saw the interaction between you and that Heath fellow. I am so sorry, Charlotte. I had absolutely no idea that there was anything going on between the two of you. If I had, I swear I would never have dropped you in it like that.'

Charlotte tried to say that there was nothing between her and Heath but the only noise she made had more in common with a wailing banshee than human speech.

Suzie sighed. 'I know we've had our differences in the past but I'd never deliberately ruin things for you.'

Sitting down on the bed she patted Charlotte's shoulder awkwardly and offered her a tissue.

'I had no idea you guys were an item. In fact, and this is going to sound really stupid and paranoid now, I thought there was something going on between you and Richard. You must think I'm an idiot!'

Charlotte felt terrible, especially seeing as Suzie was being so sweet to her. She was glad she was too upset to talk. What on earth was she supposed to say? Her personal life was turning into an episode of *The Jerry Springer Show* and she didn't like it one bit.

'I've always been a bit intimidated by you, if I'm honest,' Suzie confessed. 'The way you never normally show any emotions is pretty scary – it's quite a relief to see you actually do have them.'

'Oh, I have them, all right,' Charlotte croaked.

'I can see that now! But I thought you were really odd when Richard and I got together on Valentine's Day. You never showed any emotion at all! You were really cold about it.'

Charlotte stared at her. 'You got together on Valentine's Day. Are you sure?'

'Of course I'm sure. It's our anniversary; I'm hardly likely to forget!' Suzie's eyes narrowed. 'Why are you looking at me like that?'

The truth, ugly and bald, but actually rather unsurprising now she was confronted with it, was suddenly dawning. Rather than the draining grief she'd wallowed in all afternoon, Charlotte felt a spark of anger.

That was more like it!

'Suzie,' she said slowly, 'I didn't break up with Richard until Easter. I remember it clearly because he wanted to start trying for a baby on his birthday which is—'

'April the sixteenth,' finished Suzie, looking horrified. 'Oh my God! Charlotte, I swear to God I had absolutely no idea about any of that. Richard promised me everything was over between you guys!'

'I don't doubt it for a moment,' Charlotte said grimly. 'But before you start to beat yourself up about it, there's something else you should know.'

Taking a deep breath, Charlotte told her exactly what had been going on between her and Richard, finishing off with the proposal.

'So I'm equally as guilty as you of being the other woman,' she sighed.

But Suzie didn't seem at all bothered about that, she was more interested in finding out what the ring looked like. *Everyone deals with betrayal in their own way*, Charlotte told herself. *Maybe the ring is the final straw?*

'I can show you,' she told her, digging into her pocket and pulling out the ring. 'Rich wanted to get it resized but I needed to have it with me, just to help me make my mind up.' She held it aloft, making lamplight rainbows dance across the ceiling. 'It's pretty, isn't it?'

Suzie's eyes were like big blue saucers.

'I'll say it is. That's my ring!'

Charlotte gaped at her.

'It's been in the family for years. Richard was supposed to be getting it resized for *me* so it could be *our* engagement ring!'

They stared at each other, united by fury and disbelief.

'He was supposed to do it on the day of the awards ceremony, right?' said Charlotte slowly. 'Except that he forgot, and you had a big row?'

'And then he didn't come home until the next day,' recalled Suzie. 'I don't win any prizes for guessing where he stayed, do I?'

Charlotte hung her head. 'I'm so sorry. He stayed at my place – although nothing happened. He was in the spare room. But he did propose the next day.'

Suzie jumped up from the bed and began to pace up and down the room. Charlotte felt disappointed and angry but, unlike Suzie, she'd had a long time to come to terms with Richard's failing as a partner and human being in general. The sad thing was that probably nothing he did now would surprise her. He was weak and pathetic and, more than anything, she pitied him.

'I need a drink,' said Suzie, finally stopping pacing and gazing longingly at the minibar. 'Do you fancy joining me?'

Charlotte nodded. 'I think a drink's the least we deserve. What Richard deserves, though, is something quite different.'

Richard might have proven himself worse than the rat she'd originally thought he was but, oddly, that didn't upset her half as much as it ought to.

But the thought of Heath thinking badly of her and never wanting to see her again . . .

Well, that was another matter entirely.

17

Libby's eyes were huge with disbelief and her mouth was open so wide that everyone else in the pub could see her tonsils.

'Oh. My. God!' she exclaimed.

Charlotte told them how Richard had said that Suzie was lying, said he'd quit his job, begged for her to take him back, told her that he loved her.

'Well, I don't love you,' she'd said slowly.

And with this parting shot she'd placed the receiver back in the cradle, cutting him off mid-protest. Taking a long and deep breath she'd waited for the sadness to kick in.

And waited.

And waited.

Days later, she was still waiting.

It was totally out of character for Charlotte, but calling Zoe and arranging to meet up with the girls had definitely been a good idea. Zoe had been furious, Fern staggered, and Priya's reaction turned the air blue. As she listened to Priya describing exactly what punishment should be dished out to cheating men and as Fern retold one of her many dating disasters, Charlotte realised there was nothing like female friends to lift you out of your gloom and make you see the funny side. She decided she didn't want to keep things to herself any more, she wanted to talk about them with people who cared.

'He was never good enough for you,' Zoe was saying firmly. 'You're such a strong, independent woman, Charlie, and Richard's always been really weak. You need a man who knows his own mind. Someone who you know you can totally rely on and who can take care of you.'

For a split second Charlotte saw Heath's face, radiant with relief when he heard that Ruby was safe, and again felt his arms close around her as they sheltered from the moorland mist and was stabbed with a regret so sharp that she almost cried out. She shouldn't be more upset over losing Heath's friendship than she was at finding out about Richard's deceit.

That didn't make any sense!

'Who cares about being taken care of?' Libby said dismissively. 'As long as he's got an enormous knob!'

'That's where I went wrong,' Charlotte sighed. 'Richard *was* an enormous knob.'

'Dick by name, dick by nature.' Fern grinned. Raising her glass to Charlotte she said, 'Here's to better luck next time!'

'No way,' Charlotte insisted. 'I'm going to nail myself to my shelf because that's it. I'm sworn off men for good.'

'I thought the same once too,' Priya told her, 'but I

was wrong. Love took me totally by surprise. When you find the right one you'll know.'

'Pass me a bucket,' said Libby.

'You will find him,' Priya insisted. 'Won't she, Zoe? You knew when you met Steve, didn't you?'

'Never mind me and Steve, we're talking about Charlotte,' Zoe said quickly, neatly avoiding the subject of her own relationship. Was she worried about being a smug married woman or was there a problem between her and Steve? Charlotte frowned and made a mental note to call Zoe another day when they could have a private conversation. 'Love will come to you, Charlotte . . . through hope alone.'

The girls giggled at Charlotte's prophecy.

But what was the point in relying on hope when everything looked hopeless?

At nine-thirty the next morning, Charlotte's head still felt like it had a pneumatic drill inside it.

'My God! You look terrible,' Suzie commented, perching on the edge of her desk and staring down in concern. Unlike Charlotte, whose deathly white face and stringy hair made her a dead ringer for a plague victim, Suzie was all sparkly and bright-eyed. Dumping Richard seemed to agree with her.

'Are you OK?' Her eyes narrowed. 'You haven't been up all night crying over Arse Face, have you?'

Arse Face was Richard's new name. Suzie had called him that all the way back from Yorkshire and it seemed to have stuck.

Actually, it kind of suited him . . .

Charlotte shook her head, wincing as her brain swivelled in her skull. 'I'm fine. I just had a bit of a heavy night out with some friends.'

'Good for you.' Suzie looked approving. 'Anyway, enough of Arse Face for now. I've just had an invitation from *Hope* inviting us to a Viking Festival. Val . . . Valhal something or other. Would you like to be the one to go?'

'The Valhalla Festival,' Charlotte finished for her, remembering all too well the preparations she'd witnessed. But Charlotte wanted to face Paul and Elise again as much as she wanted to play more drinking games with Libby. The scorn on their faces was tattooed on her retinas as it was; seeking them out was just masochistic. And as for bumping into Heath . . .

That idea was just unbearable.

Thinking quickly, or as quickly as she could when this hungover, Charlotte pointed out that if they visited York especially to see Hope it could make them seem biased against YORC.

'Don't worry about that,' Suzie said cheerfully. 'Heath Fulford's emailed to say that he's withdrawing his application for funding, which means the board will give Hope the money now and you're free to visit them as much as you wish.'

Charlotte was horrified. Heath had been desperate for that funding. Without it there was no chance of YORC being able to continue their projects. He must really be determined to never lay eyes on her again to have withdrawn his application.

If she hadn't felt sick before she certainly did now.

'Come on, Charlotte, this isn't like you,' Suzie said briskly. 'Look how you came in every day regardless when Richard and I first got together. Surely facing Heath what's-his-name can't be anywhere near as difficult as that?'

Charlotte stared at her. Facing Heath would be a million times harder than having to face Richard. She'd wanted to kill Richard but when it came to Heath all she wanted to do was fling her arms around him and tell him how sorry she was, how she'd never set out to deceive him over the funding.

And then it struck Charlotte with all the force of a force-ten gale; she was totally and utterly in love with Heath. Any feelings she'd once had for Richard were mere shadows in comparison.

She loved Heath. How the hell had that happened?

Closing her eyes, she said, 'I'll go.'

'My goodness, I had absolutely no idea this was going to be so professional!' Priya exclaimed, looking around the York Play House in awe. 'I was expecting a church hall or something, not a proper theatre.'

It was Saturday evening and, against her better judgement, Charlotte was in York for the opening night of *Wuthering Heights*. Along with Priya, who was up for a few days to film a documentary about the charity, and her cameraman Ray, she was now sinking into the plush red seat and settling down to watch the performance.

'YORC do amazing work,' Charlotte reminded her. 'They've spent weeks polishing this and the kids have worked really hard.'

'And Heath, of course.' Priya grinned, digging a bony elbow into her ribs. 'With any luck you'll be able to congratulate him.'

Charlotte was glad it was dark in the theatre because her cheeks felt suspiciously warm. The thought of seeing Heath again was terrifying and wonderful all at the same time.

Once the play began, all thoughts about Heath were forgotten as Charlotte found herself mesmerised by the performance. Everything was so professional, from Justin's amazing scenery right through to the costumes that had been lovingly made by Kylie. And if Heathcliff was wearing Reeboks and Edgar Linton spoke in Ebonics, it really didn't seem to matter because they were just so convincing. But the real star of the night was Ruby. She played Cathy with such passion and conviction that Charlotte found she had tears rolling down her cheeks. The awkward and unhappy teenager had vanished and in her place was a confident young woman who owned the stage and acted like a pro-fessional. When the curtain call came and Ruby stood hand in hand with Justin, smiling radiantly as they took their bows. Charlotte thought she would burst with pride and clapped so hard that her hands felt sore.

Ruby and Justin looked so close, she thought, with a

big surge of happiness. Everything was going to work out for the best, she was sure of it.

Once the cast had taken their final bow, to rapturous applause, Charlotte excused herself to Priya and Ray and made her way backstage where she congratulated the kids and hugged the beaming Ruby.

'You were amazing!' Charlotte told her. 'I knew you were good, but I had no idea just how good.'

'She's mint, isn't she?' Justin said proudly, draping an arm around her shoulders and pulling her close. 'Heath's gonna love it when he sees the film I shot.'

'Heath's not here?' asked Charlotte in dismay.

'Joel was being sick, so Heath had to rush back home,' explained Ruby.

Charlotte's heart sunk right into her boots. She'd come all this way, taken a huge risk, driven like a maniac up the M1, to confront the man she loved, to bear her soul . . . and it was all for nothing. Heath Fulford was as far out of her reach as the stars twinkling above the Play House.

Maybe it was time that she admitted that some things just weren't meant to be?

Charlotte was grateful it was the Valhalla Festival the next day because it was impossible to feel down when you were surrounded by such colour and amazing costumes. The streets were filled with Vikings: some sporting huge horned hats, some with beards and some tiny ones waving tinfoil swords and shields. Bright banners and flags fluttered high above her in the breeze and the smell of roasting pork hung in the air. Priya and Ray were off filming somewhere, which left her free to explore at her leisure.

I should have dressed up, Charlotte decided, feeling conspicuous in her decidedly un-Viking get-up of jeans and a green fleece. As usual, she was apart from everyone else, feeling like she didn't quite fit in, only this time the feeling was literal as well as metaphorical.

'Arrah! Got you!' A small Viking stabbed Charlotte in the leg with a cardboard sword and jabbed her out of her melancholy mood. Glancing down Charlotte laughed when she realised that it was Isla. She joined in the game and crumpled to the floor clutching her leg and groaning. Shrieking with mirth Isla parried a few more times until a pair of strong hands grasped her little waist and lifted her up into the air.

'I think you've well and truly beaten Charlotte!' Paul laughed. Putting his excited daughter down, he helped Charlotte up and then kissed her on the cheek.

'What's that for?' she asked, surprised. The last time she'd seen Paul, he'd been the colour of Kermit; a kiss was completely unexpected coming from him – a smack in the face was what she deserved for pulling such a thoughtless stunt.

But Paul didn't look angry. Far from it. He was beaming from ear to ear like a Halloween lantern.

'That's for getting me and Elise back together,' he told her. 'Granted, I think I would have preferred it if you'd found a way to do so on terra firma, but it did the trick.'

Charlotte hung her head, 'I had no idea you were afraid of heights. I'm so sorry, Paul; it never even occurred to me.'

'Why would it?' He grinned. 'But who cares? It worked! Seeing how worried Elise was and how furious she was with you made me realise just how much she does love me . . . so I may have exaggerated a little.'

Her mouth fell open. 'You were putting it on?'

Paul winked. 'Just a tiny bit. You can't blame a guy! Anyway, ssh! That's between you and me.'

Promising to keep in touch, she kissed them goodbye, blinking back tears because she really would miss Isla. She retraced her footsteps through the crowded narrow streets. There was no point staying now. She'd said her goodbyes and it was abundantly clear that her time in Yorkshire was drawing to a close. She was just deliberating whether to call a cab or try and make her way to the hotel on foot, when her mobile rang.

'Where are you?' demanded Suzie when she answered.

'I'm at the Viking Fair.' Charlotte wedged the phone between her ear and her shoulder and elbowed her way through the throng of people in what she hoped was the direction of the hotel. 'But I'm leaving now. Do you need—'

'You can't leave yet; I've just taken a call from Heath,' her boss said quickly. 'He's desperate to find you.'

'Did he say what he wanted?'

'He said he had to see you. He sounded absolutely frantic. It must be really important.'

Charlotte's mouth dried. Was it something to do with Ruby? *Please God*, she thought, *don't let anything have happened to her!*

'You'd better try and find him,' Suzie said and then, oddly, wished her luck.

Charlotte tried to call Heath on his mobile but there was no response. She would have to search for him through the crowds and hope she could spot him amongst the hundreds of other men who were dressed as Vikings. This was easier said than done when the streets were this busy and the daylight starting to fade.

Charlotte swallowed. She wanted nothing more than

to see Heath again but she was scared, too. She'd upset him the last time he saw her and she didn't think she could bear another blast of his wrath. Now she didn't have a choice. There could be far more at stake than her broken heart.

Squeezing her way through the crowds she scanned the press of bodies for that familiar frame, almost weeping with despair when every adult Viking turned out to be someone else. Yet, when she did finally catch sight of Heath, there was no mistaking that chiselled face and thick golden mane of hair and her heart filled with joy. She hadn't known just how badly she'd missed him until that second.

'Heath!' Charlotte shouted, waving frantically. 'Heath!'

Heath turned and she thought he saw her but then a procession of elaborate floats, crammed with people dressed as Norse gods, cut between them. When it had passed there was no sign of him and the only evidence he'd ever been nearby was the racing of her pulse. *This is hopeless*, thought Charlotte in despair. *I'll never reach him in such a crowd.*

Feeling utterly defeated, she was just heading towards the spot where she'd seen him when a strong hand grasped her elbow.

'It's traditional for Vikings to abduct beautiful maidens, carry them away to their ships and ravish them,' a tall blond Viking said, pulling her into his arms and holding her tightly against his chest. 'I'm afraid I don't have a ship, just a rather tatty old Land Rover! But

I'm sure it's perfectly adequate for ravishing . . . if you're up for it?'

His face was masked by a heavy metal helmet framed with golden curls, but there was no disguising that deep midnight voice or the sparkling emerald eyes. As though suddenly possessed of a mind of their own, Charlotte's hands rose up to touch the light stubble of his cheeks before rising higher and pushing the helmet away from his face.

'Heath!' she gasped, unable to believe that she'd actually found him, and that he was smiling down at her with that stomach-flipping crinkle-eyed smile. 'It's you!'

'Didn't you recognise me?' he teased, one hand reaching out to cup her cheek. 'How many other Vikings have come along to ravish you?'

Charlotte stared up at him. He was so tall, so broad shouldered and rugged that he looked every inch the powerful Viking warrior and she longed for nothing more than to be carried away to his longboat and ravished. If she was honest, she'd longed for nothing else since she'd first met him.

'Why were you looking for me?' she asked. 'Suzie said you were frantic. I've been searching high and low for you! Is everything all right? Is Ruby OK?'

'Ruby's fine,' Heath said softly. 'But I'm not.'

As he spoke there was such an intensity of feeling in his voice that her heart began to skitter. Afraid of what he might be about to say, Charlotte interrupted.

'Is that because you still think I betrayed YORC? Is

that why you withdrew the application for funding? It's totally selfish and childish, putting the charity and all the kids' hard work at risk just because you're mad at me! In fact I think—'

But Charlotte couldn't tell Heath what she thought because he'd wound his hands into her loose red hair and, before she had a second to protest any further, he was kissing her. At first his mouth on hers was soft and tentative, as though he were waiting for all her fire and anger to burn his lips. Just the touch of his mouth against hers made Charlotte forget everything else; the noise of the festival faded, her anger evaporated like a morning mist and, hardly aware of what she was doing, she wrapped her arms around him, threading her hands through the soft golden curls at the nape of his neck and pulling him closer. Heath's kiss deepened and his arms closed around her, his stubble rasping against her face. It was a chain reaction of desire and Charlotte's heart was beating in double time; when he finally and gently broke away, she felt giddy and disorientated, surprised to find herself back in the bustle of a busy York street because, for a few moments, nothing else had mattered more than being close to Heath. She'd been so lost in a world of sensation and longing that time and place had ceased to exist. As she gazed up at him Charlotte knew beyond all doubt that nothing from now on could matter more.

'I was looking for you because I can't bear to be apart from you for a minute longer,' he whispered. 'But I don't expect Suzie knew how to tell you that!'

Charlotte smiled. 'She did, in her own way.'

Heath's lips brushed the soft skin of her throat, his warm breath sending goosebumps Mexican-waving across her body. Burying his face in her neck he murmured, 'I thought I knew how your skin would smell, but I never imagined for a second it would be this good.'

Then he was kissing her again and this time his mouth was harder and more demanding. When they broke apart for a second time, their breathing was ragged and they stared at each other with mutual shock and desire.

'I think we'd better go to the car,' Heath said hoarsely, taking her hand and tracing the palm with his finger so slowly that her knees turned to water. 'I know Vikings are all for ravishing, but maybe not in the middle of a family friendly festival!'

Then he caught her eye and started to laugh.

'I don't think Zak or Justin would ever be so uncool as to kiss in public! They'd probably cringe at the sight of wrinklies snogging in broad daylight!'

Charlotte stretched up on tiptoes to brush his mouth with hers. 'I think I like being uncool, but on second thoughts, maybe we should go and check out that Land Rover.'

They ran as fast as they could through the throngs to get to the privacy of the car, but before they got there Heath stopped and said, 'I should never have yelled at you like that.' He pulled her close and placed a kiss on the top of her head. 'I was so angry but I knew deep down you loved both charities equally; expecting you to choose between them was really unreasonable.'

'But I didn't—'

He hushed her words with a kiss. 'I know. I always knew. The Arts Council have pulled stunts like that before. You were only doing your job. I phoned you at work to apologise for my behaviour but Suzie said you were back here for the Festival.'

'Suzie told you where to find me?'

'A bit more than that! She tore a strip off me for being out of order and pointed out that you'd been acting totally under her instructions. She said you'd been really upset when she'd decided not to tell Cass and me about the funding problem.' He squeezed her hand. 'She was furious on your behalf.'

Charlotte wasn't sure she could take the world dipping on its axis any further. Since when had Suzie gone from being her arch enemy to her staunchest ally? She supposed she had Richard to thank for that!

'So why withdraw from funding,' she asked, 'if you're not angry with me?'

Heath shook his head. 'Do you remember that Luke Scottman was at the awards ceremony?'

Charlotte nodded. 'He was extremely nice. I talked to him for ages. He was really interested in YORC; he loved the idea that acting could turn things round for kids like Zak and Justin.'

Heath stared at her. 'Well, that explains it!'

'Explains what?'

'Last week I got a phone call from Luke Scottman's

manager. It came out of the blue but, apparently, he's really interested in the work we do and he wanted to know how he could be involved.' A big smile spread across Heath's face. 'Charlotte, thanks to what you told him, Luke's setting up a bursary that'll keep YORC going for years! We don't need the Arts Council any more, so it doesn't matter if I get involved with someone who could be accused of influencing any decision!' He cupped her face in his hands and stared down at her, his eyes bright with emotion.

And then he was kissing her and spinning her around and they were laughing so much she didn't realise they had reached the car. Heath was just fishing in his Viking costume for the keys when Charlotte noticed that a black-clad figure was slumped on the floor against the wheel, hunched up and whimpering.

'Ruby?' Dropping to her knees she pushed the girl's hood from her face and was horrified to see her pretty features were all screwed up with pain. 'Heath! Quickly! It's Ruby.'

'Rubes?' In an instant Heath was at her side. 'Sweetheart, what's wrong? What is it?'

'Heath, I'm so sorry!' gasped Ruby, clutching her stomach and raising big tear-filled eyes. 'I should have told you earlier. Charlotte said I should!'

'What's the matter?' Heath tried to touch her tummy to see where the pain was but when he felt the bump beneath the baggy clothes his face paled. 'You're pregnant!'

Ruby was crying in earnest now. 'I'm sorry, Heath;

I'm so sorry. I didn't know how to tell you. I'm so sorry I've let you down.'

Heath hugged her. 'Rubes, you could never let me down. I just wish you'd told me and that I'd been able to help you.' His brow pleated as he saw her clutch at the distended stomach beneath the baggy hoodie. 'How pregnant are you, sweetheart?'

'Nearly eight months,' gasped Ruby, 'and I think the baby's coming. I'm scared, Heath; I'm really scared.'

'Eight months!' Charlotte was stunned. 'You never said you were that far along!' Looking more closely at the girl now it was so obvious she could have wept. Why on earth hadn't she noticed? No wonder Ruby had been so desperate.

Heath looked up at her and his eyes were so bleak that it broke her heart. 'You knew about this? And you never thought to mention it?'

'I'm so sorry, Heath, but it wasn't my decision to make.'

'But I'm her stepfather! Didn't you think I needed to know?'

'Yes, but—' Charlotte firmly changed the subject. 'Heath, call an ambulance.'

Leaving him to make the call she dropped down beside Ruby and put her arm around the terrified girl.

'It really hurts!' sobbed Ruby, as a contraction tore through her body.

'I know, sweetheart. Just breathe,' she advised, 'and squeeze my hand tightly when the pain comes.'

'The ambulance will be here in five minutes,' Heath said, snapping his phone shut. 'Just hang on.'

Between them Heath and Charlotte managed to keep Ruby calm, which was easier said than done because the contractions seemed to be gathering intensity at an alarming pace. Glancing at her watch Charlotte saw that there were now only three minutes between the pains and it was with enormous relief that she saw the ambulance pull up.

Thank goodness! Charlotte really didn't think she could cope with delivering a baby.

Blue lights swept across the car park and, moments later, paramedics were helping Ruby into the ambulance and offering her gas and air. Charlotte slumped against the Defender and watched the professionals take charge, feeling awash with relief that at long last Ruby was in safe hands.

Heath was climbing into the ambulance. His face was haggard and her heart twisted with love for him. She'd known about Ruby for weeks, it must have come as a shock for Heath.

'How could you not tell me?' he asked, his voice hoarse with devastation. 'You know how worried I was about her. I told you so over and over again and you knew all the time what was the matter. How could you keep that from me?'

'I'm so sorry,' whispered Charlotte.

Heath shook his head in disgusted silence.

Then he slammed the doors shut and the ambulance sped away, leaving Charlotte staring after it, with tears pooling in her eyes. The expression of disbelief and betrayal on his face was seared into her heart and she wished she could turn back time so much that it hurt.

How was it possible to go from heaven to hell so quickly?

Charlotte dabbed her eyes with the corner of her sleeve. What on earth had she been thinking to even dream things could ever have worked out between her and Heath? For weeks she'd been keeping a huge secret from him and this, added to the funding complications, didn't exactly show her in the most open and honest light. No wonder he was so angry and so hurt. *I don't blame him one bit*, she thought sadly.

There was one person who she did need to speak to, though. Urgently. Making her way back through the streets towards the press of stalls and fairground rides, Charlotte searched everywhere until she finally found Justin, queuing with some of the other lads for burgers.

Seeing her worried expression Justin instantly abandoned his friends. 'What's wrong?' he asked. 'Is it Ruby?'

Charlotte nodded. 'She's gone into labour, Justin. Heath's with her but I really think you should be there too.'

Justin turned so pale that his freckles stood out like bruises. 'Of course,' was all he managed to say.

'I'll get you a cab,' Charlotte said, catching sight of one across the street and signalling to the driver.

Justin clutched her arm. 'Will you come with me? Heath will go mental when he finds out it's my fault Ruby's in this mess. You could stop him from killing me.'

Charlotte was pretty sure that the sight of her was the one thing guaranteed to make Heath flip but, touched by Justin's pleas, she agreed to accompany him and, moments later, they were speeding away from the city towards the general hospital.

'I'm scared,' Justin whispered when the cab drew up outside the maternity unit. 'I don't know if I'm ready to be a dad.'

She reached forward and took his trembling hands in hers. 'The truth is, Justin, I don't think *anyone* is ever ready to be a parent. Believe you me, lots of people older than you are just as scared as you are right now.'

'Really?'

'Really.' Charlotte squeezed his icy fingers.

'The baby's early,' Justin worried, biting his lip. 'Ruby said it isn't due until next month. Will it be OK?'

'I can't make any promises but I don't think your baby's dangerously early. And they'll have the best possible care waiting.'

Justin took a deep and shaky breath before squaring his shoulders. 'Come on. Ruby needs me.'

The maternity ward was packed and the medical staff rushed off their feet but, once Charlotte had told the nurses who Justin was, he was quickly ushered into the delivery suite and she was left alone in a waiting room.

Turning off her phone as instructed, she sank on to a plastic seat and closed her eyes. The drama and extremes of emotion of the past hour had left her weak and trembling. She remained slumped in the seat for a good ten minutes until eventually her heart rate slowed and her pulse returned to normal.

The recollection of Heath's haunted expression when he realised what was wrong with Ruby broke her heart. Heath would be crucifying himself for not working it out and blaming himself that Ruby hadn't been able to turn to him. He couldn't have loved his stepchildren any more if they'd been his own. Heath was always there for the kids.

But who was there for him?

Charlotte longed to be able to put her arms around him and smooth the worries away, but she was the last person he'd want to see. Maybe she should go? She wasn't needed. Justin and Ruby were together and Heath was with them. But she couldn't leave though, not until she knew that Ruby and the baby were safe.

Whether Heath liked it or not she was too involved now to just walk away. She had to wait until the baby was born. She couldn't abandon Ruby and Justin, she just couldn't.

Time passed painfully slowly as Charlotte paced the room, torturing herself by reliving the myriad ways that she'd messed up. As the light faded from the sky and the night nurses relieved the day staff, Charlotte flicked through dog-eared magazines, drank gallons of disgusting coffee and slipped into fitful dozes. Her dreams were punctuated by snatches of Heath's angry words or Ruby's terrified face, which jolted her awake.

Charlotte had just nodded off again when a gentle hand touched her shoulder.

'I thought you'd want to know that Ruby's had her baby,' said a midwife. 'It's a little girl, six pounds five ounces. Mum and baby are doing fine.'

'Thank goodness!' Charlotte felt as though she'd been holding her breath, even in her sleep. She could practically taste the relief. Standing and picking up her bag, she said, 'Thanks so much for letting me know!'

'You're not going to leave without seeing the baby, are you?' the nurse asked, looking surprised.

'This is a time for family,' Charlotte told her as she donned her jacket.

'But you've waited all these hours! I'm sure they'd love to show you the new arrival.' Before Charlotte could protest any further she was being propelled down the corridor and into a side room.

Ruby looked exhausted, but she and Justin were beaming at the smallest and newest baby she'd ever seen. They looked so happy.

Heath, Charlotte noticed – with both sadness and a sense of relief that she'd been let off the hook – wasn't present.

'Charlotte!' cried Ruby in delight, beckoning her over. 'Look at her! Isn't she amazing?'

'She's perfect,' added Justin, and the pride in his voice as he said this brought tears to Charlotte's eyes. Gone was the cocky lad she'd first met all those weeks ago and in his place was a proud new father. Putting down her bag, she joined the young family, crying in earnest when she saw how beautiful the new arrival was. She had ears like little pink shells, a rosebud mouth and the softest, freshest skin Charlotte had ever seen. One tiny hand with minute pink nails was curled around the hospital blanket as she slept, the jet-black lashes fanned against her round cheeks. It blew Charlotte away; here was a whole new life, breathing, yawning, moving on its own. It was absolutely awesome.

'She's exquisite,' she told them, reaching down and brushing her forefinger across the baby's soft cheek. 'Well done, both of you!'

'We're going to keep her,' Ruby said, looking across at Justin and smiling. 'I couldn't give her up for adoption. Not any more!'

'I know we're young, but we're going to try our best to make a go of things,' he added, raising his chin a fraction just in case anyone tried to argue with him. Charlotte loved him for his determination to do what was right, which was something lots of men way older than he was couldn't manage.

'You're going to make brilliant parents. She's a very lucky little girl to have you both,' she said warmly.

'That's just what Heath told us,' Ruby said, reaching out to caress the baby's head.

Charlotte's heart beat triple time at the mention of his name.

'Where is Heath?' she asked, hoping her voice sounded steadier than it felt.

'Gone to make some phone calls, I think.' Justin shrugged. 'You must have just missed him. He's been brilliant. I seriously thought he'd skin me alive but he was OK about it, wasn't he, Rubes?'

'It's too late to tell us off now,' gulped Ruby. 'But you're right, he was amazing. He could hardly put her down.'

Charlotte wasn't at all surprised to hear this. She strongly suspected that the new baby was going to have a doting step-granddad. Kissing Ruby and Justin goodbye she felt sad because she had a hunch she wouldn't be returning to Yorkshire in a hurry. She probably wouldn't see them again. Heath had obviously done a vanishing act because he knew she was in the hospital and didn't want to be in the same space as her. He probably couldn't wait for her to leave.

Outside the warm, airless fug of the hospital, it was a sharp and clear autumn night, with a slice of moon and a glittery sprinkling of stars against the black sky. All she wanted was to get back to the hotel and the privacy of her room where she could weep for Heath all night long.

She'd have to call a cab. She rummaged in her bag for her mobile.

'Have you lost something?'

Charlotte's breath caught in her throat. Looking up slowly she saw Heath standing in front of her. He had a huge teddy bear under one arm and a massive bunch of velvety red roses under the other. She braced herself for the impact of his anger, but it never came. Instead, Heath was smiling that crinkly eyed smile while his dimples played hide and seek in his cheeks. *Of course he was smiling*, Charlotte told herself sternly. Hadn't Ruby just said that he was every inch the doting grandfather?

For a moment they stared at each other as the silence between them seemed to swell and grow like a living entity.

Charlotte drew a shaky breath. 'Congratulations. She's absolutely gorgeous.'

Heath's smile grew even wider. 'I know, I know! She's breathtaking. Ruby was so brave and Justin was fantastic.'

'They're both amazing,' Charlotte agreed. Then, before he had a chance to say anything further, she continued in a choked voice, 'I'm so sorry I didn't tell you it was Ruby who was pregnant. I wanted to, I really did, but it wasn't my place. I was horrified when I realised she was your stepdaughter. I know you'll never forgive me for keeping it from you. There's no one who wishes more than I do that things had worked out differently. I wish I'd behaved differently! I should never have come to York!'

Her eyes stinging with unshed tears, Charlotte made to turn away but Heath caught her arm and pulled her back to face him.

'You have nothing to apologise for,' he said fiercely. 'I'm the one who needs to be apologising for the appalling way I treated you earlier. I was shocked, but that was no excuse for taking it out on you. It's not your fault that I've been too busy to notice what was happening under my nose.'

Charlotte closed her eyes in defeat. 'I still should have said something.'

'No.' He shook his head vehemently. 'You were totally right to keep her confidence. I know that. I was just so angry . . . with myself, mainly. You were there for Ruby. There is no one I'd rather she'd spoken to about it.'

She opened her eyes and saw that Heath was smiling at her. So she really was forgiven. Things might be ruined between them but if Heath didn't hate her she might one day learn to live with this biting disappointment.

Heath held the roses out to her. 'These are for you.'

Red roses? For her? In spite of everything that had happened Charlotte's heart floated upwards like Picton Fair's hot-air balloon. Maybe there was hope for them yet.

'Thank you for being such a good friend to Ruby.' Heath paused. 'Well, to all of us.'

Oh. Thank-you flowers. That hot-air balloon popped and Charlotte's heart shattered into a thousand disappointed fragments. The roses were to say *thank you*. Of course they were. What a fool she was to think they meant to say anything else.

'That's kind, but you didn't need to,' Charlotte said, her throat tight with grief as she took them. She buried her face in the soft petals to hide her tears. 'I'll leave you to get back to Ruby and the baby. Good luck with everything.'

Dragging up what pride she had left she turned away from him. Walking away from Heath Fulford was the hardest thing she'd ever had to do. But there was no way she wanted to embarrass him by causing a scene.

But then again . . .

Wasn't being in the arms of the love of her life worth the risk of embarrassment? Didn't she owe it to herself to take the chance and tell him how she felt, for once in her life?

Charlotte turned back to him. 'They were *thank-you* flowers, weren't they?'

Heath shook his head. 'And before you ask they're not *sorry* flowers, either!'

That was all she needed to hear. Before she knew what she was doing Charlotte was running back to Heath and, in the boldest move of her normally cautious life, she flung herself into his arms and drew him close to her heart. Then her mouth found his and she was kissing him as though her life depended upon it, which was exactly the case. Without Heath, without his fire and passion and energy, she was only leading a half-life. Yes, it was a safe life where she didn't take risks and wouldn't get hurt, but it wasn't living. Without Heath she was merely existing and that just wasn't enough any more. When he kissed her back with equal feeling Charlotte knew that Heath felt exactly the same way.

Finally they broke apart, their breathing loud in the silent air and their eyes wide with wonder.

'Does this mean you might like me a bit?' asked Heath, smiling down at her.

Her own lips curved upwards in answer. 'A bit. A lot. I've certainly never done that before!' She kissed him softly again. 'I love you, Heath.' And oddly enough, saying these words out loud didn't terrify her at all.

Heath buried his face in her hair and whispered against the top of her head. 'From the minute I first saw you, standing outside Archie's hotel in the autumn sunshine, I loved you. Your hair looked like flames and I soon realised you were every bit as fiery. It makes no sense, but I've loved you from that moment and for every moment since. I love the way you challenge me, the way you're so natural with the kids and the way you give one hundred per cent to everything you do. But most of all, I love you for just being you.'

Heath loved her for being her? Spiky, difficult Charlotte . . . and after all the silly mistakes she'd made?

Maybe miracles did happen after all . . .

Heath tilted her chin up with his forefinger and kissed her tears away. 'No more crying,' he whispered. 'I know I've got crazy stepchildren, a mad dog and I live a million miles from you, but if you'll have me, I promise I'll make you happy every day for the rest of our lives.'

Her tears had turned to tears of joy.

'I can't think of anything I'd like better,' she told him, leaning her forehead against his and smiling into those rock-pool eyes.

'Now,' he murmured tenderly, 'how about we go back inside and we tell the rest of the family?'

Family! Charlotte's eyes widened and she felt her lips curl into a smile of amazement. That was what she and Heath would be now. Along with Ruby and Justin and the new baby, Ruby's brothers, Tilly the dog and maybe, one day, even children of their own.

'Of course you do realise this brand-new baby will make you a step-granny?' teased Heath.

'Well, Granddad, I would be honoured. Even if "step-granny" makes me sound terribly old,' she laughed.

Heath took her hand, threading his fingers through hers before brushing her palm with his lips. 'Shall we go back in and see her?'

There was nothing she'd like more than to see the baby again. Maybe Ruby might even let her have a cuddle.

Hand in hand they made their way back towards the hospital, stopping to kiss again at the door. Charlotte cupped Heath's face in her hands and shook her head in wonder. It was weird but she had the oddest sensation that the final pieces of a puzzle were somehow falling into place.

'This baby is special in so many ways,' Heath was saying, 'but none more so than because she brought us together at long last. When she's old enough we'll have to take Hope out for a drink to say thank you.'

Charlotte gaped at him. 'Say that again?'

'Hope,' Heath repeated softly. 'They've called her Hope. Isn't that a great name?'

And as his lips met hers in a gossamer-soft kiss

Charlotte had to agree. The final piece of the celestial puzzle had fallen into place and she smiled to herself.

Impossible as it seemed, Angela had been right all along!

Hope had brought her love after all.

Pick up a *little black dress* – it's a girl thing.

978 0 7553 4743 8

ITALIAN FOR BEGINNERS
Kristin Harmel
PBO £5.99

Despairing of finding love, Cat Connelly takes up an invitation to go to Italy, where an unexpected friendship, a whirlwind tour of the Eternal City and a surprise encounter show her that the best things in life (and love) are always unexpected . . .

Say '*arrivederci*, lonely hearts' with another fabulous page-turner from Kristin Harmel.

THE GIRL MOST LIKELY TO . . .
Susan Donovan
PBO £5.99

Years after walking out of her small town in West Virginia, Kat Cavanaugh's back and looking for apologies – especially from Riley Bohland, the man who broke her heart. But soon Kat's questioning everything she thought she knew about her past . . . and about her future.

A red-hot tale of getting mad, getting even – and getting everything you want!

978 0 7553 5144 2

Pick up a *little black dress* – it's a girl thing.

978 0 7553 3731 6

THE BALANCE THING
Margaret Dumas
PB £4.99

Becks Mansfield has never put much effort into her relationships with men, but now she's lost her hot-shot job as well. Surely it's more important to sort out her career than her love life? Or is life trying to tell her she needs a little more of *The Balance Thing*?

SIMPLY IRRESISTIBLE
Rachel Gibson
PB £4.99

Georganne Howard knows she's irresistible, but when she's rescued by John Kowalsky he proves impervious to her charms and packs her off after one night.

Ten years later, she's back and this time Georganne is playing hard to get. She's also hiding a very big secret . . .

978 0 7553 3742 2

You can buy any of these other
Little Black Dress titles from your
bookshop or *direct from the publisher*.

FREE P&P AND UK DELIVERY
(Overseas and Ireland £3.50 per book)

TO ORDER SIMPLY CALL THIS NUMBER

01235 400 414

or visit our website: www.headline.co.uk

Prices and availability subject to change without notice.